SCALLYWAGS

JAMES J. JENKINS

outskirts
press

Scallywags
All Rights Reserved.
Copyright © 2024 James J. Jenkins
v2.0

This is a work of fiction. Names, characters, businesses, places, events, locales, and incidents are either the products of the author's imagination or used in a fictitious manner. Any resemblance to actual persons, living or dead, or actual events is purely coincidental.

The opinions expressed in this manuscript are solely the opinions of the author and do not represent the opinions or thoughts of the publisher. The author has represented and warranted full ownership and/or legal right to publish all the materials in this book.

This book may not be reproduced, transmitted, or stored in whole or in part by any means, including graphic, electronic, or mechanical without the express written consent of the publisher except in the case of brief quotations embodied in critical articles and reviews.

Outskirts Press, Inc.
http://www.outskirtspress.com

ISBN: 978-1-9772-7639-1

Cover Illustration by Victor Guiza © 2024 James J. Jenkins.

Outskirts Press and the "OP" logo are trademarks belonging to Outskirts Press, Inc.

PRINTED IN THE UNITED STATES OF AMERICA

*Dedicated to
my mom,
Joan Easterly*

1

My brother's funeral was not as much fun as he wanted it to be.

Once when we were kids, Ray told me what he wanted his funeral to be like. I must have been around twelve, so Ray was probably fourteen at the time. He said he wanted to have fireworks, loud heavy metal music, girls in leather boots dancing in cages, and maybe even a trained elephant or two. Of course he had most likely outgrown those specific things when he turned thirty-four, but then again, who knows?

The point was he wanted his funeral to be a celebration, not some depressing cryfest. Too bad that when the time came it didn't happen the way Ray had wanted. My mother made all the arrangements for Ray's funeral and did things her way. She always did things her way.

I sat in the front row of the church staring at the floral arrangements surrounding the casket. Their scent, mixed with Mother's perfume, lay oppressively heavy in the air. My mother sat stiffly on my right, clutching an unused white handkerchief that contrasted with her black dress and pillbox hat and veil perched atop her short gray hair. Emily sat on my left, fidgeting as if she were anxious for this all to be over. Her dark ponytail swept across my shoulder when she turned to the woman beside her, asking for a tissue so she could clean her butterfly-framed glasses.

Behind us were about two dozen mourners dressed in black, crying and whispering to each other with solemn voices. The minister gave his eulogy in a monotone that became an annoying buzz. I had no idea what he even said. He lost me after "dearly beloved." Ray deserved a better funeral than he got.

I snapped my eyes open, fighting to stay awake for the fifth time. I looked up and thought I saw Ray standing over his coffin looking down at his own lifeless body. But something wasn't right with him. He seemed to be translucent, more like a reflection on a car windshield than an actual person. I rubbed my eyes, and when I looked again, he was gone. I glanced around wondering if anybody else noticed him, but no one gave any indication that they had seen anything. I dismissed it, assuming I had dozed off for a moment and dreamed it.

Then the pirates arrived.

They entered through the large double doors, laughing and chatting among themselves. After a half-dozen steps into the church, they stopped and became silent, as if they noticed the gathered people for the first time. The leader, a tall, dark-haired man with a goatee that stuck out in a point, loudly whispered an apology to the minister. The group, about nine in all, squeezed past several parishioners to take their seats in the pews. Once they settled in, the minister continued, except everyone was trying to get a look at this new bunch in their outlandish attire. The parishioners probably assumed the new people were all extras in the latest pirate movie filming down the road.

The minister asked if anyone cared to say a few words. It was to be Mom's moment. She had requested that the minister ask the question so she could express how much she missed Ray. What she really wanted to do was to feed off everyone's sympathy. Before she could respond, though, the pirate leader rose.

"I would like to say a few words, if you please," he said.

The comment caused some chattering among the attendees. No one expected anyone other than Mom to say anything

The man in the long red coat and black bandana tied around his left arm had already squeezed past the few people seated beside him and was striding up to the pulpit. "Thank you, Reverend," he said.

The minister stepped back from the pulpit to allow him to speak.

"Friends," he began, "most of you don't know me, so allow me to introduce myself. I am Captain Willow." He gestured toward the other members of his group. "And this is my crew. We are the Scallywags of Cannon Lake."

The seated pirates all said, "Arrgh!"

"We come here today," Captain Willow continued, "to pay our respects to our dear friend, Longbucket."

The pirates gave another chorus of "Arrgh!"

"Of course most of you don't know him as Longbucket. Funny story that..."

Several pirates noisily cleared their throats, giving a signal to their captain.

"But I digress." Captain Willow waved his hand, dismissing what he had been about to say. "Most of you know this fine fellow as Raymond Potts. Raymond was one of my crew. In fact he was my quartermaster.

"For the past four years we, as a crew, got together and attended various pirate festivals throughout Florida. This year we planned to take our first cross-country trip to the Palo Alto Pirate Festival in California. Longbucket himself made the arrangements and mapped out our journey. Sadly we begin our journey tomorrow without our beloved quartermaster. And I'll tell you this much: it won't be the same without him. He was the best among us. Can I get an Arrgh?"

The pirates sang out, "Arrgh!"

Everyone else remained silent.

"Fare-thee-well, mate," Captain Willow said to Ray who lay in his casket. "May you always have a fair wind at your back, spiced rum in your cup, and a pretty wench on your lap. To our shipmate, Longbucket."

"To Longbucket!" the pirates cried out. They stood and drew their daggers in salute.

The other attendees gasped. Fear filled their eyes as they scrambled to get away. The pirates realized their mistake and sheathed their daggers, offering apologies.

Captain Willow turned to the minister with a deep bow and a sweeping gesture. "It's all yours, your Reverend-ship." He stepped down from the pulpit and returned to his crew, again squeezing past the same parishioners, repeatedly asking them to pardon him.

The minister returned to the pulpit and asked if anyone else would like to speak, looking at Mom as he did so. She sat still with a sour look on her face. The moment was gone. Ruined. She would not speak. Not now. No one else would either.

After the service the pallbearers carried Ray's coffin out

through the double doors of the church and placed it in the waiting hearse. We all followed. Everyone went to their respective cars. Mother, Emily, and I had a limousine waiting for us. As my mother climbed into the back, I watched the pirate band clambering aboard a rusty old school bus with a wooden figurehead of a mermaid fastened to its front and the words The Ship painted on the side.

Captain Willow remained at the open door, leaning out with one hand on his hip, surveying all the other cars. I half expected him to pull a spyglass from his pocket and start charting a course for our little fleet.

The procession crawled along to the cemetery. The burial took little time, and soon my mother and I were shaking everyone's hand and receiving their condolences. The pirates were the last in line. It was the first time I had a chance to look at them individually. They were a motley crew. Among them was a large man with a shaved head and a big red handlebar mustache, a small-framed man with a crooked back, a grizzled old man, an Asian woman wearing spider-shaped jewelry, and a barrel-chested man with a menacing scowl.

And then *she* stood before me. Her cinnamon-colored eyes were bewitchingly beautiful. It felt as if someone had punched me in the chest. I instantly regretted having eaten three doughnuts that morning and sucked in my gut to try to hide my belly. Her full lips parted, and as she spoke my heart melted. She then turned and sauntered away. My gaze followed, only to be met by my girlfriend's narrowed eyes. I smiled apologetically and turned to see Captain Willow standing in front of me.

"I am very sorry about your brother, me hearty. He will sorely be missed," he said, shaking my hand. "He and I shared many an adventure together. Why, there was that one time in St. Augustine—"

"I'm sorry, but Ben and I must leave," my mother interrupted. "We have a great deal to do, you understand."

"Yes, of course." Captain Willow tipped his hat. "I do ramble on."

"If you will excuse us." Mom took me by the arm and dragged me away.

Emily followed.

"Ah, I almost forgot," Captain Willow called after us. "There is something—"

"Perhaps later. Thank you for coming." Mom shoved me into the back of the limousine.

As the limo drove out of the cemetery Mom gave the little huff she always made when she was annoyed. Emily rolled her eyes. My mother could be a challenge to deal with at times, but I knew enough to wait out the storm; it would pass after a few minutes.

"What a bunch of weirdos," Mom began. "And that man is the worst of the lot. Of course that was Ray for you. He always associated with the weird ones. I can only imagine the kind of illegal activity they got into. Probably sold drugs. It's that Newton boy all over again. He used to get Ray into all kinds of trouble."

"Ray was six years old when he and Peter Newton were friends," I said.

"Yes," she continued, "and remember what they did to the Perkins's cat? I'll never forget. They ruined a perfectly good electric razor too."

The limo driver dropped us off at Mom's house. Emily and I helped Mom get the place ready for the friends and family members who would soon be arriving from the funeral. Mom was her usual controlling self. I was used to it and mustered as much patience as I could. Emily, however, was clearly on edge. Luckily Aunt Sherry and Aunt Terri arrived to pitch in, which helped ease the burden, or so I thought.

When the guests began arriving and the house started getting overcrowded, I caught a glimpse of my mother chastising Emily about something in the kitchen. Emily waved her hand as if to say she was done. She left the kitchen, grabbed her purse, and stormed out the front door.

I chased after her.

Outside dusk made its regular appearance as the sun sank below the horizon. The rumbling of a lawnmower came from half a block away. From the opposite direction an automated garage door hummed open, welcoming its weary residents home from their long day at work. The neighborhood birds chirped incessantly as they settled in the trees and on the power lines above.

"Emily, wait," I called.

She had already reached the end of my mother's walkway and turned left onto the sidewalk.

I was about to cut across the lawn to catch her, but remembered my mother didn't like it when people walked on her grass, so I jogged down the walkway to the sidewalk and came up behind Emily. "Listen." I reached out, but she pulled her arm away. "I know Mom can be difficult. She has her ways, but you don't have to leave because of her."

"I'm done with this, Ben," she said over her shoulder. "I'm done with all of it. I came here today because I wanted to be there for you, but I can't do this anymore."

"Whatever it is, we can work it out. I'll talk to my mother."

"It's not just her." She spun around to face me.

"What is it? What happened?"

"Nothing's happened." Her arms shot out to both sides. "That's the problem."

"I don't understand."

"Ben, we've been dating for three years, and the only reason we started dating was because I asked you out." She massaged her forehead with her thumb and middle finger, her way of trying to calm herself. "It's usually the guy who asks the woman out, but that's okay. I liked you and was okay with asking you out."

She was being truthful. I never was good at asking women out. I lacked the confidence.

Emily continued, "but I'll be damned if I'm going to be the one to ask you to marry me. I mean, come on. It's been three years, and you still haven't even given the slightest hint that you might propose to me."

"If that's all it is." Shoving my hand into my pocket, I pulled out a small jewelry box. The lid refused to open at first, causing me to fumble and almost drop it. Finally I opened it and held it out to Emily. Inside the box was an engagement ring, the best I could afford, which wasn't saying a whole lot, but in my opinion, it was nice.

I got down on one knee, smiling up at her. "Would you do me the honor of becoming Mrs. Benjamin Potts?"

Emily's facial expressions were sometimes hard to read. While I kneeled, smiling up at her, she looked at me with a wooden expression that could have meant any number of things. I hoped it meant she was too surprised to speak.

"Okay," I said, "I know the timing is a bit weird, what with the funeral going on and the problems with my mother and everything, but I've thought about asking you for a while now. I bought the ring after we went to Sanibel Island that one weekend. Remember?"

"That was like a year ago."

"Yeah, I know." I rose to my feet. "I could never find the

right time to ask you, and I had to make sure Mom was okay with it."

She cocked her head to one side and stared at me with brow furrowed and mouth agape. "You had to get your mother's approval?" she asked.

"You know how she is with change, and me getting married is a big change."

"Ben, no, I'm not marrying you." She shook her head as she reached into her purse. "I care about you; you know that. I've always cared about you. But you let your mother control your life."

"No, I don't."

"Yes, you do." Her eyes shot a rebuking glare at me before she continued digging through her purse. "I can't deal with it anymore. Besides, I'm seeing somebody else now."

"Somebody else?" The pinot noir and shrimp canapes I had consumed earlier started to creep up the back of my throat. I swallowed hard and managed to keep them down. "What do you mean?"

"I'm sorry." She pulled her keys from her purse and then dropped them. We both bent down to retrieve them and bumped our heads together. We pulled back.

The top of my head throbbed, but I still managed to pluck the keys from the sidewalk.

"I should have told you sooner." She rubbed the crown of her head. "We met a few weeks ago and started dating. I meant to tell you, but after your brother passed away, I didn't have the heart to."

"You're dating someone else?" I handed her the keys.

"He's a really great guy. You'd like him." She walked around her car to the driver's side.

"Sure, maybe the three of us can hang out sometime."

"Actually, that might be a bit awkward."

"I was being sarcastic." I frowned at the ring I still held. I couldn't even look at Emily.

Behind me a vehicle pulled up to Mom's house sounding as if every gear and engine part were about to break down. I knew exactly what vehicle it was by the sound. I looked over my shoulder to see the pirate crew climb off the old school bus with the mermaid figurehead still clinging to the front grill. I continued to watch them as Emily spoke.

"I think I should go." She unlocked her car and opened the door. Pausing a moment, she leaned on the car roof. "I hope you meet the right woman one day. But do yourself a favor. When you do meet her, don't be so afraid to tell her. And who knows? It just might be her."

I turned back to Emily. "Her? Who her?"

"Her." Emily pointed at the young woman with the captivating eyes and enticing lips among the pirates as they filed into Mom's house. "The one dressed like a pirate or a gypsy or whatever she's supposed to be."

"I don't even know her."

"I saw the way you looked at her earlier. For once in your life, Ben, take a chance."

Emily got into her car and drove away. I stood by the road feeling empty, watching her car turn the corner and disappear from sight.

There was some commotion at the front door. I didn't hear it at first, but eventually it caught my attention. The pirates were being unceremoniously escorted out of the house by my aunts. Aunt Terri even wielded a broom, waving it like a club. Captain Willow held up his hands, attempting to reason with my aunts, but to no avail. The group gave in and marched back toward their bus.

Captain Willow stopped and looked in my direction. "Potts," he called. He walked over to me. "Brother of Potts. There you are."

"What is it?" I stuffed the jewelry box with the ring into my pocket.

"It would appear your mother does not care for our company. We were ordered to vacate the premises under no uncertain terms."

"Yeah, Mom never did care for any of Ray's friends."

"No hard feelings, eh?" He wrapped his arm around my shoulders and pulled me to him. "We go now to the nearest tavern and drink to your brother's memory. Come. What say you, Potts? Have a drink with us?"

"Thank you," I said, "but no. It's been a rough day, and I should be getting home."

"Some other time, then. It was good to meet you, Potts."

"Thank you," I said. "I'm sure Ray appreciates that you came...even if my mother doesn't."

"Yes, Old Longbucket is in a better place now. Ye can be assured of that. Alas, I must be off. You take care of yourself."

"You too."

He shook my hand and started walking to the bus. Halfway there he stopped and turned back. "Once again I almost forgot." He reached into his coat pocket and pulled out a letter-sized envelope and held it out to me. "This is for you. Longbucket, I mean Ray, gave it to me the last time I saw him. He asked me to give it to you."

"Ray gave you this?" I asked, taking the envelope. It had my name on it.

"He was always about the melodrama, you know. Everything had to be big and dramatic. There you go. Good night, Potts, brother of Potts."

I watched him climb aboard the bus. I had no idea what to make of any of it. Too much had happened all at once; Ray died, Emily broke up with me, and the pirates made it all feel like some surreal dream. I stood with Ray's letter in my hand. When the old school bus pulled away, I noticed one of the pirates standing under a streetlight several houses down, watching me. I couldn't understand why he wasn't on the bus with the others until I realized it wasn't one of Willow's crew. It was Ray. He wore pirate garb and held a goblet in one hand, his other hand on his hip. He looked right at me. After several moments he raised his goblet, smiled, turned, and vanished.

2

I had a dream that night. Ray and I were aboard a pirate ship. We were caught in the middle of a huge storm that kicked our vessel around like a soccer ball. Ray stood at the helm wearing the same pirate garb I saw him wearing on the street corner. He laughed and mocked the storm. I scrambled along the railing trying to reach him, struggling to keep from being swept overboard. When I called out, I barely heard myself over the storm.

"Look at it, Ben," Ray cried. "This is it!"

"This is what?"

"Life. This is life. You never know what life will throw at you, but you can't be afraid. You have to meet every challenge head on, laughing at it the whole time."

"I don't know how to do that."

"Don't worry." He looked at me with that self-assured smile of his.

Then there was silence. The storm still raged around us, but it made no sound, as if someone had pressed the mute button.

Ray's voice came over the silence, like a voice from the heavens. "I'll teach you," he said. "Follow my instructions and be at the Brantley Motel at noon tomorrow."

I woke up in my bed at home. There was no storm, no pirate ship, and there was no Ray. The clock on the nightstand displayed 11:57. I sat on the edge of the bed and switched on the light. Next to the clock on the nightstand lay the envelope Captain Willow had given me alongside the engagement ring Emily had rejected.

The envelope was what interested me then. My name was written on it in Ray's handwriting. I recognized his big swooping P that looked like it was about to eat the other letters. From the drawer in the nightstand I took out the sword letter opener Ray had given me for Christmas a few years earlier and cut open the top of the envelope. When I pulled out the letter, a key fell out and landed on the floor. I picked it up and noticed it had D11 engraved on it. I placed it on the nightstand and read the letter.

Dear Ben,

If Captain Willow has given you this letter, I must be dead. Trust me, my death was not unexpected, but I refuse to let fear and psychic predictions control my life.

There is something I need you to do for me. Actually it's not just one thing, it's five. Go to the Stanley Self Storage Facility on 53rd Avenue. Find unit D11. I've put the key to the unit inside the envelope with the letter. Inside the unit you will find a chest. Inside the chest you will find five envelopes and five items. Each envelope is marked with a specific town. Do not open the envelopes until you arrive in their designated towns.

Yes, I need you to travel across the country for me and deliver the five items. The letters in the envelopes will tell you where to deliver each item.

To save yourself some money all you have to do is travel across the country with Captain Willow and the Scallywags. Tell Willow it's for me, and he'll help you. They'll be traveling to the Palo Alto Pirate Festival, and the route they follow will bring you to each of the towns along the way.

One more thing.

You never know what life will throw at you, but you can't be afraid. You have to meet every challenge head on, laughing at it the whole time.

Take care,
Ray

In the morning I was tempted to stay home from work, but I went anyway. I sat at my desk unable to concentrate on my job. I kept reading and rereading Ray's letter and examining the key. I couldn't figure out how Ray knew to write me a letter like that and give it to Willow before he died. Ray had died in a small plane crash. How did he know? What was this stuff about psychic predictions? And if he knew he would die, why would he get on the plane?

I thought about the dream I had the previous night, seeing Ray at his own funeral and later on the street. Nothing made any sense. I needed to talk to someone about it, and the only person I felt I could trust was my coworker, Chantal, who sat at the desk next to mine. I thought it best not to mention that I may have seen my brother's ghost, twice, but I did tell her about Ray's letter and how he wanted me to deliver five items to different people across the country and to do it by traveling with the Scallywags of Cannon Lake.

"Are you crazy?" Chantal's gold bracelets jingled as she waved her fingernail file at me. Her short, plump, dark-skinned form filled her office chair like a freshly baked muffin filled a pan.

Our offices occupied the third floor of a four-story building. Eight of us, not including management, worked on the east end of the building inside eight individual cubicles. Management, of course, had its private offices, three of them, on the north side of the building. Chantal and I often worked on projects together, so our desks were separated by a half panel.

"I didn't say I was going to do it." I held my coffee mug up, about to take a sip. The steam from the coffee caressed the tip of my nose like a heated feather.

"Riding across the country with a bunch of wackos? Not me." Chantal snatched one of the three powdered doughnuts I had gotten from the breakroom. "You'd never catch me doing something like that."

"Maybe I can mail the stuff to the people." I considered the possibility. I preferred to make things as easy as possible. "I mean they'll still get it, wouldn't they?"

"What kind of stuff we talkin' about?" Powdered sugar coated her lips as she ate the doughnut. "Is it big stuff? Is it heavy? If it is, you'll end up payin' a fortune on freight charges."

"I haven't actually seen what it is yet." I offered her a napkin.

"If my brother asked me to travel across the country," she took the napkin and wiped her mouth with it, "to deliver some stuff to people I didn't know, I'd say uh-uh, baby. You should'a thought of that while you was still breathin'. No offense, Ben."

"None taken."

"I ain't gonna be nobody's delivery service. You know what I'm sayin'?"

"I know."

A head popped up above the partition to my right. It sported slicked-back brown hair and a used-car salesman grin. Danny, who worked in the next cubicle, peered over the partition at Chantal and me.

"Are you getting another job, Ben?" he asked.

"It's none of your business," I muttered into my coffee cup.

"No, Danny, he's not getting another job." Chantal took another bite of her doughnut.

"I thought I heard you talking about working for a delivery service."

Every time Danny spoke, he reminded me of the snake in Rudyard Kipling's *The Jungle Book*.

"He ain't talkin' about working for no delivery service." As much as I liked Chantal, her biggest flaw was that she didn't know when to keep quiet.

"Then what are you talking about?" spoke the snake.

"When the man's brother passed away—" Chantal began.

"It's none of his business," I told her.

"He left a last request." She couldn't stop at that point if she had wanted to. "He wants Ben to deliver some stuff to some people, like he was a UPS truck or somethin'." She harrumphed at the idea.

"Is there money involved?" Danny asked.

"Money? No, there's no money involved," I told him. "He wants me to travel across the country and deliver some stuff."

"Travel across the country? You'd never do that."

"That's right. He ain't gonna do that." Chantal had finished the doughnut and was licking powdered sugar from her fingers.

"I haven't decided yet."

"What's there to decide?" Danny said. "Your mommy would never let you travel so far from home."

"Oh no, you didn't." Chantal held up her index finger and drew it horizontally. "I know you didn't just bring the man's mother into this."

"I'm right, and you know it. She would never give him permission to do something like that."

"I don't need my mother's permission," I snapped at Danny more harshly than I intended.

"And besides," Danny added, "Old Man Ferguson would never give you the time off."

"I think I've got some vacation time saved up."

"But you would never have the nerve to ask him."

"That sounds like a dare to me," Chantal said. "Ben, don't you go lettin' Danny push you into doin' somethin' you're not comfortable with. Mr. Ferguson is not someone you want to mess around with."

"Mr. Ferguson is a reasonable man. I bet he'd give me the time off if I told him it was my brother's last request."

"Okay, here's your chance to find out." Danny pointed to a short, balding man in large glasses and a blue three-piece suit coming our way.

"What's going on here?" Mr. Ferguson asked as he approached us. "It's not break time yet. You're here to work, not lollygag around. You can lollygag on your own time."

"Yes, sir, Mr. Ferguson." Chantal furiously typed away on her computer keyboard.

I turned my attention to my work as well, but Danny had other ideas.

"Sorry, Mr. Ferguson," Danny said, "you're absolutely right. We were telling Ben how sorry we were about his brother."

"Ben?" Mr. Ferguson turned to me as if he had just noticed me. "Ah, yes. Ben, on behalf of the entire company, we were sorry to hear about your brother's passing."

"Thank you, Mr. Ferguson," I said.

"If there is anything I can do for you, don't hesitate to let me know."

"Yes, sir. Thank you."

"Actually, Mr. Ferguson," Danny said, "Ben was saying there was something he wanted to talk to you about."

"Is that so? What is it?"

"I don't want to trouble you, sir."

"No trouble at all. Speak up."

"Well, uh..." Behind me I could hear Chantal's disapproving mumbles. I looked over at Danny, who was smirking, expecting me to make a fool of myself.

Mr. Ferguson stood there drumming his fingers on the top of the partition while rocking back and forth on his heels.

To be honest I wasn't sure if I wanted to take the time off from work. Plus I didn't like the idea of leaving home on such short notice. Of course, since it was Ray's final request, I wanted to respect it, but at the same time, the idea of traveling across the country with people I didn't know was terrifying. Maybe if I had enough time I could find another way of fulfilling Ray's final request, one that wasn't so inconvenient.

"It's nothing, sir," I said. "It can wait."

"Very well then," he said. "Let's get back to work, shall we?" He turned and walked toward his office.

"I knew you couldn't do it," Danny said.

"You hush, Danny," Chantal said. "It's okay, Ben. You're better off. You don't want to get yourself into some crazy situation."

"Yeah," Danny said. "Play it safe like you always do. Stay

home where you're close to your mommy." He chuckled as his head sank behind the partition.

As much as I despised Danny, he was right. I had always played it safe. Ray had been the daring one. He never let fear hold him back. That's why he and I drifted apart. While he was off having adventures, I stayed home where I was comfortable. I had always regretted that decision. I didn't know what Ray wanted me to deliver or even why it was important to him, but I couldn't let him down again. I also had to prove Danny wrong.

I got up from my chair and strode toward Mr. Ferguson's office. I knew if I didn't do it right away, I'd chicken out. I knocked on Mr. Ferguson's door, and he motioned through the window for me to enter.

"I'm sorry, Mr. Ferguson." I closed the door behind me. "I was wrong. It can't wait."

"What can't wait?" he asked.

"When my brother Ray passed away, he left a letter for me. In the letter he asked me to do something for him, a final request. The problem is that for me to carry out his final request, I would need to take the week off."

"The entire week?"

"Yes, sir. I have some vacation time saved, and I figured I could use that, and I'll be back next Monday, one way or another. But it's really important that I do this."

"I see. So what is it he wants you to do?"

"He wants me to travel across the country to deliver some things to some people." As the words left my mouth I realized how crazy it sounded.

"I see," Mr. Ferguson said again, slowly. "And who are these people you're supposed to deliver these things to?"

"I don't know."

"And what are the things you'll be delivering?"

"I don't know."

"So you want me to give you a week off so you can travel across the country to deliver some things to some people when you have no idea what those things are or who the people are. Is that correct?"

"Yes, sir."

"You do know how strange that sounds, don't you?"

"Yes, sir."

Mr. Ferguson leaned back in his chair with his fingers interlinked across his chest. He looked at a framed photo on his desk with a blank expression.

I prepared myself, knowing he was about to kick me out of his office, telling me to get back to work and never waste his time with such nonsense again.

"You know," he said at last, "I had a sister." He picked up the framed photo and showed it to me. An attractive woman in her mid-fifties kneeled next to a litter of puppies and their mother. She cradled one of the puppies as she smiled for the camera.

"She died about twelve years ago. She made a last request of me as well. She wanted me to adopt a dog. My sister was a big animal advocate. Me, I was never big on animals. Even though my wife and kids were always begging me to get a family pet, I refused. Too much work, in my opinion. But when my sister lay on her deathbed and asked me to adopt a dog, how could I refuse? So against my better judgment we adopted a dog, a beagle. The dog died almost a year ago. I cried when we buried him. Never in my life did I think I would cry over a dog, but that dog had become a part of my family. Three months ago we decided to adopt another dog. A puppy this time. Cutest thing you ever saw. I never would have experienced any of that if I hadn't carried out my sister's final request."

He sat still for a moment staring at his sister's photo with a smile on his face.

"All right, Ben." He placed the framed photo back on his desk. "You can have the week off, but make sure you're here next Monday, on time, and ready to work."

"Yes, sir. Thank you. I will."

"Now get out of here." With a wave of his hand he dismissed me, then picked up a nearby file.

"Yes sir." I opened the office door to leave.

"Oh, and, Ben," he said.

"Yes, sir?" I paused halfway out of the office.

"If you ever tell anyone the story I told you, you're fired."

I wasn't sure whether or not he was serious. "Of course, sir. I won't tell a soul." I held up three fingers like we used to do in the scouts.

"I'll see you next week then." He returned to his work.

"Yes, sir." I closed his office door behind me. On my way out I gave both Chantal and Danny the thumbs up.

Chantal told me to stay safe and not get myself into any questionable situations. Danny watched me leave with his mouth hanging open.

Half an hour later I arrived at the Stanley Self Storage Facility on 53rd Avenue, standing in front of unit D11. All the questions flying around inside my head needed answers. Maybe I would find some here. I unlocked the unit door and opened it.

Inside was empty except for what appeared to be an old

pirate treasure chest. I knelt before the chest and opened it to find five business-sized envelopes sitting on top of five different objects, a small stack of old baseball cards bound together with a rubber band, a DVD with For Sam written on it in permanent marker, a wooden puzzle box, a cardboard shoebox containing a brand-new pair of shoes, and a gold locket on a chain. I had no idea why Ray wanted me to deliver any of that stuff, but I felt it was something I needed to do, both for Ray and myself. I couldn't explain it. I had what you'd call a gut feeling.

I took the treasure chest home, packed a bag for a week-long trip, and called a cab. When the cab arrived, the driver helped me load my stuff into the trunk, and I told him to take me to the Brantley Motel.

The cab driver prattled on about one thing or another, but I didn't hear a word he said. I started thinking about Emily. I still had the engagement ring with me, twirling it between my fingers while I looked out the window and thought about the night before. I decided I needed to talk to her before I left, so I called her on my cell phone. Her voicemail picked up.

"Emily, it's Ben. Listen, I'm going to be out of town for the next week, but I've been thinking about last night, and I'd really like a chance to talk things over with you. Look, call me when you get this, please. We'll talk, okay? Hope you have a great day."

The cab dropped me off in front of the motel with my bag and Ray's treasure chest. At the far end of the parking lot Willow and his crew were loading their things onto the old school bus. They laughed and bickered like some dysfunctional family of demented vagabonds. The mean-looking pirate dressed in black chased after a young kid pirate who whooped as he disappeared behind the rear of the school bus, only to reappear, still laughing, at the front end moments later. The mean-looking pirate sneered at him, which only made the young kid pirate laugh more.

I couldn't believe Ray actually expected me to travel with these people for the next week. My brain screamed, *No! Don't board that old pile of junk they call a school bus.* Only someone as crazy as they were could spend the next seven days with them. An overwhelming urge to run away came over me. I frantically searched for a place to hide somewhere until they left. A large red pickup sat in a nearby parking spot. I grabbed my bag and the chest and started dragging them over to it.

"Potts, brother of Potts!"

Too late. Willow had spotted me.

"What brings you to these parts?" He crossed the parking lot toward me.

I stared at him, trying to come up with some excuse to get out of an uncomfortable situation. Nothing came to mind.

"That letter you gave me." I resigned myself to my fate. "Ray wants me to deliver some things for him, and the letter said I should ask if I could travel with you."

"To California?"

"Ray requested it."

"And you are a damned fine human being to be willing to fulfill your brother's dying request."

"I don't know about being a fine human being, but I'm here, so I guess I'm doing it."

"Good man. Let me ask my crew." He turned to the others. "Ahoy, mateys, Potts, brother of Potts, has requested the privilege of joining us on our voyage to Palo Alto. What say ye?"

The crew gave a half-hearted response in the affirmative. No one seemed to care one way or the other.

"There you are," Willow said to me.

"Great. Thanks. I'll put my stuff on board."

"One moment, please," Willow put his hand on my shoulder. "We have some rules."

"What rules?"

"Rule number one." He held up his index finger. "No one boards The Ship in civilian clothing. You must be properly appareled."

"Really? You're saying I have to dress like a pirate?"

"It is our way, Potts."

"Okay, I guess. Anything else?"

"Rule number two." He held up two fingers. "No free rides. You must contribute."

"That's fine. How do I contribute? Money? Work? Clean the bus?"

"We all have assigned duties aboard The Ship, yes. But at the pirate festival there will be a competition between us and another pirate crew, a rival crew, if you will. You will be required to participate in your brother's stead."

The thought concerned me. Ray was way much more athletic, and I was supposed to take his place in some sort of competition. I didn't like it. "What kind of competition?" I asked.

"I'll fill you in on the details later, but trust me, you'll love it."

"That's what worries me."

"Are we agreed then?" He put his arm around me and gave me a comradely half embrace.

"As long as you help me with delivering the stuff Ray requested I deliver, then yes, we're agreed."

"Good man." He patted me on the back. "Now let's get you outfitted for the voyage."

"Okay, I guess."

"All Hands on deck!" Willow called out.

The members of his crew paid no heed. Then a single pirate who looked like he belonged in high school walked toward us. He was heavily tattooed, with long sandy-brown hair braided and beaded, with a few feathers stuck in for good measure, topped by a green stocking cap. Light peach fuzz covered his chin. He wore a tan shirt with brown vest and breeches that came down below his knees and sandals made of hemp. A green sash was wrapped around his waist. He had a set of bongos cradled in his arm.

Willow put his arm around the young man's shoulders. Both men grinned at me.

"Potts," Willow said, "I'd like you to meet All Hands Murphy."

"Pleased to meet you." I shook his proffered hand.

"All Hands," Willow said, "our friend here needs to be properly fitted out for our voyage. Do you think you can help him?"

"Aye, aye, Captain." All Hands saluted, then turned to me. "Right this way, mate."

"Worry not, Potts," Willow said as I followed All Hands. "Redjack will stow your gear."

All Hands led me to the back of the bus, the whole time drumming his bongos with his fingertips. "Sorry, what was your name?" All Hands asked.

"Ben."

"You're Longbucket's brother, huh? Never knew he had a brother. Any other brothers or sisters, maybe?"

"No, it was just me and Ray."

"What about your parents? I saw your mom at the funeral. What about your dad?"

"He passed away some years ago."

"Too bad. Too bad about Longbucket too. He was a good old salt."

"What about you? Why do they call you All Hands?"

"It's what the ladies say about me. I'm all hands." He wiggled his fingers at me for emphasis.

The little man with the crooked back danced up to us playing a mandolin. The smile on his face revealed a missing tooth beneath a barely noticeable mustache the color of dead leaves. He wore a faded blue shirt over white cotton breeches and a gold fringed sash around his waist. As he pranced around us playing his mandolin, I wondered how his rope sandals didn't fall off. All Hands joined in with his bongos, as they both pranced around.

"What say you, All Hands?" the little man said. "Shall we play a song of welcome for our guest?"

"Sounds good to me, Jake."

The two danced, playing a song for me. Luckily it was a short song.

"Ben," All Hands said, "meet Jake."

"Crooked Jake, they call me." He held out his hand. "Pleased to meet you."

I shook his hand. "Crooked Jake? Because you're..."

"Because I cheat at cards."

"He does," All Hands confirmed. "Don't ever play for money with Jake. He'll take you for every red cent."

"Ben? Is that your name?" Jake asked.

"Yes," I said. "Ben Potts."

Jake played his mandolin and danced around while he sang "Ben, Ben, Ben, his name is Ben, his name is Ben."

With that he danced away, still singing and playing his mandolin.

All Hands opened the emergency exit door at the back of the bus to reveal an entire rack of pirate garments. He climbed up to stand inside the door. "So," he said, "what kind of pirate do you see yourself as?"

"I didn't know there were different kinds."

"Aye, it's all about the image you want to project. We all project different images. Like me and Jake. Since we're musicians and we entertain, we don't want to project anything too menacing. Now Crenshaw, he wants to be seen as menacing, so he put together his wardrobe to create a dark, sinister persona. Not that he needs much help with that. Then there's Captain Willow, who prefers a more stylish look. Everybody's different, even the women. Spider Lau dresses to show off her jewelry and give the appearance of a black widow spider. Maggie likes color, so she always has colorful outfits. And Celeste has her own style, which is kind of a combination of a pirate and a flower child."

"To be honest," I said, "I don't really care. Give me whatever you have."

"Okay, I can give you the basic seaman look, and we can develop your image later."

"That's fine. Whatever."

All Hands handed me a linen shirt, sailor slops, a red sash, and a red bandanna.

"Am I supposed to change out here on the street?" I asked.

"Retaining our dignity, are we?"

I raised one eyebrow.

"Okay," he said with good humor. "Come on."

He pulled me onto the bus, and I changed in a small corner behind a curtain. Once I was properly dressed in my pirate gear, he handed me a pair of sandals and clapped a tricorn hat on my head. I jumped down onto the pavement to get a better look at my outfit.

All Hands looked at me from the emergency exit door. "I like it," he said. "Simple yet effective, but I think something is missing."

"What? Sanity, maybe?"

"Oh, there's no sanity here. Give me a second." He looked through the nearest window and called out, "Spider? Do you have a moment?"

Spider Lau walked over to us, and All Hands was right when he said she projected the image of the black widow spider. Her entire outfit was as dark as obsidian, except for a scarlet corset. A spider-shaped pendant necklace hung around her neck. Bracelets and rings with arachnid designs adorned her wrists and fingers. Long jet-black hair shimmered beneath a crimson silk bandana and an ebony tricorn hat.

"Spider," All Hands said, squatting inside the emergency exit. "What can you offer our newest recruit?"

She studied me a moment then said, "His ears, for a start. I would put four rings in his left ear and three in his right. A nose ring would work, even an eyebrow ring. Maybe both."

"Wait a second," I stammered. "You're not talking about piercings, are you? I'm not getting any piercings."

"Pirates are famous for their piercings," Spider said.

"We all got 'em," All Hands said.

"I don't."

"You must free your mind," Spider said. "Embrace the pirate that is in you."

"How about one piercing?" All Hands asked.

"I can do one piercing," Spider said. "And if you do not want it to be so obvious, I can do it where it is not so readily noticeable."

"Where would that be?" I asked.

"I can do a small piercing on your genitalia." She shrugged as if it were no big deal.

"No, no thanks. I'm good. I'll keep things the way I have them, thank you." I started backing away from Spider but found my way blocked by the rear bumper of the bus. She stood there laughing.

All Hands seemed to be amused by it all as well.

"To your stations, mateys," Willow called out. "The tide waits for no one. Time to weigh anchor."

Spider walked away laughing. All Hands closed the emergency exit door and disappeared inside the bus. I wondered if I had made a bad decision. I thought maybe they were having a laugh at my expense, so after a moment I walked to the entrance of the bus.

"Welcome aboard, Potts," Willow said when I climbed onto the bus.

The driver grinned at me with a mouth missing half its teeth. His unkempt yellowish beard and bony cheeks made me think he had to be the oldest man on the planet. I could only hope he didn't keel over and die while driving. "Better take a seat, matey," he said, "cuz we're about to set sail."

"There's a seat available next to Crenshaw." Willow pointed to it.

I looked over at the seat he indicated. The barrel-chested man dressed in black with an eye patch over his left eye sat there next to the window. He methodically sharpened a large knife while looking at me. I had no desire to sit next to him but saw no other option, so I sat down and gave him my friendliest smile. "Hi," I said, "I'm Ben."

He looked at me and then turned his attention back to his knife, peering down the cutting edge.

"Helmsman," Willow said to the driver, "keep her nose to the wind and her tires to the pavement."

"Aye aye, Cap'n," the old driver said, and we were off.

The bus lurched forward. I said a quiet prayer, asking for the trip not to turn out to be a big mistake.

"Have you ever killed a man, Ben?" Crenshaw asked in a deep, husky voice.

"N...no, I haven't." I hoped I didn't sound too frightened.

"Are you trained in any of the martial arts?"

"No."

"It's important to be able to protect yourself, Ben. How are you going to protect yourself from an attacker if you're not properly prepared?"

"I don't know."

"Have you ever read *The Practical Art of Killing Your Opponent* by Mirumu Oko?"

"I'm not familiar with it, no."

"Get it. Everyone needs to read that book. You never know when you may have to kill a man."

"Okay."

"You never know." He leaned closer, his face mere inches from mine, and then he returned to sharpening his knife.

I spent the next few hours praying like I'd never prayed before.

3

Later that evening we stopped at a campground outside Mobile, Alabama. The ride had been long and uncomfortable. Crenshaw finished sharpening one knife, produced another, and began sharpening it. Every once in a while he would pause to tell me why it was important to keep your knives sharp or how to kill a man with some common household item like a toilet brush or a coat hanger. He even told me how to take someone out using a spatula. I don't think breakfast will ever be the same for me again.

At the campground everyone's first objective, naturally, was to use the restroom. We all hurried off the bus and across the grounds to the facilities. It became a bit crowded in the men's restroom, but we managed to work things out. Afterward I thought it might be a good idea to call my mother, so I trotted off to an area that offered some privacy and called her on my cell phone.

"Hello?"

"Mom, hi, it's Ben."

"Ben, where are you?"

"I'm at a campground outside Mobile, Alabama, actually."

"Alabama? What are you doing in Alabama?"

"I'll be gone a few days, Mom. There's something I have to do."

"Something you have to do? What do you have to do in Alabama?"

"Nothing. I don't have to do anything in Alabama. I'm on my way to California."

"Now you're going to California? Why are you going to California?"

"I have to do something. I said that. It's something Ray wanted me to do."

"Ben, what does Ray want you to do? It has to do with those no-good friends of his, doesn't it? Are you with that bunch of hoodlums? They're not making you take drugs, are they?"

"No, Mom, I'm not taking drugs."

"You need to get away from those people, Ben. Please, come home."

"Relax. Everything is okay. I just called to let you know where I am. If you need anything, just call one of the neighbors, okay?"

"When will you be home?"

"I don't know. Not before Sunday."

"Sunday?"

"I'll call you tomorrow, okay?"

"Ben, oh, Ben, I just lost your brother. I don't want to lose you too."

"You're not going to lose me. Everything will be okay. I'll call you tomorrow."

"You make sure you call me."

"I will. I'll talk to you later. Bye."

After I hung up I started back to the campsite, when I spotted Celeste walking toward me. The moment I saw her I felt as if I had been jolted with a nine-volt battery to my chest. She walked like she hadn't a care in the world. Her hunter-green skirt swayed with each step. The burgundy bodice with golden flower brocade that she wore fit nicely over her frilly white blouse. From the hem of her eggplant-colored sash around her waist jingled golden coin tassels.

"Hey," I said.

"Hey, yourself," she said as she approached.

"Where're you off to?"

"Going for a walk." Her chestnut hair beneath her eggplant-colored bandana showed hints of honey blond.

"Want some company?"

"Nope." She walked away like a wild cat determined to get into mischief. Her left leg poked out from the slit in her skirt revealing a rose and dagger tattoo on the back of her calf. I watched until she turned a corner and her shadow slipped away. I was tempted to follow but decided it might be a bad idea.

When I returned to the campsite, I found Redjack, Crenshaw, and All Hands in the process of building a campfire. Jake and Maggie were cooking a pot of stew on a portable camp stove, and Willow walked from one crew member to the next, passing around a bottle of rum so each of them could take a swig.

"Potts," Willow called, "come join us."

"The stew will be ready soon." Maggie stood over the pot. Her right hand grasped the stew ladle; her left hand was on her hip. From under a broad-brimmed straw hat long chestnut-colored curls loosely fell onto her shoulders. A white blouse with puffy short sleeves beneath a crocheted lavender vest struggled to contain her ample bosom. Her long gold-and-black floral skirt swayed about her ankles.

"Here, Potts." Willow held the bottle of rum out to me. "Have some."

"No, thank you," I said.

"Oh, come now." Willow waved the bottle from side to side in his extended hand. "You are one of us now. Drink."

The pirates began chanting, "Drink, drink, drink."

I gave in and took the bottle. The chanting continued until I took a good swig. The pirates all cheered.

We sat around the fire, some in canvas chairs and others on logs and tree stumps. I mostly listened while they talked and laughed and told stories. Most of the pirates were gathered around the fire. Maggie and Jake were busy preparing the stew, and I noticed Crenshaw off to the side throwing knives at a nearby tree.

I leaned over to Willow and whispered, "Is there anything I should know about Crenshaw?"

"Why do you ask?"

"Because the entire bus ride he was sharpening his knives and telling me about the many ways there are to kill a man."

"Oh that." Willow nodded. "Don't worry, it's just his character. He's created this persona for our pirate outings. It's his way of having fun."

"He's not going to go bananas and try to cut me up into little pieces?"

"Certainly not. It's role-playing to him; he'd never actually hurt anyone."

"I'm glad to hear that."

"Of course there is that one thing," Willow said in a way that made me concerned.

"What one thing?" I asked.

"It's nothing, really."

"Don't tell me it's nothing. You said there's one thing. What is it?"

"It's just," he leaned in closer to me and whispered as if we were co-conspirators in some nefarious scheme, "never ask him about Tortuga. It's a very touchy subject with him."

"Why would I ask him about Tortuga?"

"I don't know. Like I said, it's nothing, but a couple years ago there was this one landlubber who asked him about Tortuga, and it sent Crenshaw into a maniacal rage. The poor fellow ended up in the hospital."

"Why? I mean what happened in Tortuga?"

"I don't know. You'd have to ask Crenshaw."

Jake announced the stew was ready, and Willow leaped to his feet to be the first in line. We each grabbed a tin plate and spoon, and one by one we helped ourselves. I was beginning to enjoy being with the Scallywags. I unwittingly got sucked into their camaraderie as they laughed, joked, and told funny stories. It had been a long time since I had that much fun.

Celeste returned and joined the group without ceremony. She grabbed a plate of stew and sat next to Spider. I tried to act as casual as I could, but my eyes were drawn to her like a magnet.

"So, Potts," Willow said, "are you looking forward to the pirate festival?"

"I've never been to one," I admitted. "I wouldn't know what to expect."

"Never been to a pirate festival?" Willow sounded shocked. "Potts, dear fellow, you've no idea what you've been missing."

"It's like another world." All Hands wiggled his fingers as he moved his hand to draw a circle in the air. "A world of pirates."

"They got all kinds of things," Jake said. "Music and artwork, different people displaying and selling different stuff."

"And food." All Hands chopped the air with his hands. "Lots and lots of food."

"We'll be performing there," Maggie said, pulling Jake and All Hands to her. "We've been practicing for months, and we sound damn good."

I nodded, watching as Jake and All Hands helplessly allowed their faces to become buried in the large woman's fleshy armpits.

"And I'm sure Belasco and his crew will be there too," All Hands said after Maggie released him and Jake from her clutches.

Willow leaped to his feet, his face twisted into a scowl. "Don't ever mention that blackguard's name in my presence again."

"Sorry, Brian," All Hands said.

"And you will address me as Captain."

"Aye, Captain. Sorry."

Willow turned to me. "Potts," he said, smiling as jovially as ever. "What is it exactly that old Longbucket wants you to do?"

The group turned to look at me expectantly.

"He wants me to deliver some stuff," I said.

"Couldn't he have used UPS or something?" Jake asked.

"He is using UPS," All Hands said. "Us Poor Scallywags."

Everyone laughed.

Celeste covered her mouth with her hand when she laughed. She turned to me, and our eyes met for a brief moment.

"May we ask what the items are?" Willow said.

"I don't know." I shrugged. "It's in that box that looks like a treasure chest."

"You mean this?"

I looked up.

Redjack stood there holding the chest. I never even saw him go to retrieve it. For a large man, he moved quietly. He set the chest on the ground next to me and returned to his seat.

"Open it up," Maggie said.

"Yeah," All Hands agreed. "Let's have a look."

Everyone cried "Arrgh!" in agreement.

"All right." I gave in. "But it's nothing, really. I don't know why anyone would even want any of this stuff."

I took out the key, unlocked the chest, and opened it so everyone could see inside. They moved in closer as if they might see some great treasure, but there it all was, the shoe box, the locket on the chain, the DVD, the baseball cards, and the wooden puzzle box. I removed the five envelopes so they could get a better view.

"What are those?" Willow asked.

"Some envelopes. Probably notes or something."

"May I?"

He held out his open hand, and I passed him the envelopes. He shuffled through them, reading each one in turn.

"'Do not open until you are in San Antonio, Texas.' 'Do not open until you are in Albuquerque, New Mexico.' 'Do not open until you are in Bakersfield, California.' Interesting."

"We'll be in San Antonio tomorrow," Maggie said.

"I guess we'll find out more then," I said.

"No, no, come on," Jake said. "Let's open that one now and see what it says."

"Arrgh!" several of the pirates concurred.

"I can't do that," I protested. "Ray's instructions are to wait until we reach San Antonio."

"I don't think Longbucket would mind," Maggie said.

"Nah, he wouldn't mind at all," Jake said.

"He'd be good with it," All Hands said.

"I'm sorry," I told them. "I'm not going to go against my brother's wishes."

"I have to agree with Potts," Willow said, provoking several of the crew to express their disappointment. "Now," Willow added. "I realize you all want to know what's in the envelopes, as do I, but Longbucket was one of us, and we must respect his wishes. We'll open the first envelope tomorrow as soon as we get into San Antonio."

"Thank you, Captain," I said.

"No need to thank me, Potts. For now why don't we close up the chest, lock it, and let Redjack stow it away?"

"Fair enough."

Willow returned the envelopes to me. I placed them inside the chest, closed the lid, and locked it.

Redjack started to get up from his seat but paused. "Correct me if I'm wrong, but wasn't it a plane crash?" he said.

"What's that?" I asked.

"Longbucket died in a plane crash, if I'm not mistaken."

"Yeah, he did."

"So what I'm wondering is how did he know enough to put these things together and write you a letter?"

"Good question," Maggie said.

"I don't know," I admitted. "That's something I'm trying to figure out myself."

"A mystery is afoot!" Willow exclaimed, slapping his knee.

"Maybe he was psychic," Jake offered.

"Psychic? No way. That's all bilgewater," Maggie said.

"Jake may have a point," I said.

"What? You think Longbucket was psychic?" Maggie asked.

"I don't know," I told them. "But when our dad died Ray

did have a dream the night before. I must have been five at the time. Ray woke up and said something happened to Dad. Mom didn't believe him, but that afternoon the cops showed up at our door."

"You think Longbucket foresaw his own death?" All Hands asked.

"I don't know." I shook my head at the thought. "I'm just saying."

We sat in silence for the next few minutes.

Willow took a last swig of the rum and handed me the bottle. "We'll want to get an early start tomorrow," he said as he rose to his feet. "Maybe we'd best turn in."

He set his used tin plate and spoon beside me and walked away saying good night to everyone. Redjack stood, set his plate and spoon on top of Willow's, picked up the chest, said good night, and carried the chest away. One by one all the others rose, set their plates and spoons next to me, said good night, and went to claim their sleeping spots.

Finally Celeste walked over, set her plate and spoon with the others, and smiled at me.

I gladly returned her smile.

"Make sure you clean them thoroughly," she said. "None of us wants to eat off a dirty plate. Good night." She too then walked away, leaving me with a stack of dirty plates and spoons.

4

We sat at a corner table in a dark, dank dockside tavern. Rough-looking seamen filled every corner of the place, drinking and carousing. Two guys got into a fist fight. I don't even know what it was about. I looked at Ray across the table, a cup of rum in his hand.

"Are you scared?" Ray asked.

"Yeah, of course. I mean, I'm traveling across the country with a group of people I know nothing about. I'm beginning to think every single one of them is nuts, especially that Crenshaw guy."

"Fear isn't a bad thing, Ben. It's all a question of how you use it or if you let it use you."

"Are you supposed to be Yoda now?"

"I was trying for the Dalai Lama, but whatever."

"What's with all this stuff you want me to deliver, anyway? Who am I supposed to deliver it to?"

"Just open the first envelope when you get to San Antonio. You'll get the idea."

"Why me? Why am I your errand boy?"

"You're doing it, aren't you?"

"I'm trying to honor your last request."

"You're doing it because deep inside you know it's something you need to do. Not just for me, for yourself."

"I don't know."

"Come on, Ben. You're a pirate now. Act like one."

"I'm no pirate."

"You're one of us, Ben."

In an instant dozens of sneering pirates crowded around us, pressing in as close as they could, chanting, "You're one of us. You're one of us."

Ray disappeared into the fold as if the group had swallowed him.

One of the pirates leaned in closer to me. It was Crenshaw. He showed me the gleaming blade of his knife. "You never know when you may have to kill a man," he said.

I awoke at the campground in Mobile, looking up at the star-filled sky. The quarter moon grinned down at me like the Cheshire Cat. I wondered why *Alice's Adventures in Wonderland* came to mind. Maybe because I felt as if I had fallen down my own rabbit hole.

Not ten feet away the scruffy old bus driver snored like a cheap kitchen blender grinding gravel. The others were scattered around on the ground, tucked away inside their sleeping bags, except for the women, who slept inside the bus. By the dying campfire a lone silhouette sat with his back to me. I couldn't see his face, but I recognized Redjack and wondered why he would be up and about at such an hour. It wasn't my concern, so I curled up and tried to go back to sleep. I then realized I had to use the bathroom.

Reluctantly I climbed out of my sleeping bag and walked across the dark campground to the public facilities. After I finished I washed my hands, returned to the campsite, and noticed Redjack still sitting at the campfire, which was nothing more than a few smoldering embers by then. What I hadn't noticed earlier was the band around his head with a small light shining down on the book he was reading. With his right hand he lifted a pipe to his mouth, puffing on it every now and then.

My curiosity got the better of me, so I approached him. "Can't sleep?" I asked.

He looked up and switched off the light on his forehead. "I sometimes have bouts of insomnia."

"Mind if I join you?"

"By all means."

"Thanks." I sat on the log. The smell of the campfire rushed at me, reinforcing the smoky scent that still lingered in my hair and clothes from earlier in the evening.

"What about you?" Redjack asked.

"I had to use the restroom." I thought it best not to tell him about my dream, at least not yet. "Now I'm wide awake."

"Do you want something to help you get back to sleep?"

"No, I'll be okay, thanks."

I sat for a few minutes looking up at the sky, with its Cheshire Cat-like smiling moon and all the millions of stars. I had never seen so many stars. "It's kind of nice out here," I said. "So many stars."

"The night sky is something many people take for granted," he said. "Sailors, pirate or honest, used to navigate by the stars. Now we've got GPS."

"I don't get to see the stars often. I'm usually busy with stuff."

"You should get away from the city every now and then."

"Yeah, sure, just go out and look at the stars." Such an idea seemed almost alien to me.

"Why not? I do."

"Really?" I chuckled at his comment. Going out to look at the stars wasn't something I would normally think of doing. "You actually run off somewhere to look at stars?"

"Sure. Stargazing is one of my hobbies." He set his book down on the seat next to him. "In fact I have my telescope on The Ship. I'm planning on catching a meteor shower Thursday night. You're welcome to join me if you like."

"Sounds interesting." I wasn't sure if it was something I wanted to do, but I figured there was no harm in playing along.

"Believe me, it's much more than interesting." He pulled a half-charred stick from the almost lifeless campfire and stirred up the embers until their edges glowed a bright red.

"It must be late." I instinctively looked at my wrist and then realized I hadn't worn a watch in years. "What time is it?"

"A little after one, I'd say." Redjack looked up at the sky as if there were a giant celestial clock above us.

"Hmm, Monday night." Thoughts of what I would normally be doing came to mind. "I missed tonight's episode of *Crackdown: Miami*."

"TV show?"

"Yeah, it's pretty good." Grabbing a nearby stick I began doodling in the dirt at my feet. "You ever see it?"

"No, I don't watch much television."

"Tomorrow night there's another show, *Clinical Error*. Wednesday I usually watch *The Ambassadors*, Thursday, *Foolproof Plan*."

"You watch a lot of TV?" He took a moment to examine the bowl of his pipe.

"Not as much as I used to." I drew a series of shapes, circles, squares, triangles, in the dirt as I talked. "Movies and TV were always my way of escaping, I guess. I think it's like that for most of us. Books too. You read a lot?"

"As a matter of fact I do." He tapped his pipe against a nearby rock, knocking out the used tobacco from the bowl.

"What book is that?" I pointed at the book Redjack had been reading.

"*A Comprehensive History of Metallurgy.*"

"Really?" I stopped doodling in the dirt and looked up at him. "And you suffer from insomnia? After reading stuff like that?"

"It's actually quite interesting."

"I'm sure it is."

A loud snort caught our attention. We both looked over to see the old bus driver turning over in his sleep. Redjack looked at me and gave a little humph, which I took to be a chuckle.

"Do you usually read books like that?" I asked.

"I read a lot of books on sword smithing, some on science, some on history." He reached into his vest pocket and pulled out a small pouch and then, dipping his pipe into the pouch, he scooped out some tobacco.

"How about a good novel?"

"I typically don't read novels, no."

"What about *Treasure Island*?" I smudged out my most recent dirt drawing with my foot. "You had to have read that."

"No, I've never read it." He shook his head as he returned the pouch to his vest.

"Come on. With all this pirate stuff you guys are into? You've never read the most famous pirate novel there is?"

"No," he finally said. "I never got around to it."

"So what got you into this pirate stuff, anyway? The swords and stuff, huh?"

"The weapons, yes." He used a twig to press the tobacco into his pipe. "I forge swords and daggers and sell them at these festivals."

"Really? You're a blacksmith?"

"A bladesmith, actually."

"You make swords?"

"And daggers." He drew a small dagger from its leather sheath on his belt and held it out to me pommel first. "I made this one," he said.

I took the dagger and looked at it, turning it over in my hand. A metallic squid with menacing eyes wrapped its tentacles around the handle. The tips of the tentacles gave way to a straight double-edged blade. "Wow," I said. "You made this?"

"Yes, there's actually a story behind it."

"What story?" My interest was piqued.

He picked up the stick he had used to stir the embers of the campfire. Its tip glowed orange. He blew gently on its smoldering end, causing it to burn hotter. He dipped it into his pipe, lighting the tobacco as he puffed until it began smoking. After returning the stick into the fire, he puffed on his pipe to get it going. "A few years ago," he began, "I was selling my swords at a pirate festival in North Carolina. A red-headed woman came up to me and showed some interest in my work. She asked if I could make a dagger with a sinister-looking squid on the handle. I told her I could. She asked me to make it for her, and she would buy it the next time she saw me."

"What happened to the woman?"

"I never saw her again."

"But you kept the dagger." I handed the dagger back to him.

"What else can I do with it? I suppose I could sell it to someone else, but it wouldn't feel right."

"The only thing I've ever made was a handprint in a glob of clay. That was back in preschool, I think."

"Creativity is a form of expression. You're just expressing yourself, and everyone has a need to express themselves."

"I'm not so sure about that."

"When the time comes, you'll find it."

"Maybe." I stifled a yawn, beginning to feel sleepy again. "I'd better try to get a little more shuteye. It'll be time to leave in a few hours, and if I don't get my sleep, I'm an awful grouch."

"Is there any such thing as a good grouch?" He studied me through the smoke drifting up from his pipe.

"I'll see you in the morning, Redjack."

"Good night." He picked up his book and set it in his lap.

"By the way, how did you get your name? Redjack?"

"Because of my mustache."

"Your mustache?"

"I named it Jack," he said and wiggled his rust-colored mustache. One corner of his mouth curled, almost becoming a smile. He switched on his headlamp and, taking a few puffs from his pipe, returned to his book.

I walked back to my sleeping bag beside the snoring bus driver, slipped in, curled up, and covered my ears, trying my best to fall asleep.

In the morning I awoke and nearly jumped out of my sleeping bag when I discovered Willow crouching over me.

"Good morning, Potts," he said. "It's seven a.m. Not too early, not too late. We've got a long drive ahead of us, so time to be on our way."

"All right," I said. "I'll be ready as soon as I can."

I wanted to roll over and go back to sleep but thought that considering the group I was traveling with, I might run the risk of being stranded. I had no choice but to get up and get ready for the long drive ahead.

After a quick shower I brushed my teeth, dressed myself as a pirate once again, and joined the rest of the crew on the bus. I hoped for the chance to sit next to Celeste. I wanted to talk to her, get to know her. I wanted to find out if my attraction to her was more than just physical. As luck would have it, though, she and Maggie sat together in the back.

Once again my one option appeared to be the seat next to Crenshaw, who sat next to the window with a rope in his hand. He appeared to be tying it into a noose.

I took my seat and smiled at him in hopes that he would return the smile. "Good morning," I said.

He glowered at me, holding the noose up to my face. "Have you ever seen a man hung by the neck with one of these?" he asked.

Both my smile and hope faded.

"Everyone aboard?" Willow stood at the front of the bus facing us. "Everything stowed away?"

"Aye, Captain," several of the crew called out.

"Helmsman," Willow said to the driver. "Keep her back to the wind, a foot on the pedal, and full speed ahead."

"Aye, aye, Captain," the driver cried, and off we went, heading for San Antonio, Texas.

5

I had never experienced anything like riding on a bus with a group of people playing at being pirates. Several times when we came upon another vehicle traveling in the same direction Willow cried out, "Fire a warning shot across their bow," at which point the old bus driver honked his horn a couple times, drawing the attention of the people in the other vehicle. All the pirates then crowded around the windows and gave the other car their fiercest pirate yell.

The pirates did their best to convince me to join in, but the idea of yelling at people in another car seemed like a bad idea, especially when there were kids in the car. Their wide-eyed looks of terror concerned me. I wondered what they thought of us. Maybe they thought we were actually going to attack them and rob them or something. I don't know, but the pirates all laughed, and the bus continued on its way.

After I refused to participate the third time, Willow sprang to the seat across from me, pushing All Hands into Jake, crushing Jake against the window.

"Come, Potts," Willow said. "Why must you be so uncooperative? You are one of us now, a pirate. Time to join in the fun."

"I'm sorry," I told him, "but I fail to understand how scaring people is fun."

"Scaring people?" Willow seemed to be taken aback by the idea, but after thinking about it for a moment, he said, "I suppose we might be scaring them a bit. But it's like going to a haunted attraction at the carnival. People like being scared, don't they? They enjoy being a little frightened at times. I'm sure they all have a good giggle about it afterwards."

"But they're not at an amusement park. They're driving down the highway. People don't want to be scared when they're driving down the highway."

"Hmm, you may have a point. Nevertheless, Potts, you must learn how to let loose every once in a while. Allow yourself to be a pirate."

"I don't get this pirate stuff. I don't get any of it. Why are we dressed like pirates? Why can't we wear jeans and a T-shirt or something? None of this makes any sense to me."

"Jeans and a T-shirt? Did Blackbeard wear jeans and a T-shirt when he confronted Lieutenant Maynard and the English Navy? I think not. Did Captain Henry Morgan wear jeans and a T-shirt when he ransacked Panama? I think not. We wear pirate gear because we are pirates. If we wore jeans and a T-shirt we would be no better than Sha-Na-Na."

"I like Sha-Na-Na," I said.

"Actually, I like Sha-Na-Na too," All Hands said.

Willow glared at him over his shoulder. All Hands whistled and turned his head in the other direction.

"That's neither here nor there," Willow continued. "All right, Potts, you want to know why we're pirates? Then we'll tell you why we're pirates."

Willow jumped to his feet, allowing All Hands and Jake enough room to un-crush themselves.

"Attention, crew," Willow announced to the entire bus. "Our newest recruit, Mr. Benjamin Aloysius Potts—"

"Allen, not Aloysius," I said.

"Wants to know why we are pirates," Willow continued, ignoring my remark. "And not some other non-piratical thing, like a nineteen-fifties singing group. I believe it is time for a few testimonials."

"Hear hear," Maggie cried. "Testimonials; let's have some testimonials." Several others expressed their agreement, but no one louder than Maggie. "Give us some testimonials."

"Who would like to go first?"

"I would," Spider said. She sauntered to the front of the bus, grabbing each of the seat backs to pull herself forward.

"Thank you, my dear." Willow bowed to Spider and sat down.

"I was raised a poor orphan," Spider began, "in the cruel city of Beijing. My parents had been savagely murdered by a Mongol warlord."

"What?" I said, trying to remember if there were any Mongol warlords still around.

"When I was only nine years old, I had to steal food to survive. Then, when I was twelve years old, the great pirate Chang Shih took me aboard his pirate ship to be his concubine. I was loyal to him, and he taught me how to fight with a sword and navigate a ship. When Chang Shih was killed in battle, I took command of the ship. I became the Black Widow of the China Sea. I terrorized the shipping lanes for five glorious years."

"Is any of this even true?" I asked, looking around for someone to back me up, but the entire crew kept their attention on Spider, enraptured by her tale.

"After a prosperous pirating career in the China Sea, I decided it was time to sail new waters, so here I am, terrorizing the western world, the Black Widow of the Atlantic Ocean, the Pacific Ocean, and any other ocean you got."

The pirates all cheered Spider. She threw her hands in the air as if she had won a decathlon. The bus hit a little pothole, and Spider grabbed the nearest seat back to keep herself from falling.

"Sorry," the old bus driver shouted over his shoulder.

"Impertinent dog," Spider snapped at the bus driver.

"Saucy wench," the bus driver returned.

"Barnacle-encrusted, bilgewater-slurping offshoot of a cowfish."

"Hmm," the old bus driver said. "That's pretty good. Got me there."

Spider held up her hands in another claim to victory.

Willow popped into the aisle, directed Spider back to her seat, and asked, "Anyone else care to testify?"

"Me," Jake said. He squeezed past All Hands to stand in the aisle. He clung to the seat backs, his head bent toward me, but he looked at the others.

"As a young man," he said, "I joined the British Royal Navy. 'Sail for adventure,' they said. 'See the world,' they said. What I mostly saw was the business end of a cat-o'-nine-tails. If I didn't scrub the deck right, I was flogged. If I didn't climb aloft fast enough, I was flogged. Once I was caught picking my nose, and you know what happened?"

"You were flogged," the pirates cried out together.

"Aye, I was flogged. 'Twas the floggings made me what I am today, a poor bent old sailor. 'Twas the floggings what did this to me." Jake shoved his thumb over his shoulder at his back. "But I won't be flogged no more, I tells ya. Because I deserted the Royal Navy, and now I sail as a pirate with Captain Willow and you lot."

The pirates cheered. Jake pumped his fist in the air just as the bus hit another pothole and caused him to fall into my lap.

"Sorry," the old bus driver called out.

"Blast ye," Jake said to the bus driver. "Ye steer this vessel like a landlubber."

"Oh, shut your blowhole," the bus driver responded.

"I'll skewer your gizzard, you rusty old lice-infested cuttlefish."

"Not bad. Not bad."

Jake started to squeeze past All Hands to return to his seat next to the window but changed his mind and gave All Hands a gentle backhanded slap on the shoulder to get him to move over. All Hands obliged but returned the slap. The two got into a playful bout of slapping like two restless adolescent brothers in the back seat of the family car.

"So, Potts," Willow said to me from across the aisle. "What do you think?"

"They were making up stories," I told him. "None of it was true."

"Not true?" he gasped. "Not true, you say?"

"My story was one hundred percent true," Jake said. "I should know—I did my research."

"Research?" I said. "Why do you need to do research if it really happened to you?"

Jake started to speak, stopped, started to speak again, and again stopped, and then said, "I was flogged, I tells ya, flogged like a common criminal."

"You ain't no common criminal," All Hands said. "You're the most uncommon criminal there is."

"Thank'ee, mate," Jake said.

"Don't mention it."

I pointed at him. "You were never in the British Royal Navy, were you?"

"I—" Jake stammered.

"Port-o-call, Cap'n," the bus driver called out. "Fuel's gettin' low."

"Make for the nearest anchorage, Helmsman," Willow replied. "We must see to The Ship's needs. And if anyone is in need of the facilities, we can see to that as well."

"We'll be granted shore leave, Captain?"

"Aye, All Hands, that ye will. However, it must be a brief shore leave. We've still a long voyage ahead of us."

"I want to get me some of those chocolate cupcakes they have and a grape soda or something."

"I'll go with you," Jake said. "I could go for some beef jerky."

"You two will die from junk food poisoning," Maggie told them.

"Then let me die with a candy wrapper in my hand and cream filling on my face," All Hands said.

We pulled off the expressway somewhere in Louisiana and pulled into one of the large, modern service plazas. The bus driver guided the bus next to a pump. As soon as he opened the doors, everyone charged outside as if raiding an East Indiaman. Crenshaw leapt from his seat next to me and shoved my knees aside to get out. I had to press myself against the back of the seat to keep from getting trampled.

When I finally found the courage to look, I discovered the others had left me alone on the bus. I thought it might be a good idea to take advantage of our stop and try to call Emily again. I had hoped she would have returned my call by then but considered she might have been busy or unable to call me for some reason. When I called, however, the phone rang a couple of times and went to voicemail. "Emily, hi. It's Ben. I hadn't heard from you. Hope everything's okay. Right now I'm somewhere in Louisiana. I'll be home next week, but I thought it'd be a good idea to maybe make plans before then. You know, decide what day and time we can get together to talk. I'm open. Give me a call and let me know when you're available. Okay. Looking forward to hearing from you. Bye."

After I left the message I figured it'd be a good idea to use the facilities while I had the chance. I entered the station and passed the cashier. An elderly woman who had just finished her transaction dropped her change purse. Some money and identification cards fell out onto the floor. I stopped to help her pick everything up. When I stood up, I noticed Celeste watching me.

"Thank you, young man," the woman said, taking my hand.

"Not a problem, ma'am," I said.

The elderly woman left the store. I looked for Celeste. She headed toward the beverage coolers in the back, so I crossed to the restroom, which, upon entering, prompted my mind to scream, *Don't touch anything!*

Several minutes later when I left the restroom, Willow appeared as if from nowhere and wrapped his arm around my shoulders. "Potts," he said. "We need to talk. Come, I'll buy you a slushie."

An overweight fuzzy-bearded baseball cap-wearing guy sucking soda from a large plastic cup through a red straw approached us. "Hey," he said, "what are you guys supposed to be?"

"What are *you* supposed to be?" Willow asked in return.

"No, seriously, are you supposed to be pirates or something?"

Willow studied the guy a moment and then called out, "Crenshaw!"

Crenshaw appeared, also as if from nowhere, and stepped in between us and the guy sucking on his soda. Crenshaw growled at the guy.

"I withdraw the question," the guy said and scurried away.

"Much obliged, Crenshaw," Willow said. He led me to the slushie machine. "Red or blue?"

"I really don't want—"

Willow never let me finish. "Very well," he said. "Blue it is. I'll have the red."

I thought it best to let him have his way. I began looking around. I caught several people staring at us. Like the fat guy with the soda, they were all gawking at our pirate outfits like they'd never seen a pirate get a slushie before.

"Awesome. Pirates," someone said.

I turned to see a young freckle-faced redheaded kid smiling at us with one of those big toothy grins. "Mom," he called to a woman at the other end of the aisle behind him. "Mom, look, pirates. Can you take my picture with them?"

I never did like standing out in a crowd. I never liked wearing costumes or being paraded out in front of others. I never liked being gawked at, stared at, or even being looked at. I always preferred to blend in; it made me feel safer, but then some kid wanted to have his picture taken with Willow and me because we were dressed like pirates. Damn it, Ray, what did you get me into?

The kid ran to his mother, a short, plump woman in a flowered muumuu, whose grin and hair were identical to her kid's. He tugged on her sleeve while pointing at us and pleading with her to take his picture with us.

His mother looked our way and nodded, getting her

cell phone out of her purse. "Excuse me," she said as she approached.

"Ah, good morrow, fair lady," Willow said in his usual jovial manner. "How may we be of service?"

"My son would like to have his picture taken with you. Would you mind?"

"Not at all, not at all." Willow scanned the area for some of the other crew. He called their names as he spotted them. "Crenshaw. Redjack. Spider. Come, we're having our picture taken."

"Oh, thank you," the boy's mother said when the other three came over to pose for the photo.

"I'll hold the slushies," I said to Willow, who still held the two cups of frozen beverage.

"Nonsense, Potts," Willow said. "You must be in the photo as well."

"That's okay," I told him, taking the slushies. "I've never been comfortable in front of a camera."

"Very well, Potts, have it your way."

Willow, Crenshaw, Redjack, and Spider gathered around the young boy as the boy's mother aimed her cell phone at them.

"Come, mates," Willow said. "Give us your best 'Arrgh!'"

They all said, "Arrgh," including the boy, and his mother took their picture. She asked for another, and they did it once more.

Willow tousled the boy's hair. "What be your name, lad?" he asked.

"Zach," the boy told him.

"Zach, ye'll make a fine pirate one day. That ye will."

Willow reached into his pocket and produced a small piece of black plastic with a nylon string attached to it. "Here," he said, handing it to Zach. "Have an eye patch."

"Thank you so much," Zach's mother said to Willow. "Let me give you some money." She began digging into her purse.

Willow stopped her. "No need for that, dear lady. Allow me to kiss your hand, and that will be payment enough." He took her hand in his and with a grand gesture, kissed it.

"Oh my, aren't you the charmer?" She blushed.

"Now then, Potts," Willow said as he reclaimed his red slushie. "Let us speak of things."

"Like what?" I asked.

"For starters," he said, placing his hand on my back, guiding me to walk with him. "You don't seem to be getting the hang of being a pirate."

"Because I'm not a pirate."

"You're dressed like a pirate."

"You made me dress like a pirate." We emerged from the building and stepped out to the asphalt yard where dozens of vehicles maneuvered this way and that around each other, entering and exiting the service plaza, pulling in and out of parking spaces, and searching for any available gas pump. "You said I had to dress like a pirate to get on the bus," I said as we crossed to the old school bus.

"The Ship, Potts, The Ship."

"Whatever." To me it was just an old school bus.

"There, Potts." Willow wheeled around to stand in front of me, his outstretched finger jammed into my chest. "That's what I'm talking about. We must work on your attitude. First I want you to give me your best 'arrgh!'"

"I'm not going to say 'arrgh.'" I tried to step around him, but he sidestepped to block me.

"Come now, Potts, just one 'arrgh.'"

"No, I'm not saying it."

"A little one." He held up his thumb and forefinger and, in an almost whisper, said, "arrgh."

"Why do you want me to say 'arrgh?'"

"Because you'll feel so much better once you do. It's a release. A tiny little 'arrgh,' and you'll feel like a new man, I promise."

"If I say it, will that be the end of it? We can get back on the bus and go?"

"The Ship, Potts, The Ship."

"Fine, The Ship."

"Give me one little 'arrgh,' and we'll return to The Ship and cast off to continue our voyage."

"Arrgh," I said halfheartedly.

"Ah well, it needs a little work, but it will do for now."

"That's it. Let's go." I quickstepped to the old school bus that Willow insisted on calling The Ship.

"Do you feel better, Potts?" Willow asked as he trailed behind me.

"Not really, but the slushie's pretty good."

"Wait until we add rum."

6

We arrived in San Antonio later that evening. As soon as the Welcome to San Antonio sign came in sight Maggie, All Hands, Spider, and Jake began begging me to get the envelope and open it. I thought about it, not sure when I should open it. Should I wait until we get to our stop? Is it okay to open it now? The envelope still lay in the chest, and I figured we would have to dig the chest out from the back of the bus before we could get to it.

Redjack solved that problem. He reached behind the curtain that hung at the back of the bus where they stored everything and pulled out the chest. He set it in the aisle right next to me. I closed my eyes and thought, *Ray, is it okay to open the envelope now?* I didn't expect any response, but I sort of hoped for some sort of confirmation.

"Well, Potts," Willow said, "what's the verdict? The instructions were to not open the envelope until we were in San Antonio, Texas, and here we are."

"I guess it's all right to open it." I still felt apprehensive about the whole thing. I reached down to open the lid of the chest. Everyone's eyes bore into my back, as if two dozen assassins had their laser sights targeting me. I hoped the old bus driver at least kept his eyes on the road rather than on me. Luckily, I didn't have to dig for the anticipated envelope since it sat on top of everything else. I picked up the envelope, closed the chest lid, and opened the envelope. Inside I found a yellowish piece of paper folded into thirds, so I pulled it out. I unfolded the parchment to reveal a drawing of a map with a large black X marking a specific spot. Something had been written in the upper left corner: Give the shoes to Louis Peck. Below it was the number 520.

"Who's Louis Peck?" I asked.

"Louis Peck?" All Hands echoed.

"No idea."

"Don't know."

"Uh-uh."

Those were the only responses I got.

"It says to give the shoes to Louis Peck," I said.

"And how are we supposed to find this Louis Peck?" Willow asked.

"Is there an address or phone number where we can reach him?" Maggie asked.

"No, just three numbers. See?" I held up the parchment for everyone to see.

"That looks like a treasure map," Jake said, pointing at the parchment over All Hands's shoulder.

"You think it will lead us to some treasure?" All Hands asked.

"If I'm not mistaken," Redjack said, "we already have the treasure."

"What?" All Hands asked. "This stuff? This is supposed to be treasure?"

"I have often heard it said that one man's trash is another man's treasure."

"So we are giving the treasure away," Spider said.

"The note does say give the shoes to Louis Peck," Redjack said.

"So if this is the treasure, instead of finding treasure we are to find the people to give the treasure to."

"A reverse treasure hunt," Willow said. "I like it."

"Then X must indicate where Louis Peck is," Celeste said.

I had not heard her speak since the night before. Now that she had, my thoughts were no longer on the map. I could see nothing but Celeste. Being near her was like being on a roller coaster with a best friend, scary and glorious at the same time. My mind filled with images of me taking her into my arms, gazing deep into her almond-shaped eyes, and tasting her delectable lips.

"Potts." Willow poked my shoulder.

"What?" My daydream vanished.

"Maggie asked what location the X is indicating."

"Oh, sorry." I looked at the map. There was a drawing of a building off-center on the map. It appeared to be a stone church or something. Below the drawing were what appeared to be two roads that ran almost parallel to each other. A third road connected them, forming a sideways crooked H. A large X was positioned off-center of the third road.

"What is this building? It looks familiar, but I can't quite place it. Any of you have any ideas?" I held up the parchment, offering it to anyone who might be able to figure it out.

Redjack took the map and examined it. All Hands tried to get a closer look, but Redjack pushed him away like a father moving a child aside.

After a moment or two Redjack grunted and tapped the parchment with his finger. "The building on the right," he said, "is the Alamo."

"The Alamo?" Jake said. "Isn't that in Houston?"

"No," All Hands said. "It's in Dallas. That's where J.R. was shot."

"The Alamo is here in San Antonio, guys." Celeste rolled her eyes like a teenage girl tired of patiently explaining things to her little brothers.

I started to go into another fantasy moment but snapped myself out of it.

"In order to find this Louis Peck, we must first find the Alamo," Willow said.

"That shouldn't be too hard," Maggie said. "It's a national monument. There should be signs all over the place to tell us where it is."

"Then we must watch for the signs." Willow reached inside his coat and produced a spyglass. "All Hands," he said, "get up in the crow's nest and keep a lookout for a sign."

"Aye aye, Cap'n," All Hands saluted and accepted the spyglass. He almost flew toward the center of the bus where a small ladder led up to the crow's nest. He climbed into the metal basket, unlocked the hatch, and pushed it open. He stood inside the crow's nest with the top third of his body sticking up through the hatch. Using the spyglass, he scanned for a sign that would direct us to the Alamo.

"Do you see anything?" Jake called to him.

"I just got up here," All Hands called from the hatch. "Give me a chance to look, will ya? Geez."

"I'm just asking."

"What about the numbers?" I asked. "Does anyone know what they might be?"

"Maybe it's a street address," Crenshaw offered over my shoulder.

"I have to agree with Crenshaw," Redjack said. "We just need to find out what street the X is marking, and most likely that's the precise address."

"Now this is teamwork," Willow said. "We shall solve this puzzle in no time."

"Sign, ho," All Hands called from the crow's nest. "The Alamo."

"Which exit?" Willow called back.

"The next one, I think," All Hands said.

"Helmsman," Willow called out. "Bring us to starboard."

"Aye, aye, Cap'n."

Traffic had slowed to a crawl. Despite the difficulty, the driver managed to get The Ship into the right-hand lane and make the exit. At long last, after numerous stops and starts and waiting at traffic lights, we came into view of the Alamo itself.

"Alamo, ho!" All Hands cried out.

I leaned close to the window to get a better view of the historic building. How I wished we had time to do some exploring. There stood the famous mission where Davy Crockett, Jim Bowie, and Colonel William Travis made their final stand against Santa Ana's army. I remembered reading the stories and watching the movies. I wanted to see it all, every crack, every crevice, every stone, but we had a more pressing matter and no time, so I made a mental note of adding it to my bucket list.

"Remember the Alamo!" All Hands belted out from the crow's nest.

"Remember the Alamo!" Jake echoed.

"Remember what we're here for," Maggie said.

"Right ye are, m'dear," Willow agreed. "Potts, where to next?"

I pointed at the indicated spots on the map. "If the Alamo is here, then we need to go here."

"And where might that be?" Willow gave me a questioning look.

"Hmm." I looked at the map, looked out at the road, and then back at the map. "I'm not sure. I mean, the roads on the map aren't identified."

"So what shall we do?" Willow asked. "Travel in circles until something presents itself?"

"Maybe we should park somewhere and search on foot," Jake suggested.

"A capital idea. Glad I thought of it. Helmsman, prepare to drop anchor."

"Aye aye, Cap'n," the old bus driver said. "If I can find a spot to anchor her."

"Yes," Willow said, gazing out the windshield. "That does seem to be a bit of a problem."

"Never any parking when you need it," Maggie said.

"Why don't ye disembark here?" the old bus driver suggested. "I'll find anchorage and come back to pick ye up when you're ready."

"Brilliant," Willow said. "We shall disembark here."

We pulled alongside the curb, the bus driver opened the door, and we all filed out.

"Give us thirty minutes," Willow told him, "and meet us back here."

"Aye aye, Cap'n."

The bus moved off while we spread out.

"Hey, look at this," All Hands said, pointing at a large statue in the center of the square. "That must be all the guys who were killed at the Alamo."

"That's the Alamo Cenotaph Monument," Redjack said.

"Come on, Jake. I'll be Davy Crockett; you be Jim Bowie."

"All right, I've got my knife." Jake held up his hand as if holding a knife.

"That's not a knife," All Hands said.

"What do you mean it's not a knife?" Jake protested. "I'm Jim Bowie, and this is my Bowie knife."

"That's not a knife, I tell ya." All Hands whipped his hand out as if holding a knife. "This is a knife."

"All right, Crockett, you've had this coming for a long time." Jake waved his imaginary knife and the two began circling each other. "Nobody insults my knife."

"Your knife don't scare me, Jim Bowie." All Hands tossed his imaginary knife from one hand to the other. "Why, I killed a bear when I was only three."

"Except it wasn't a bear." Jake tossed his imaginary knife high into the air and caught it in his teeth when it came down. He took the knife from his teeth before speaking. "It was your mother's ratty old fur coat, and it wasn't even real fur."

"I'll have your gizzard for that, Bowie." All Hands threw his imaginary knife like a boomerang, catching it under his leg when it returned.

"All right, you two." Maggie stepped in. "Enough fooling around. We've got to find this place we're looking for."

"Potts," Willow said, "what exactly are we searching for?"

"According to the map," I said, studying the parchment in my hands, "the address we're looking for is five twenty something."

"Do we know which street?" Maggie asked.

"Not exactly," I said. "But looking at the street position on the map, it's very likely this one here."

"Houston Street?" Celeste asked.

"I think so."

"Our best option," Redjack said, "might be to walk down the street and look at the numbers on the buildings."

"I think you're right, Redjack," Celeste said.

"What are we waiting for?" Maggie said. "Let's start walking."

"And who made you captain?" Willow glared at Maggie with folded arms. "Or are you challenging me for the position?"

"My apologies, Captain." Maggie curtsied to Willow. "I was out of line. We await your orders."

"Apology accepted." Willow bowed, tipping his hat with a flourish. "Now then, Scallywags, let's start walking."

Willow led the way down Houston Street. As often was the case, we passed a lot of people who stared at us. None of the Scallywags paid any mind to the stares, but it made me feel self-conscious. I tried to put it out of my mind, but it wasn't easy.

"Ben," Redjack said. "Did you say the number was five twenty?"

"Yes." I double-checked the map to make certain.

"Could this be the place?"

"Maybe," I said.

Willow read the numbers above the door. "Five two oh. This would appear to be our destination."

We stood before a small old-fashioned restaurant with large storefront windows. A neon sign overhead read The Davy Crockett Diner. On the door a plastic sign read Closed, but two people were still inside. A short, rotund, gray-haired woman in a blue waitress uniform stuffed paper napkins into napkin holders. Her bouffant hairstyle made her look like she had stepped out of the 1950s. A small, middle-aged, black man in white T-shirt and slacks vigorously mopped the floor. We knocked on the glass door.

"We're closed," the man mopping the floor exclaimed without even glancing in our direction.

"We're looking for Louis Peck," I said through the glass door.

"He ain't here," he said. "We're closed. Go away."

The woman filling the napkin containers turned, looked at us, and gasped. She still stared at us when the man looked up at her, and he turned to look at us. He whipped his mop around as if to fend us off.

"What do you want?" he shouted.

"We want to know where we can find Louis Peck," I said. "That's all. We've got something for him."

"Go away, now." He shooed us as if we were a group of pesky children. "I don't know who you people are, but I ain't opening no door for you."

"Louis," the woman said. "Should I call 9-1-1?"

"Bea," he said, "hush."

"Are you Louis Peck?" I asked. "I was asked to give you something."

"Why're you people dressed like that, huh? Why're you dressed like pirates? There some costume party 'round here or somethin'?"

"It's a long story," I said. "Look, open the door so I can give this to you." I held up the shoe box.

"I don't want nothin' you got." He returned to his mopping.

"It's from Ray Potts. You knew Ray, right?"

"Ray? Yeah, I know Ray."

"I'm his brother, Ben. He asked me to give you something when he died."

"Ray's dead?" He stopped his mopping and peered up at me.

"Yes, he died about two weeks ago."

"I'm sorry to hear that." He slowly shook his head.

"Thank you. But like I said, he wanted me to give you this."

His gaze met mine and he studied me and then he scrutinized each of the Scallywags in turn. His face scrunched up as if he were thinking over his options. Finally his shoulders sank and he seemed to relax a little. "Okay," he said, "but if this is some trick to rob me, I know some people who'll put a serious curse on all o' y'all."

"We're not here to rob you," I told him. "Just please open up so we can talk."

"I ain't lettin' all y'all in here. I'll let two o' you in."

"That's fine," I said.

"Redjack and I shall go in," Willow said.

"What?" I protested. "I've got the box. Ray wanted me to give it to him, not you."

"Very well," Willow conceded. "You and I shall go in then."

The man inside the diner leaned his mop against the wall, walked over, and unlocked the door with a loud clack. He warily opened the door so Willow and I could enter.

"You be careful of my clean floor, hear?" he warned as we entered.

"Not one iota of dirt shall we leave," Willow said.

"Mm-hmm."

"Are you the proprietor of this quaint little tavern?" Willow asked. "I must say what it lacks in ambience, it makes up for in tawdriness."

"What are you talkin' 'bout? This here's a diner, not no tavern."

"Never mind him," I said. "You knew Ray?"

"Yeah, he came in here whenever he was in town. Took a lot of pictures for the tourist magazines and such. First time I met him, that's what he was doing, taking pictures of the Alamo.

Came in here for lunch and we started talkin'. He came here a bunch of times since then."

"So you're Louis Peck."

"Yeah, I'm him."

"Ray wanted me to give you this."

I handed Louis the shoe box, and when he opened it, he gave a look as if he were about to cry.

"What is it, Louis?" the woman in the waitress uniform asked.

"Ray told me about these shoes. He promised me he'd get me a pair. I never would'a thought he was serious about buyin' 'em for me though. This is somethin' else."

"Are those the shoes he was always talking about?"

"Yeah, this is them."

"Put them on. See how they fit."

"All right. I sure hope they the right size."

"Oh, I'm sure they are."

Louis sat down on the edge of one of the seats in a booth and took his shoes off.

"Hi, my name's Ben," I said to the woman in the waitress uniform.

"I'm Bea," she said.

"Pleased to meet you, Bea."

Willow stepped up beside me biting into a French fry.

"What's with the shoes anyway?" he asked. "I've never seen anyone get emotional over a pair of shoes."

"Louis is on his feet twelve hours a day," Bea explained, "and is always complaining that his feet hurt. Ray told him about these shoes that are supposed to be extremely comfortable. The problem was they're so expensive. I think Louis is more emotional about the idea that someone would actually buy the shoes for him."

"Where'd you get that French fry?" I asked Willow.

"From that Styrofoam container over there."

"Are you eating my French fries?" Bea demanded.

"I only ate one. They smelled so good I couldn't help myself."

"That's my dinner."

"Terribly sorry." He stuffed the remainder of the French fry into his mouth and held his hand up to try to hide his chewing.

Bea let go a disapproving groan and turned back to Louis, who had put the shoes on.

Louis rose from the seat and walked around. "Man, these sure feel different," he said.

"Are they comfortable?" Bea asked.

"They much more comfortable than the shoes I was wearing."

"Walk around some more. Give them a little workout."

"I'll do better than that." Louis began dancing a soft-shoe routine.

"There you go." Bea clapped.

"Now those are some fancy moves," Willow said.

"I could do this all night."

"You can't dance all night," Bea said.

"I could," Louis argued. "Maybe I will."

"Louis, you have to finish mopping the floor."

"Okay, then," Louis said, "I'm gonna finish mopping the floor in my new shoes." He took up his mop and twirled it around as if he were dancing with a partner. He resumed his mopping, but his steps had a much lighter and happier air about them.

After Louis finished mopping the floor, he shut off the diner lights and locked the doors. We gathered outside with the others and said good night to Louis and Bea.

The bus returned and pulled up to the curb.

"Your brother was a good man," Bea said as she hugged me. "I know you're a good man too."

"Thanks, Bea. It was a pleasure meeting you."

"And you." She pointed at Willow. "Stay away from my French fries."

"I shall make every effort to do so in the future," Willow vowed.

Bea gave him a playful pat on the cheek and walked to her car with her dinner in hand.

Louis stood grinning at us in his new shoes. He had his old shoes inside the shoe box tucked under his arm. "If either of you fellas find yourselves around here again," he said. "Make sure you stop in for a visit. Oh, and some of our sweet potato pie."

"We will, Louis," I said as I shook his hand.

Louis started walking toward his car but paused next to the trash dumpster. He turned the shoe box over in his hand, studying it for a few seconds. "Guess I won't be needing these anymore," he said, tossing the shoe box into the dumpster. He waved to us and continued to his car.

"It's late," Willow said. "I think it's time we find our campsite for the night."

The other Scallywags gave a hearty "Arrgh" and began filing onto the bus.

Before I followed them, I glanced back and noticed someone sitting at the counter inside the dark diner. I looked closer and recognized Ray. He still wore his pirate garb and held a coffee cup. He raised the cup to me.

"You coming, Benny?" Jake called to me.

"Benny?" I said, annoyed. "Nobody ever calls me Benny. I hate Benny."

"Fine. Would you care to join us, Benjamin?" he said in a mock British accent.

"I'm coming," I said. I turned back to the diner, but Ray was gone.

7

I stood in the middle of a street I had never seen before. Candle lanterns mounted on wooden poles provided what little light they had to offer. Half-naked heavily painted women lined the balconies of the buildings, waving to the men passing along the street. The men, all dressed as pirates and seafarers and unquestionably drunk, waved back. Every now and then one of the men saw a particular woman he took a liking to and charged into the building to claim his prize.

"Ben, what do you think of Port Royal?" Ray came up beside me with two mugs of rum in his hands. He handed one to me.

"Jamaica?" I asked.

"Yeah, Jamaica," he said. "Port Royal was one of the most famed pirate havens. They would come here to spend their loot on women and drink. It was one big party."

"I still don't get any of this, Ray," I said. "I mean, it was nice you bought those shoes for Mr. Peck, but what is all this about? Why am I having these dreams? Why do you want me to deliver these things? Why am I dressed like a pirate?"

"Why, why, why. All these whys. Ben, I'll be honest. I could tell you why, but then I'd have to kill you."

"What?"

"I'm kidding," he said and laughed his big, boisterous laugh. "Take a joke, will you?"

"Answer my question."

"I can't answer your questions. That's the whole point. You have to find the answers to your own questions."

"What does that mean?"

"Stick with it. And tell Caitlin I'm sorry."

"Who's Caitlin?"

The earth began to tremble beneath my feet. A thunderous roar drowned everything else out. It continued to grow in volume.

"What's happening?" I screamed.

"Did I forget to mention?" Ray's voice came over the thunder. "Port Royal was destroyed in an earthquake."

"An earthquake? Get me out—"

The earth opened under my feet, and I fell into a deep, dark pit. Pitch blackness engulfed me as I fell deeper into nothingness.

I awoke with a start, reaching out for something to grab and catch myself, but realized I wasn't falling. I lay in my sleeping bag at a campground outside of San Antonio. Dawn began to make its appearance, and night eased out of its way. I sat up. The others still slept soundly. Even Redjack, who had a bout of insomnia the night before, slept peacefully. I felt the need to talk about my dream and considered waking one of the others but decided against it.

Not far away, Celeste appeared. She was walking down a dirt path leading away from the camp. I wondered where she was going. I wanted to follow her, to talk to her, maybe even get to know her a little, but approaching beautiful women was never something I was good at, so following Celeste made me feel a bit stalkerish. I mean, I had no idea how to start a conversation with her. I knew whatever I said would come out as awkward, but it beat lying in my sleeping bag, staring up at the sky, trying to fall back to sleep.

The path led to a small pond. When I caught up, I found her sitting on a bench with a sketch pad and pencil. Her gaze dropped to her sketch pad then rose to the scene before her as the pencil in her hand capered across the pad. I thought I should approach her as casually as I could so I wouldn't startle her. I took a few steps forward intending to say something witty or clever but couldn't think of anything, so I turned and retraced those few steps. I tried to imagine what I could say to her.

Are you an artist? I bet you'd make a better model than an artist. No, that's terrible. Maybe you could draw me sometime, or I could draw you. Horrendous. They say a picture is worth a thousand words. How much is that one worth? Good lord, I really suck at this.

"Are you going to pace back and forth much longer? It's very annoying." She peered over her shoulder.

"Sorry." I honestly had not been aware of my pacing. I took a few steps toward her.

"Is there something you wanted?" she asked.

"Um, well...beautiful morning, isn't it?"

She stopped sketching, turned around, and frowned at me. "You really need to work on your social skills."

I thought about how to respond, but nothing came to mind. Instead I crossed my arms and kicked at the grass. Some ducks quacked as they waddled toward the pond. I thought about diving into the water with them and sitting on the bottom of the pond until the planet exploded. Again I tried to think of something to say, but my mind was a blank.

"Do you have a javelin?" she asked.

"A what?"

"A javelin. You know, like a spear?"

"Why would I have a javelin?"

"Maybe you're out hunting wild boar."

"Wild boar?"

"Never mind. Stand over there." She pointed to a spot at the edge of the pond. "And pretend you're about to throw a javelin."

I walked down to the spot where she indicated and pretended to throw an imaginary javelin. "Like that?" I asked.

"No, silly, I want to sketch you. You have to stand still."

"You want me to pose for you?"

"That's the idea."

"Okay." I struck a pose to look like I was about to throw a javelin. "How's this?"

"You have to take off your shirt."

"Take off my shirt? Why?"

"Have you ever seen anyone throw a javelin while wearing their shirt? It isn't done. They always take their shirts off before they throw the javelin."

"What Olympics have you been watching?"

"Who's doing the sketch? Take your shirt off, please."

"Can I leave my pants on?"

"Yes, please."

"Okay." I took my shirt off and resumed my pose.

"Hmm," she said with a disapproving look.

"What's the matter now?"

"You don't have much muscle tone, do you? You're a bit flabby."

"I'm terribly sorry, but I work behind a desk all day, and I don't get much chance to go to the gym."

"And you're a little pale."

"I come from a fair-skinned family. We burn easily."

"Your brother had a pretty good tan."

"Ray was different. There were times when I wondered if we were even brothers."

"Maybe you were adopted."

"Me? No, if anyone was adopted, it was Ray. Talk about your black sheep. You've met my mother, haven't you? Neurotic, possessive, controlling. It's a wonder I didn't turn out to be Norman Bates or something."

"Stand still, will you?"

"Sorry. My father wasn't much better. He was obsessive-compulsive. I mean, I never really got to know him very well. He died when I was a kid, but what I do remember…there was that one time, I must have been six or so… You know what? Forget it. I don't even want to talk about it. It really isn't something I need to get into right now. But believe me, they were something else, my parents. Both of them. And my mother, what a piece of work she is."

"Stop moving, will you?"

"Sorry. Sorry. I get a little agitated when I talk about my family."

"Just so long as you don't move."

"I won't. I'm done moving. No more moving. But it wasn't easy growing up in that house. Oh, it was easy for Ray. Ray was good in school, always got good grades. I worked twice as hard as him and never got above a C average. Ray was good at sports. I sucked at any sport I tried. He got all the girls and had all the cool friends. The only friend I ever had was Dickie Barber, and he smelled like Lysol and always had a runny nose. Strange kid. But see, that's the thing, I was always the outsider. Ray was the favorite."

"You're moving."

"Sorry." I had been babbling nonstop, so it took a while for me to register something she had said. "Wait, what do you mean Ray had a good tan?"

"He wasn't pale like you."

"But how do you know that? Did he pose for you?"

"Sometimes."

"Did you and Ray…I mean, were the two of you—"

"Sometimes."

Her answer was oddly nonchalant.

"You and Ray slept together?"

"Will you keep your voice down, please? And stand still."

"You and Ray had sex? I should have known. You and Ray actually had sex. How many times was it? I know it wasn't just one time. How many times? Twice? Three times? Five times?"

"You know what? I'm not having this. What Ray and I did is really none of your damn business, all right? We're done here. I'll see you on The Ship." She gathered her pad and pencil, shot up from the bench, and started back toward the camp.

She was right. It wasn't any of my business. The problem was I felt jealous. I liked her, I felt good when I was near her, but finding out that she had been with Ray sucked. Still, she was right, and I felt like a jerk for reacting the way I did. I owed her an apology.

"Wait," I said. "I'm sorry. I didn't mean it like that." I started after her and then remembered my shirt. I went back, grabbed my shirt, and tried to put it on while I raced after her. My arm kept getting caught in the sleeve, though, which had gotten twisted. I had to stop to untangle it, and then I hurried toward the camp, only to run into Willow.

"Potts," he said, "I must speak with you."

"Not now. I have to talk to Celeste."

"My point exactly. Come, let us confabulate."

"What?"

"Converse, tête-à-tête, you know, talk."

"Can this wait?"

"Potts, there comes a time in every man's life when he must choose between bologna and liverwurst. Now let us be honest, no one likes either, but they are relatively cheap, and a cold glass of good beer can make almost anything palatable."

"What are you talking about?"

"That's probably a bad analogy."

"Look, I really have to go talk to Celeste."

"Ah yes, about that, I think it might be best if you gave her some space right now."

"Wait a second, how much of our conversation did you hear?"

"All of it. Well, most of it. Okay, I caught that last part when you yelled something about how Celeste and your brother had sex."

"I wasn't yelling. My voice may have gotten a little loud, but I wasn't yelling."

"Potts, people in Peoria are talking. You woke up Crenshaw. Nobody wakes up Crenshaw."

"I didn't realize I was that loud," I said, wondering if it meant Crenshaw's mood would be worse than usual.

"It does no one any good to dwell on the past; however, keep in mind that Celeste must mourn Longbucket's death in her own way."

"Were they really that involved?"

"Potts, that is in the past. You and I must discuss the future."

"You mean when we arrive in Albuquerque?"

"No, I mean the future, like when we're all driving around in flying cars. That would be spectacular, wouldn't it?"

"Can't you take anything seriously?"

"Origami."

"What?"

"Origami, the Japanese art of paper folding."

"I know what origami is."

"I take origami seriously."

"Origami?"

"My family has practiced it for centuries. Well, since the 1970s, anyway. My mother taught me. Oh, the swans we made."

"Okay, I have to go apologize to Celeste."

"I thought you wanted to hear about my origami."

"Some other time. I said something to Celeste that upset her, and I need to apologize."

"You could do that, but sometimes it's best to leave things alone."

"This is not one of those times."

"Potts, I know Celeste better than you. Trust me when I say you should leave it alone."

"I can't do that."

I walked away and headed back toward the camp. As the campsite came into view my cellphone rang. My mother was calling.

"Hi, Mom," I said with some guilt.

"Ben? Ben, where are you? I've been worried sick about you. You were supposed to call me yesterday, and you didn't.

I've been sitting here all alone worrying that something might have happened to you."

"I'm fine, Mom. Sorry I didn't call you."

"Don't you ever do that to me again, Ben. You need to call me and let me know you're all right. You could have been lying dead in a ditch somewhere, full of bullet holes, and I would never know."

"Mom, I'm still alive. Everything is okay."

"Where are you?"

"I'm in Texas."

"Texas? Why are you in Texas? What are you doing there? I thought you were going to California."

"We are going to California."

"We? Ben, are you still with those hoodlums who dress like pirates?"

"Yes, Mom, I'm traveling with them on their bus."

"A bus? Who takes a bus to California? Why are you taking a bus? They do have airplanes, you know. Why take a bus when there are perfectly good airplanes that can fly you to California faster?"

"This is what Ray wanted. He asked me to travel with the Scallywags."

I watched Willow join the others to help load the bus—correction—The Ship.

Mother continued, "Ben, this is too much for me. I can't deal with this right now. It's too traumatic. I'm going to be traumatized the rest of my life because you're going all the way to California on a bus full of hoodlums who dress like pirates. I'm going to hang up now. I need to lie down."

"Okay, Mom, you take care, and I'll call you tomorrow."

"You'd better call me tomorrow, Ben. Do you hear me? God help me if you don't. I'm going to get on a plane, not a bus, Ben, a plane, and I'm going to fly out to wherever you are, and I will smack you in the head so hard in front of all your hoodlum friends. Do you understand me?"

"Yes, Mom, I understand."

"Good. I swear, I can't take much more of this. I can't." The phone clicked.

I turned toward the camp. Celeste crouched near the long-extinguished campfire packing several small bags. I forgot everything Willow had said and walked as fast as I could to offer my assistance. In my head I rehearsed what I would say to her. I was no more than ten feet from her when Maggie and Spider stepped into my path, cutting me off.

"Good morning, Mr. Potts," Maggie said. "Kind of you to join us and help with the loading of gear."

"Umm," I wasn't sure what to say at first. Celeste had finished packing the bags and was carrying them to the bus. "Yeah, that's what I'm here for, to help out."

"Good," Spider said, pointing. "You can take that cooler over to Redjack in The Ship's cargo hold."

"No problem," I said. I rubbed my hands together, grabbed the handles, and lifted the cooler off the ground for less than a second. It refused to stay lifted and returned to the ground with a crash. I stood up straight, smiled at Maggie and Spider, and chuckled. Once again I took the handles of the cooler and lifted it with all my strength. Slowly I started toward the bus's front door.

"Not that way, Mr. Potts," Spider said. "To the cargo hold. Aft." She pointed to the rear of the bus.

"You got it." I smiled on the outside, but inside I cursed them for keeping me from Celeste. I had to accept the fact that I would have to wait to talk to Celeste after I carried the cooler to the back end of the bus.

I found Redjack at the rear emergency exit handing things up to All Hands, who stood inside the bus, packing things away.

"Ben," All Hands said, "you shouldn't be carrying that by yourself."

"It's okay, really." I grunted, struggling with the cooler. My fingers began to lose their grip, but I would never admit that I needed help.

Redjack reached for one of the handles.

"I got it," I insisted.

"Let me help you."

He stood between The Ship and me, and my fingers couldn't take much more, so I let him take one of the handles, and I held the other handle with both hands. Together we carried the cooler to the back door and lifted it into the opening. All Hands helped us slide it in the rest of the way.

"I know Willow spoke to you," Redjack said to me once we had the cooler on board. "Nothing against you. We're looking out for what's best for everyone involved, so it'd probably be best if you let Celeste be for now."

"I need to apologize to her," I told him. "I can be an idiot sometimes, and when I am, I try to apologize for it."

"I can appreciate that, but this time you really should let it go."

I couldn't let it go, and since all the Scallywags seemed determined to prevent me from apologizing to Celeste, I became more determined to do so. I was also curious why they didn't want me to talk to her.

"So, why don't—" I started to ask.

"I think it's time to board The Ship," Redjack said. He gave me a firm pat on my upper arm and walked away.

All Hands closed the emergency exit door and disappeared inside the bus.

"Prepare to weigh anchor," Willow called out.

I walked around and climbed aboard the bus—The Ship. Willow watched me with a raised eyebrow. I made my way down the aisle feeling every eye on me, with the exception of Celeste, who stared out the window, chin cupped in hand. I looked at her for a few seconds and started to walk toward her, but then Jake sprang up in front of me.

"Morning, Ben," Jake said. "The thought just occurred to me that All Hands, Maggie, and I have yet to give you a sample of our music. We shall have to remedy that oversight this evening."

"Yeah, sure," I said. "Sounds good."

"We'll be looking forward to it."

"Yeah, me too."

"We're setting sail, mates," Willow announced. "Helmsman, set course for Albuquerque, New Mexico, and don't spare the sails."

"Aye aye, Cap'n."

I again tried to get past Jake, but Crenshaw grabbed the back of my pants and pulled me into my seat. "Best take a seat, mate. We're shoving off."

I reluctantly succumbed, glancing back at Celeste, who remained gazing out the window with her chin in her hand.

"Have I told you the history of the cat-o'-nine-tails?" Crenshaw asked me.

"No, but I'm sure you're about to."

As the bus, a.k.a. The Ship, pulled away, Crenshaw began filling my ears with a long-detailed history of the notorious cat-o'-nine-tails. Most of which, I suspect, he manufactured on the spot.

8

After the first hour of driving, everyone else sat in silence, keeping to their own thoughts, but Willow began fidgeting about. He slid to the inner edge of his seat then slid back against the window and leaned back, putting his feet up onto the seat. He looked around the bus at the other members of the crew, got out of his seat, stood beside the bus driver, and gazed out the front window at the road ahead. With a quick spin he turned around, facing the crew. "I cannot tolerate this any longer," he announced. "It must end now. Prepare to fire the cannons."

The bus driver chuckled, and everybody got ready to spring into action. I swung my legs into the aisle and pressed myself against the seat back, fearing Crenshaw might trample me. Without warning the bus swerved into the left lane and sped up to come alongside a brown Cadillac.

"Enemy ship to starboard," the bus driver called.

"Fire a warning shot across her bow," Willow ordered.

The bus driver honked his horn, and when the people in

the Cadillac looked in our direction, all the Scallywags ran to the windows and yelled "Arrgh!"

I didn't want to have anything to do with any of it and could only imagine the looks of horror on the people's faces.

When the bus passed the Cadillac, the old bus driver cut over into the right lane and sped up to come alongside a black SUV.

"Enemy ship to port, Captain," the bus driver cried out.

"Fire a warning shot across their bow!"

Again the horn honked, and all the Scallywags ran to the left side of the bus. All Hands and Jake were practically climbing on top of me to get to the window.

"Arrgh!" they all roared.

Willow laughed and danced a little jig in the aisle. He turned to the crew and said, "Arrgh. This is more like it. The firings will continue until morale improves. What say ye, Scallywags?"

"Arrgh!" they all roared again.

The bus driver continued to pull up alongside various vehicles, calling out "Ship to starboard," or "Ship to port," depending on which side the vehicle came up on, and the Scallywags charged to the windows on that side and yelled "Arrgh," at the vehicle.

At one point Jake almost fell into my lap trying to get past me. He reared up his head and said "Arrgh" to my face in a joking manner. All Hands took it upon himself to give me his best "Arrgh," and Jake came back, trying to top All Hands. They continued to alternately say "Arrgh" at me, making the most ridiculous faces until I couldn't help but laugh.

It had been a long time since I had laughed that hard, and it felt good.

Crenshaw then got in my face and gave me his meanest

"Arrgh," and I laughed at that. His "Arr" became louder and more menacing, so I decided to give him an "Arrgh" in return. Crenshaw roared, "Arrgh!"

I roared, "Arrgh!"

All the members of the crew stopped where they were and gaped at me.

"Potts," Willow said, "that's a damn fine 'Arrgh' ye've got there."

"Where've you been keeping that?" Jake asked.

"What say ye, mates?" Willow said. "Let's give Potts three cheers. Hip hip…"

"Huzzah!"

The crew's cheering made me feel kind of good about myself.

I must have drifted off to sleep sometime later because suddenly Maggie's laughter startled me awake. I looked to the back of the bus to see her, Celeste, and Spider huddled together, whispering and giggling. Well, Celeste and Spider were whispering and giggling. I don't think Maggie was capable of either.

Next to me Crenshaw practiced tying a noose. Across the aisle from me, All Hands and Jake were playing a game of cards and accusing each other of cheating. Behind me Redjack sat lost in one of his metallurgy books. Willow leaned against the window, hat over his eyes, arms crossed over his chest, legs spread out into the aisle. From the looks of it, he too had fallen asleep.

When I turned my head to look out the window, a sharp pain in my neck made it clear that sleeping on the bus seat was a bad idea. I got up, stepped over Willow's feet, and walked up to stand beside the bus driver. "Where are we?" I asked as I worked out the kinks in my neck.

"Outside Pecos, Texas," he said. "We should be hitting New Mexico in about an hour."

"Will we be stopping soon?"

"We'll be making a port o' call in a few hours. If you have to use the head, you'll have to hold it for now."

"No, I'm good. I would like to stretch my legs, though."

"Isn't that what you're doing now?"

"I mean I'd like to walk around some."

"Ye can walk up and down the aisle if you like."

I considered the possibility but looked back to see Celeste still chatting with Maggie and Spider in the back of the bus and thought it might not be such a good idea to go anywhere near them. "I'll be okay," I said. "Next stop should be good."

I started to return to my seat but saw Crenshaw still practicing his noose and feared another long lecture on the many ways to strangle an enemy. "You mind if I hang out here for a few minutes?" I asked the bus driver.

"No skin off my nose. Do what you like."

"Thanks..." I wanted to address him by name but realized that I didn't know it. "I don't even know your name. I've only heard the captain refer to you as helmsman. What is your name, anyway?"

"Helmsman," he said, a big grin spreading across his face. "Marty Helmsman."

"That's an unusual name."

"I'm an unusual person."

"You're with the right group of people then."

"You got that right."

I chuckled at the old bus driver and then turned my attention forward. A little plastic saint on the dashboard caught my eye. Getting a closer look at it, I noticed it had an eye patch painted over one eye and a skull and crossbones painted on its hat. "What's with the plastic saint?" I asked.

"That's Saint Nicholas, patron saint of pirates, prostitutes, sailors, and thieves, among a bunch of other types of people."

"Patron saint of pirates? I've never heard of that."

"Oh yeah, he started as the patron saint of sailors. In certain ports if a sailor wanted to wish another sailor luck, he might say, 'May Saint Nicholas hold the tiller.'"

"Interesting."

"Then I suppose he became the patron saint of pirates because he was also the patron saint of thieves. He would offer them redemption and a second chance, you see."

"That's something I never knew."

"Oh, I know a lot of things about pirates you probably never heard before. Do you know where walking the plank actually came from?"

"Didn't pirates make people walk the plank?"

"Actually it came from Blackbeard's dog."

"I didn't even know Blackbeard had a dog."

"Yep, vicious little cur too. Blackbeard's crew hated that mutt. He was always barking and biting the men. Blackbeard knew his crew hated the dog and sometimes used that fact to discipline them. Any of the crew got out of line, Blackbeard would make 'em take the dog ashore to do its business. Any man who took the dog ashore was bound to get bit."

"Okay, but I don't get the connection."

"Blackbeard named his dog Plankton, Plank for short. Blackbeard ever got mad at you, he'd make you walk the Plank." Helmsman roared with laughter.

Behind us Willow snorted. He lifted his hat and looked around in a state of half-sleep, mumbling, "What? What?"

"S'okay, Cap'n," Helmsman said to him. "All's well. You can go back to sleep."

With a harrumph and a sigh, Willow lowered his hat and sank back onto his seat to resume his slumber.

"You really had me going," I told Helmsman.

"One of my favorite jokes."

"Yeah, I got that impression."

"You know any pirate jokes?"

"Can't say I do."

"What about landlubber jokes?"

"Nope."

"How 'bout I tell you one?"

"That's fine."

"Okay. A landlubber walks into a dockside tavern full of pirates and says to the tavern keeper, 'Do you have any tea?' The tavern keeper says, 'No, we ain't got no tea. What kind of place do you think this is?' The landlubber says thank you and leaves. The next day the landlubber goes to the same tavern and asks the tavern keeper, 'Do you have any tea?' The tavern keeper yells at him, 'I told you yesterday we ain't got no tea. We ain't never had no tea.' The landlubber says thank you and leaves. The third day, the landlubber goes to the tavern and before he can say anything, the tavern keeper says to him, 'I'm warning you, shipmate, ask me if we have tea one more time, and I'll nail your bloody ears to the bar. You got me?' The landlubber says, 'I understand.' The tavern keeper says, 'All right. Now, what can I do for you?' The landlubber asks, 'Do you have any nails?' The tavern keeper says, 'No, I ain't got no nails.' 'Good,' says the landlubber. 'Do you have any tea?'"

Helmsman laughed so hard at his own joke that Willow awoke with a start, looking around him for the cause of his disturbance. Helmsman laughed even harder.

When we entered the city limits of Roswell, New Mexico, neither Jake nor All Hands could keep their seats. They moved about the bus looking out one window and then another. All Hands climbed up into the crow's nest at least five times to take a quick look around. Both he and Jake were like little children on Christmas morning. Their eyes lit up as they told us stories of UFO sightings and alien autopsies.

Willow dismissed it all. "True pirates don't care for such rubbish. Bartholomew Roberts was never concerned with unidentified objects, flying or otherwise. He identified his prize and went after it."

"You know," All Hands said, "if Bartholomew Roberts had been abducted by aliens, he would have been the first pirate in outer space."

"He would have been a space pirate," Jake said.

"Good God," Willow muttered as his brow dropped onto his fist.

Once we got into town, All Hands's and Jake's expressions went from childlike anticipation to complete disappointment.

"It looks like any other town," Jake said.

"What did you expect?" Maggie asked. "Buildings shaped like spaceships?"

"Yeah," All Hands said, "we did."

"It could at least look a little more futuristic," Jake said.

I found nothing unusual or even impressive about the town of Roswell. It looked like any other place in the middle of the desert. It had stores and churches and parking lots like any other town. Then a large sign displaying the letters UFO came into view.

"There it is," Jake cried out, pressing his fingertip against the window, pointing at the sign.

"Where?" All Hands asked, looking where Jake pointed.

"Right there. The UFO Zone."

"What's the UFO Zone?" Maggie asked.

"That's the store Jake and I want to check out while we're here."

"Despite your disenchantment, we shall be stopping here for about twenty minutes to get fuel." Willow spoke from the front of the aisle, facing us. "You may look around, but don't be at it too long. We need to get to Albuquerque."

The bus, I mean The Ship, pulled into a small, unimpressive service station on a small, unimpressive street corner. An overweight station attendant with a crewcut, a long straggly beard, and a sweat-and-oil-stained uniform stood outside the station door eating a candy bar. He watched us pull in, making no attempt to approach or offer any assistance.

"Look," Maggie said. "An ice cream shop. Who's for ice cream?"

"Oh no you don't," Jake said to Maggie. "All Hands and I are going to the UFO Zone, and you can't stop us."

"Why would I want to stop you?" Maggie asked. "I'm just saying I want some ice cream."

"You know how much All Hands and I love ice cream," Jake said.

"Yeah, you're trying to tempt us away from our mission," All Hands said.

"Go to your spaceship store or whatever," Maggie said. "You're free to do as you please."

"But you gotta admit," All Hands said to Jake, "ice cream does sound good."

"No," Jake protested, "we've been planning this for weeks now. Don't give in."

"Look," Maggie offered, "why don't I buy the two of you ice cream, and you can eat it after you go to your store?"

"Nothing wrong with that, Jake," All Hands said.

"Tell me what you want," Maggie said.

"Rocky road," All Hands blurted out.

"Jake?"

Jake stared out the window for a moment and then muttered, "Cherries jubilee, double scoop."

"Ooo, I'll have a double scoop too," said All Hands.

When the bus, Ship, or whatever, came to a stop beside the fuel pumps, Willow got off first, taking his time. Jake and All Hands impatiently waited behind him. Once Willow stepped clear, the two scrambled to get off as quickly as they could and made a mad dash across the street to the UFO Zone. I hung back, letting everyone off before me.

"Is everyone else up for ice cream?" Maggie asked.

Spider, Redjack, and Crenshaw all expressed an interest in the plan. Maggie looked at Celeste.

"You know what?" Celeste said. "I think I'll pass on the ice cream."

"What?" Maggie's voice went several octaves higher than normal. "Are you sure?"

"Yeah, I'm actually curious about what this UFO store is all about."

"All right. Have it your way."

Celeste followed Jake and All Hands across the street to the UFO Zone.

"Potts," Willow said. "What say you? A little tutti-frutti strike your fancy? Some pistachio? Or rum raisin?"

"Can't," I said. "Lactose intolerant, you know. Actually I noticed a pharmacy down that way. I need to get some vitamin C. My throat's been feeling a little scratchy." I cleared my throat for emphasis. "Must be all this sleeping outdoors."

"Very well," Willow said. "Be back aboard The Ship in twenty minutes."

"Aye aye," I said, saluting.

I started walking toward the pharmacy while Willow, Maggie, Spider, Redjack, and Crenshaw crossed the street to the ice cream shop. Helmsman stayed with the bus/Ship, filling up the gas tank while the overweight station attendant watched, licking chocolate from his fingertips. Once all the crew had entered the ice cream shop, I made my own mad dash across the street to the UFO Zone.

An odd green glow filled the store inside. An eight-foot-tall alien stood at the entrance, waiting to greet each visitor with an extended hand holding a ray gun. Behind the front counter a teenage girl with black and purple hair and wearing horn-rimmed glasses flipped through the pages of some magazine.

"Welcome to the UFO Zone," she droned without looking up.

The aisles were stacked with green alien dolls, alien masks, alien bobble heads, blue and purple flying saucers, and T-shirts with pictures and slogans. A tall, skinny teenage boy with a large nose and larger teeth stocked the shelves.

"Welcome to the UFO Zone," he squawked as I attempted to slip past without being noticed. I had no desire to alert Jake, All Hands, or Celeste that I was in the store. Luckily I could hear All Hands and Jake talking the next aisle over.

"Look at this one," All Hands said. "You pull the string and..."

"Take me to your leader," a squeaky recorded voice announced.

"I think I'm going to get a T-shirt," Jake said.

"I saw some good ones over here," All Hands told him.

I peered around the corner and saw them heading in the opposite direction. I hustled to move deeper into the store. Three aisles down, I found her. She stood before a bookshelf, flipping through a large coffee-table book of aliens integrated into famous paintings. I sidled up to her as quietly as I could. "Celeste, I need to talk to you," I said in an almost whisper.

"Ben," she said, turning to me. She backed away a little, clutching the book.

"Look," I said, trying to remember the speech I had been rehearsing in my head the previous several hours. "I'm sorry. I'm an idiot. It's just that I like you and I'd really like to get to know you, and I was taken by surprise to find out about you and Ray. I was jealous. I reacted badly. I seem to do that sometimes. A lot, in fact. But I'm sorry."

She let the book drop to the floor, moved close to me, wrapped her arms around my neck, and kissed me full on the mouth. The only way I can describe it would be it was like someone who had gone years without eating pizza finally being able to eat a slice of the best pizza ever made.

"I didn't see that coming," I said when she pulled away. I wanted more, so I grabbed her by her waist, pulled her to me, and resumed our kiss.

"Excuse me," came a voice from behind me, and we separated.

I turned to see the black-and-purple-haired girl with the glasses from the front counter and the tall skinny stock boy looking at us.

"Why are you people dressed like pirates?" she asked.

"Is there a costume party or something?" he asked.

"Something like that," I said with a big grin. I couldn't stop smiling.

"Whose party is it?" the girl asked as the two clerks

approached us. "Is it Melanie Gordon's party? I bet it's Melanie Gordon, isn't it?"

"I don't know Melanie Gordon," I said.

"That's just like Melanie, throwing a costume party and not inviting me."

"You know," the skinny boy said, "you should have a parrot on your shoulder. Don't pirates usually have parrots?"

"I know why she's doing this," the girl said. "It's because of Colin. She's still mad at me because of Colin."

"Or how about a peg leg?" the boy asked, snapping his finger when the idea popped into his head.

"You can tell me, you know. It's because of Colin, isn't it?"

"I don't know Colin," I said, finding myself trapped by the two inquisitors.

Celeste, who had managed to avoid getting cornered, slowly backed away, turned, and walked away, giggling into her hand and leaving me to deal with the situation.

"I saw a video one time on YouTube," the boy said, "where this guy put his leg into this sling and walked around with a peg leg attached to his knee. It looked real too."

"Colin and I didn't start dating until after he and Melanie called it quits, so she's got no reason to be pissed off at me."

"I'm sure she doesn't."

"Don't pirates usually have eye patches and big beards? How come you don't have an eye patch or a beard?"

"I still have both my eyes, and I shave."

"Anyway, from what Colin told me, she broke up with him. So what's with that, huh?"

"Listen, it's been nice, but I have to get going. We're leaving in a few minutes."

"But wait," the boy said.

"What?" I asked.

"Can I at least get an 'Arrgh, matey?'"

My instincts alerted me that it was a setup. I thought maybe All Hands and Jake had instructed the two to interrupt Celeste and me. Why would the kid ask me to say 'Arrgh, matey,' unless the Scallywags put him up to it? They all knew how uncomfortable I was with it. Still, the kid seemed to genuinely want me to say it.

"Arrgh, matey," I said in my best pirate impression, which to me sounded more like Daffy Duck with a sore throat than a pirate, but the young stock clerk seemed happy with it.

"Yeah," he said with a head bob. "We got a pirate."

When I stepped outside the others had already gathered at the bus, or The Ship, or the bus/Ship. Hell, it was time I started calling it The Ship, even though it was only an old school bus with a cheap wooden mermaid strapped to the front, but at that point, I figured if I was going to travel with those crazy people, I might as well accept their way of doing things and call their bus The Ship.

I remembered I had announced that I needed to go to the pharmacy, which was a block over, and I didn't want to be questioned when they saw me returning from the UFO store. I looked for a way to sneak over to the pharmacy, to make it look like I was returning from there instead of the UFO store. I wasn't exactly sure how stealthy I could be, but I decided to try my best to sneak across the street.

Keeping my eyes on the group, I began walking toward the pharmacy and ended up walking into someone. I looked to see who I had bumped into, and there stood Redjack holding a half-eaten ice cream cone. It looked like some sort of mocha/nut mixture.

"I've been looking for you," he said. "We're ready to leave."

"Uh, yeah, I was heading over," I said.

"Really?" he said. "Because it looked to me like you were heading in that direction." He thrust his thumb over his shoulder.

"I was going to take a quick look at that store there," I lied.

He looked at the store I indicated.

"Are you expecting a baby?" He asked. "Because that's a maternity store."

"You always want to be prepared; you know. Just in case."

"Come on," he said, and he took me by the arm and walked me across the street to the others, who were already boarding The Ship.

"Ah, Potts," Willow said as I climbed aboard The Ship. "Did you get your vitamin C?"

"Um, actually, no," I said. "They were sold out."

"Sold out? How does a pharmacy sell out of vitamin C?"

"I don't know. Must've been a clearance sale or something. I'll get some at our next stop."

All Hands and Jake were eating their ice cream while showing the others what they had bought at the UFO Zone.

"Earthlings taste like chicken," All Hands's toy said when he pulled the string. The others laughed, and All Hands pulled the string again.

"Six a.m. Time to annihilate the human race."

They all laughed some more.

"That's pretty funny, All Hands," Maggie said.

"It says twenty-five different things," All Hands said.

"What'd you get, Jake?" Maggie asked.

"A T-shirt," Jake said, holding up a green T-shirt with a picture of a smiling alien holding up a metal rod that had lightning bolts coming out of its tip. The shirt read, "I got probed at the UFO Zone."

"Did it hurt?" Maggie asked. She laughed and elbowed Celeste.

I looked at Celeste, who met my gaze for a moment and then turned her head to look out the window, but I could have sworn I saw the slightest smile on her lips.

"Helmsman," Willow called out, "make course for Albuquerque. We've a fair wind at our back, a calm sea at our front, and a full tank of gas. Don't spare the tiller!"

"Aye aye, Captain," Helmsman said, and The Ship was underway, easing out of the service station. The same fat station attendant stood outside the station door eating potato chips. He had been joined by two other men, a short, elderly man with a green baseball cap and a slouching, rotund middle-aged man in a gray sweater vest and thick, round glasses. All three stood watching as we rolled away in The Ship.

I turned to see Crenshaw looking at me. He held the last remnants of his ice cream cone. "So, are you going to tell me all the gory details of what happens to a man's body when he freezes to death or something?" I asked him.

"Maybe after I finish my ice cream," he said. "Then again, maybe not. We'll see."

9

Once we passed the sign reading Welcome to Albuquerque, New Mexico, Redjack brought out the treasure chest and set it at my feet.

I looked up to see every eye on me, every face filled with anticipation. "I suppose you all want me to open the next envelope?" I asked.

"I believe that is the consensus, Potts," Willow said.

"All right." I lifted the lid, reached in, and pulled out the envelope that read "Do not open until you are in Albuquerque, New Mexico." I slid my finger under the sealed flap of the envelope and slowly tore the envelope open.

"Would you prefer to use a letter opener?" Willow asked.

"I've got a knife," Crenshaw offered, holding up a small, thin-bladed knife.

"I got it," I said. "I know how to open a letter, thank you." I resumed opening the envelope with my finger, only to acquire a paper cut. With an exclamation I swiftly drew back my finger and sucked on it. I always hated paper cuts. They hurt like the dickens.

"Come on, Ben." Maggie leaned in between All Hands and Jake. "We'll put a bandage on your boo-boo later. Open the envelope."

"Hang on." I took my finger out of my mouth long enough to talk. "I don't want to get blood all over it."

"We are pirates," Spider said. "We can handle a little blood."

All Hands speculated, "You know, if we were vampire pirates…"

"You be quiet," Maggie scolded All Hands and swiped at his ear.

"Ow!" All Hands exclaimed. "I was joking."

My paper cut had stopped bleeding, so I finished opening the envelope with my pinkie. I pulled the sheet of parchment out and opened it to reveal another map.

A thick, blue, curvy line ran down the center of the map. Across and off-center of the map ran two parallel lines, which crossed the blue line and then curved downward on the left side of the blue line. In the upper right quarter of the map were what appeared to be lines and boxes. A large X marked a spot in the middle of those lines. In the upper right corner was written "Give the locket to Caitlin Bishop." Below it was the number 6542. The lower right corner had a four-line poem. It wasn't a very good poem, but then Ray was never much of a poet. I read it aloud.

"Past the View,
Across the Moon,
Beyond the Earth,
Up the Stream."

Jake reached for the map. "What's that supposed to mean?"

"I don't know." I lifted my arm to block him.

"It must be a clue of some kind," Redjack said.

"Maybe once we get there, we will see something to help us understand it," Spider said.

"I think the best thing to do would be to find the general area we need to be in," Maggie said.

"Yeah," Jake said. "What's that big blue line thing? A river or something?"

"I believe that is the Rio Grande," Redjack said. "We should be crossing it soon."

"All Hands," Willow directed, "to the crow's nest. Keep an eye out for a long body of water."

"You mean like a river?" All Hands asked.

"A river would be a long body of water, yes."

"Why didn't you just say a river?"

"Into the crow's nest with ye," Willow scolded, "before I have ye keelhauled."

"Aye aye, Captain." All Hands saluted and hustled into the crow's nest.

Meanwhile, I tried my best to figure out the poem. "Past the view," it began. What view? The view of the river? And what did "Across the moon" mean? New Mexico was mostly desert. The moon is a desert. Were we supposed to cross a desert that looked like the moon? That made no sense. "Beyond the Earth." The Earth as in the planet, or as in dirt? I was baffled.

"River, ho," All Hands called out.

"Is it the Rio Grande?" Willow asked.

"I don't know," All Hands said. "What does the Rio Grande look like?"

"Like a big river."

"It's kind of big," All Hands said with a puzzled look on his face.

"Look for a sign," Willow said.

"Cactus Jack's Real Pit Barbecue," All Hands read. "Hey, can we stop for some barbecue?"

"Not that kind of sign," Willow said. "Although barbecue does sound pretty good about now."

"Sign, ho," All Hands called out. "It's the Rio Grande, all right. There's the sign that says so."

"Helmsman," Willow said, "we take the next exit once we cross the river."

"Aye aye, Cap'n," Helmsman said.

"Now then," Willow announced, "we will work together as a crew should, and find this Caitlin Bishop. All in agreement say 'Aye.'"

"Aye!" came the resounding response from the crew.

"And who's for some barbecue afterward?" All Hands asked.

"Aye!" came a second resounding response.

"That's the spirit," All Hands said.

"Very well," Willow said. "First we find Caitlin Bishop, then we get some barbecue."

"Maybe Caitlin Bishop would like some barbecue," Jake suggested.

"Perhaps," Willow said, "but let's see how the day pans out before we start inviting her places, shall we?"

The exit took us into a residential area. My mind kept busy trying to solve Ray's riddle. View? Moon? Earth? What did it mean? There wasn't much of a view, other than rows upon rows of houses, and where the Earth and Moon came into play, I had no idea.

"Potts," Willow said, "be so kind as to read the poem once more, will you?"

"Past the view,
Across the moon,

Beyond the earth—"

"Wait," Celeste called out. "Past the view. Helmsman, stop The Ship."

"I beg your pardon," Willow protested. "I'm the captain. I give the orders around here."

"Then give the order to stop The Ship."

"Helmsman, lie to, if you would be so kind."

Helmsman pressed the brake, bringing The Ship to a stop.

"Now then, what's this about?"

"The first line in the poem," Celeste said. "What is it? 'Past the View?'"

"Yeah," I said, "Past the View."

"The Spanish word for view is *vista*. We just passed Vista Grande Boulevard."

"So we've passed the view?"

"What's the second line?"

"'Across the Moon.'"

"Moon. *Luna*. There." She pointed to the next street sign. "Luna Avenue."

"Okay, so then the poem says, 'Beyond the Earth.'"

"Earth is *tierra* in Spanish. It must be the next street."

"Helmsman," Willow said. "Resume course. Keep her steady."

"Aye aye, Captain."

The Ship continued at a crawl. Everyone watched for the next street sign, but All Hands spotted it first.

"Tierra del Fuego Terrace," he called out.

"That must be it," Maggie said.

"What's the next line, Ben?" Jake asked.

"'Up the Stream,'" I said.

"Stream? Stream?" Celeste said. "My Spanish is a bit rusty."

"Is it Del Arroyo?" All Hands asked.

"*Arroyo*, yes, that's it."

"We've got Del Arroyo Avenue up here."

"That's where we need to turn," I said.

"Helmsman," Willow said. "Hard to port."

"Aye aye, Captain."

We turned onto Del Arroyo Avenue, which was lined with indistinctive houses painted in various earth tones. The yards were small and mostly composed of gravel with patches of grass and occasional flower beds. Several small trees and shrubs stood in many of the yards like sentries guarding the houses. The quiet neighborhood looked empty except for a group of children who played kickball in the street. As we approached, they stopped their game and watched us with keen interest, as most people tended to do.

I still felt uncomfortable when people stared but told myself to focus on the task at hand. I looked at the parchment for the next clue. "Six five four two," I said. "We're looking for sixty-five forty-two."

"Odd numbers to port," Redjack announced. "It'll be on starboard side."

"All eyes to starboard," Willow said.

"Six five four two, ho," All Hands called from the crow's nest. He read the numbers off the mailbox as we approached.

"Prepare to drop anchor, Helmsman," Willow said.

"Aye, aye, Cap'n." Helmsman brought The Ship to a stop in front of the house and shifted into Park.

Our search had led us to a house as brown and unimpressive as any of the other houses on the street. A dull red Nissan in serious need of a good washing sat parked in the driveway. A small flower garden looked like it had not been tended to in several weeks, and the hedge around the house suffered from neglect. I wondered if anyone lived there anymore. The place seemed lifeless.

"Listen," I said, "I think it might be too much if we all went up to the house. Remember what happened with Louis Peck in San Antonio? It might be best if there were only one or two of us."

"Right you are, Potts," Willow said. "Crenshaw and I shall handle this."

"Willow," I said. "Captain, please, I think you and Crenshaw should remain on board The Ship."

"But then who'll deliver the locket?"

"Once again, this is my task. I'll deliver the locket."

"Very well," Willow said with an air of disappointment. "Have it your way."

Celeste, a sliver of a smile on her face, asked, "Would you like me to go with you?"

I remembered the time in kindergarten when I got assigned Sheila Cummings as my line partner and I got to hold her hand. I wanted to clap and laugh and rush to the highest mountain to scream out *"Yes!"* but caught myself and changed my tactic.

"Sure," I said, "if you want."

Celeste and I walked to the front door.

Talk about being nervous, I must have cleared my throat at least five times on the way. When we got to the door, I brushed off my shirt with the back of my hand, smoothed my bandana-wrapped hair, and cleared my throat once again. "Who has the locket?" I asked. "Do you have the locket?"

"You have the locket in your left hand," Celeste said.

"Oh, okay, I've got it. Here we go." I raised my knuckles to knock, paused a moment, and then rapped on the empty air a few inches short of the door.

"It works better when your knuckles actually make contact with the door," Celeste said.

"I know," I said. I raised my hand and then dropped it again. "The thing is, I've always hated knocking on people's doors, especially people I don't know."

"For crying out loud," Celeste said and knocked on the door herself.

"Thank you," I said, feeling humbled by her assertiveness.

"It's just a door," she said.

"I know, but there was this one time when I was in the Boy Scouts..."

The door opened, and a man stepped into the gap between the door and the frame. He held a beer can in his left hand, while his right hand clung to the inner doorknob. He wobbled a bit. "What d'ya want?" he said.

"Hi," I said. "I'm sorry to bother you, but we were looking for someone named Caitlin Bishop. Does she live here? Or if not, do you know where she does live?"

"What d'ya want with Caitlin?"

"We wanted to give her this locket." I held up the locket by its chain.

He squinted at it. "What the fuck you wanna give her a locket for?"

"My name is Ben Potts. My brother, Ray..."

"Ray?" He thrust his face forward. "Ray Potts?"

"Yes, sir. Ray wanted me to—"

"Where the fuck is that piece of shit?"

"I'm sorry?"

"Where is he?"

"He's dead."

"He's what?"

I cleared my throat before repeating, "He's dead."

"Dead?"

"Yes, sir. Ray was killed in a plane crash a few weeks ago."

"He's dead!" He began laughing. "Dead!" His laughter became even louder.

He didn't react the way I expected.

"Isn't that a kicker? Ray Potts is dead."

"Okay," I said, "like I was saying, Ray wanted me to give this locket to Caitlin Bishop."

He stopped laughing and looked as if he were about to hit me. "Is that so?" he said.

"Yes." I swallowed, discovering a lump in my throat. "It was one of his last requests."

"You can take that locket, shove it up your ass, and shit it into your brother's grave for all I care. Now get the fuck off my property." He slammed the door in our faces.

"That's a bit much," I said to the closed door.

"What the hell?" Celeste said.

I stood looking at the door and then at the locket in my hand and then back up at the door. Finally I turned to Celeste. "So where is Caitlin Bishop?" I asked.

"Come on," she said. "We won't find any answers here."

When we returned to The Ship, Willow stepped down from the entryway. The rest of the crew crowded together, their heads sticking out of the windows.

"She's not there?" Willow asked.

"It doesn't look that way," I told him.

"Are you sure this is the right house?" Jake asked from a window.

"Maybe we should try the next street up or something," All Hands said.

"I don't know what to do," I said.

Then came the laughter, which sounded like a miniature chainsaw buzzing up the street somewhere, the kind of laugh someone acquired after smoking far too many cigarettes for far too many years. "Will you look at you?" a woman with a husky voice said. She came around the hedge next door, cigarette in hand. "I saw the bus and thought it's awful late for the school bus to be dropping any kids off, and what kind of school bus has a mermaid strung up on its front grill? But you ain't dropping any kids off, are you? What are you, some kind of circus act or something?"

"Madame," Willow said to her, tipping his hat. "We are pirates. I am Captain Willow, and this is my crew, the Scallywags of Cannon Lake."

"Arrgh!" the crew confirmed.

"And may I inquire with whom we are speaking?" Willow asked.

"Leonor Hudson. Everyone calls me Lee. I was over there weedin' out my garden. Gotta look after my tomato plants, you know. I plan to win at the county fair again this year. I won three years in a row, you know. Ain't nobody can grow tomatoes better'n me."

"Lee, I'm Ben," I said.

"How do?" she said. "So what are pirates doing in Albuquerque? There ain't no ocean around here. Just the Rio Grande. Are y'all robbing ships along the Rio Grande?" She laughed, which then became a coughing fit. She pulled herself together after a few moments.

"We're looking for someone," I told her.

"I hope it's not Dan," she said, waving her cigarette toward the house we were parked in front of. "Ain't nobody looking for Dan these days. Hasn't exactly been the best neighbor these past few months, you know. Always angry at the world. I'm afraid one of these days he just may end up buying a gun and either shooting himself, or someone else. Hope it ain't me."

"Dan? The man who lives here?" I asked, pointing at the house.

"That's him. Used to get along with him real good. We'd have them over for barbecues and parties and such. He ain't been the same since Caitlin died."

"Wait," I said, "are you talking about Caitlin Bishop?"

"Of course. She was Dan's wife. She was also my best friend. She and I used to get together for coffee all the time and talk up a storm. Some of the things we shared, good Lord, it ain't the kind of stuff you share in mixed company. But we talked about it in private. We sure did."

"You said she died? When?"

"Must have been a few months ago. We all went to her funeral. Dan sat in the corner the whole time eyein' everyone that came in. I know he was looking for that feller, Ray. Good thing he didn't show up though. Dan would have murdered him."

"Would that be Ray Potts?"

"Yep, Ray Potts. If Dan ever got his hands on him, he'd strangle him to death if he could. You all know Ray? If you do, you'd best tell that boy to stay as far away from here as he can. I don't need no police investigation around here. Don't want to see Dan arrested for murder neither, even though he ain't been much of a neighbor lately."

"You don't need to worry about that, Leonor," I said.

"No? Why not? Don't tell me Ray's run off and joined the Foreign Legion? Or maybe he became a priest or something? Wouldn't that be a kick? Is he Catholic?"

"No, Ray's dead."

"What?" She coughed up the cigarette smoke she had been inhaling. "Good Lord, when did that happen?"

"A couple weeks ago," I said.

"What happened?"

"He died in a plane crash."

"Dear Lord. Well, now they're both dead. Maybe they'll find each other in the afterlife and Dan can get on with his life. Although I doubt he will."

"Do you mind if I ask what happened? Who exactly was Caitlin Bishop, and how did she know Ray?"

"I don't know exactly how they met, but Caitlin was in love with Ray. I never saw nobody so ga-ga over anybody as much as Caitlin was over Ray. She used to wear out my ears telling me about all the things Ray did in his travels. Boy, that girl could talk. Never could get a word in edgewise the way she kept yammering."

"Don't you hate people like that?" Willow asked, a big smile on his face.

Leonor dropped the butt of her cigarette on the sidewalk and crushed it with her heel. She pulled out a fresh cigarette, lit it, and continued her story. "She'd been married to Dan for six years maybe. Never had any kids. She always wanted some. Kept talkin' about having kids with Ray. She wasn't happy with Dan. Never was, so she was going to run away with Ray. She told Dan, and he blew up. Had himself a real temper tantrum, you know. He never hit her or nothin'. That's one thing I'll say for him. He never hit a woman, but he did have a terrible temper. There was that one time a few years ago when he got drunk, and some guy was tryin' to give Caitlin the time of day, you know what I mean? Well, Dan wasn't gonna have none of it, and he beat that guy silly. Took four big men to pull him off the guy. He spent some time in jail for it, but he never hit Caitlin, far as I know anyway."

"So what happened with her and Ray?" I asked.

"She was supposed to meet Ray at the airport," Leonor

continued. "They was gonna fly away together, so she told Dan she was leaving. He was yelling at her, threatening to kick Ray's ass, all kinds of things. She got into her car, and he was chasing after her. She was driving down the street, and he was running after her on foot, hollerin' after her. Finally he goes back into the house, slamming the door, and starts playing music real loud. We could hear him inside breaking things, yelling all kinds o' stuff.

"We were about ready to call the cops on him. But then we thought someone had beat us to it, because about an hour later the cops showed up. But they didn't show up because someone was complaining about the noise. They showed up to let him know that Caitlin was killed in a car crash. Either she ran a red light or a truck ran a red light. I don't know exactly. Her car was hit by one of them eighteen wheelers, and she was already dead when the ambulance got there."

"That's terrible," Maggie said.

I glanced at the others. Willow leaned against The Ship, eyes down, forefinger to his mouth. Celeste looked as if she was almost in tears. She quickly turned and climbed aboard The Ship. The others leaned out the windows, murmuring to each other.

"I know. I know," Leonor said. "I was heartbroken when I heard the news too. I kept thinking there had to be something I could'a done. But it was too late."

"I don't know what to do now," I said.

"What can you do?" Leonor said. "What can any of us do? There ain't nothin' to do."

"Leonor," I said, "Ray wanted me to give this locket to Caitlin." I dangled the locket by its chain so she could see it. "Now I don't know what to do with it."

"Let me see that." She took it from me. She looked at it

closely, turning it over in her hand, examining every detail. "My, my, this locket belonged to Caitlin's great-grandmother. It's been in her family for years."

"Are you sure?"

"I'm positive. I've seen it plenty of times." She opened the locket to reveal two small portraits inside, one of a man with a large bristle mustache and the other of a woman with her hair tied in a bun. It looked like the photos had been taken more than a hundred years earlier.

"See that?" Leonor said. "That's her great-grandma and her great-grandpappy. If she had any kids, I'd say give it to them, but she didn't have any kids." She handed the locket back to me.

"It wouldn't be right for me to keep it," I said.

"Perhaps you could put it with your other buried treasure," Willow suggested. "Pirates are supposed to keep their treasure buried, you know."

"Buried?" I had a thought. "Leonor, do you know where Caitlin is buried?"

"I surely do. I go there every Thursday, weather permitting."

"Can you tell us how to get there?"

"Why sure. It ain't that hard. You may want to write it down though."

10

It took us only about fifteen minutes to get to the memorial park. Using Leonor's directions, we argued over whether we were supposed to turn left at the headstone with the cherub on it or right at the tombstone with the Virgin Mary on it. Leonor didn't seem to be quite certain herself when she gave us the directions. Eventually we found the elm tree Leonor told us to look for. Spider pointed it out. She seemed to know a lot about trees. Personally I don't know one from the next.

"Do you need a shovel?" Willow asked as I disembarked from The Ship.

"We're not robbing her grave," I said. "I'm going to dig a small hole. I can do that by hand."

Celeste followed me off The Ship.

I stopped and turned to her. "I can handle this alone."

"I started this with you," she said. "We're finishing it together."

"Is it that important to you?"

"Yes," she said as she brushed past me and walked up the

hill. I wanted to ask why it mattered to her but thought better of it and followed her to Caitlin Bishop's grave.

The headstone was a small block of marble with a plaque on the top that showed Caitlin's name, her year of birth, and her year of death. It seemed sad that she had such a simple memorial, but perhaps Dan wasn't willing to spend much on her. After all, she did leave him to be with Ray.

I stood for a few minutes looking down at the headstone, trying to decide the best way to carry out my task. I glanced up at Celeste, but she remained silent and appeared to be in thought. I decided to handle the situation the same way I would if Caitlin were alive.

"Caitlin, hi. I'm Ben. Ray's brother. I'm sorry to tell you this, but Ray died in a plane crash a few weeks ago. I know it sucks the way things turned out for the two of you. It didn't work out the way you had hoped, but Ray wanted me to give you back your locket. Anyway, if you never got your happiness in this life, I hope you find it in your next life, wherever that may be."

I squatted and dug a hole at the foot of the headstone. I placed the locket inside the hole and shoved the dirt in on top. Standing up, I brushed my hands off and sighed. "That's the best I can do, I guess."

"I'm sure it's fine," Celeste said.

"Are you all right? You seem saddened by the whole thing. I mean, you never knew her, did you?"

"No, I'm fine."

"I was thinking, since both Ray and Caitlin are, well, dead, maybe they'll be reunited in the afterlife. I mean, they obviously loved each other. Maybe they were soul mates, so they should be able to spend the afterlife together. Don't you think?"

When I turned to look at Celeste, I saw what appeared to be a tear in her eye, but I had little time to confirm my suspicions. Without warning she slapped me across the face. I reeled from the impact. She turned and walked away, leaving me to rub the sting out of my cheek, wondering what happened.

With little recourse, I walked to The Ship behind her. I didn't try to catch up. Instead I made sure to keep my distance.

Before I climbed into The Ship, something told me to turn around. When I did, I saw someone standing over Caitlin's grave. I couldn't make out any features, but I knew it had to be Ray. I felt an urge to go to him to comfort him, but I had no idea how to comfort a ghost, so I climbed aboard The Ship.

A few hours later we were at our campsite, gathered around a campfire, eating barbecued chicken and ribs, coleslaw, corn on the cob, and fried potato wedges from Cactus Jack's Real Pit Barbecue. The Scallywags seemed to be uncharacteristically content. Even Jake and All Hands, who were usually playful and mischievous, sat serenely eating their food with relish. Willow took charge of the rum bottle, making sure it got passed to everyone, especially to himself at least twice as much as everyone else.

Only Celeste remained dispassionate about everything. She took small, incurious bites of her food and the occasional sip of rum when someone offered it to her. Not a word passed her lips. She gazed into the fire and occasionally looked at the others if they spoke, but her eyes never so much as glanced my way. We had not spoken since she slapped me at the memorial park. No one mentioned the incident or even asked about it.

Other than the red mark on my cheek, it was like it had never happened.

For my part I felt no anger or resentment. I couldn't understand how she could go from kissing me in Roswell to slapping me in the face in Albuquerque. Of course, trying to figure women out was far from my strong suit. Other guys, Ray for example, seemed to have some grasp on what made them tick, but not me. Never me.

As I pondered these things, I remembered I should call my mother, another woman I could never figure out or ever hope to. I finished cleaning the meat off the chicken leg I had been eating, grabbed one of the moist towelettes that had come with the meal, and excused myself to find someplace that offered more privacy.

My mother's phone rang longer than usual, but she eventually picked up. "Hello?" Her voice sounded a little hoarse.

"Mom, it's Ben. Are you okay? Did I wake you?"

"Ben, oh Ben, the most terrible thing has happened."

"What? What's wrong? Are you okay?"

"Mr. Barker is dead." She let go a little sob.

"Mr. Barker? Who's Mr. Barker? Was he that old man who lived in the beige house on the corner?"

"No, that's Mr. Bronson. He's still alive."

"Then who's Mr. Barker?"

"You know very well who Mr. Barker is."

"I'm sorry, Mom. I don't remember any Mr. Barker."

"Benjamin, how could you be so callous? Mr. Barker was my goldfish."

"You had a goldfish?"

I had forgotten Mom had goldfish. She was allergic to dog and cat fur, and birds terrified her, so she kept goldfish. The aquarium sat in a corner of the den and, in my opinion, somehow blended in with everything else in the room. I found it boring and paid it no mind. "Listen, Mom, I'll buy you another goldfish when I get home. How about that?"

"Do you really expect me to replace Mr. Barker so easily?"

"Mom, it's a goldfish. You flush it down the toilet and buy a new one."

"How can you be so cruel to your own mother?"

"I offered to buy you another goldfish. How is that being cruel?"

"I suppose since your brother passed away, I should go out and buy a new son?"

"How can you compare Ray to a goldfish?"

"I don't know, Benjamin. Can't you tell I'm distraught? You've abandoned me in my time of need to go gallivanting across the country. I don't know what to do."

"I'm sorry. I know it's hard on you. I'll be home in a few days, and we can talk then. We'll have a funeral for your goldfish if you want."

"Don't patronize me. I am not a child. I can bury Mr. Barker myself. I'll place him among the azaleas."

"There you go. I'm sure he'll be fine there."

"Yes, Benjamin, I have everything under control. There is no longer any need for you to come home."

"Don't start that. What do you want me to do?"

"Nothing, Benjamin. Since you refuse to be here when I need you, I want you to do nothing."

"Mom, please, you know I'm not refusing to be there. I can't be there."

"I don't see the difference. Either way you're not here."

I wanted to smash my phone against a nearby tree. Instead I screamed with my mouth tightly closed, shaking the phone as if strangling it.

"Benjamin? Benjamin, are you there?" Her voice came through the phone as I put it back to my ear.

"Yes, Mom, I'm here."

"I asked if you were staying warm. I know how the chill can affect your sinuses."

"I'm fine. There's no need for you to worry about me."

"You're my son, Benjamin. I will always worry about you."

"I know, Mom. Thank you."

"It's what mothers are for."

"I know, Mom. I appreciate it."

"Benjamin, when you get home, you'll have to bury Mr. Barker for me. You'll do that, won't you?"

"Of course, Mom."

"I'll keep him in a bucket full of ice until then."

"You could keep him in your freezer."

"I certainly will not. That's where I keep my food and ice. I'll not keep Mr. Barker in my freezer."

"My mistake. A bucket full of ice should do the trick."

"And Benjamin."

"Yes, Mom?"

"I hope you're not letting your hoodlum friends talk you into doing anything illegal. I don't want a criminal for a son."

"Of course not, Mom."

"Good night, Benjamin."

"Good night, Mom." I bit my lip as I hung up. My mother had a bad habit of driving me nuts. As a way to get out my frustrations, I resorted to kicking and punching the empty air while spewing profanities until I realized I was being watched. Across the lot a family of four stood outside their RV. They stared at me with eyes wide and mouths agape.

"Good evening." I waved to them. "Nice weather we're having."

Without responding the father hustled his family into their RV, watching me over his shoulder the whole time. As soon as he closed the door to the RV, a single click informed me he had locked his family inside. All four faces appeared at four different windows, gazing out in my direction. Feeling awkward at the turn of events, I walked back to my own camp.

When I returned to the crew, my ears caught the airs of some lively tune, and I came upon a welcome sight. Jake played his guitar, All Hands tapped his bongos, and Maggie sang. Willow danced a little jig around the campfire. He pulled Spider Lau to her feet, and she danced with him while the others clapped to the rhythm of the music. I couldn't help but smile as I moved closer.

When the song ended, Jake waved me over. "Come on, Ben," he said. "We've got a special song for you."

"What's it called? 'The Man Who Ruined Our Trip?'"

"Come on," All Hands said, "don't be like that. It's called 'There's a Little Pirate in Us All.'"

The three of them began performing their song.

"I met a man in a business suit
with silver cufflinks and black leather boots.
I asked him, 'Mate, have ye been to sea?'
'No, sir,' he said, 'that isn't for me,'
Yo-ho-ho-ho, it isn't for me.'"

Willow and Spider began dancing around the fire again, until Redjack stepped up and tapped Willow on the shoulder. Willow bowed to Redjack, Redjack bowed to Willow, and Redjack and Spider danced together. Willow crossed to Celeste, extending his hand to her with a sweeping gesture. Celeste took his hand and rose to her feet. She and Willow joined in the dancing. As the song continued, the two couples danced around the fire. On their third or fourth pass, Willow and Celeste stopped in front of me.

"Potts," Willow said, gasping for breath, "would you be so kind as to take over for me?"

The request surprised me, since earlier that day the entire crew did its best to keep me from Celeste. Now Willow was asking me to dance with her. The gesture made me feel apprehensive. "I don't dance," I said. Honestly, I had always been a terrible dancer. Anytime I ever tried I ended up stepping on my partner's toes. Even when my mother sent me to a dance class when I was in the fourth grade, I often stepped on the teacher's toes.

"Potts, we have a rule here. No one may refuse a dance, so be so kind as to take over for me. I seem to be out of shape these days."

With no discernable way out of the situation, I took Celeste by the hand and did my most awkward best to dance with her around the fire. Redjack and Spider easily skirted past us. Willow sat down between Crenshaw and Helmsman, accepted the rum bottle Crenshaw proffered, took a good swig from it, and passed it to Helmsman, who tipped it in thanks.

I did my best to avoid stepping on Celeste's feet. Of course the inevitable happened, and Celeste yelped and hopped back a few steps, favoring her right foot.

I could hear the others laughing. "Sorry, sorry, sorry," I said.

"It's okay." She winced at the pain and gingerly put her foot down, shifting her weight to test the damage I had caused.

"I'm sorry. I'm a terrible dancer."

"It's fine. Here, let me show you something." She took my hands and resumed our dance position. "What you want to do is stand slightly to my left so our feet aren't lined up with each other. Okay? That way you won't step on my toes."

"You sure that will help?" I asked.

"Trust me. Stay a little to my left. You ready to try again?"

"They're your toes, not mine."

"I'll consider myself forewarned."

As uncertain as I felt, we resumed the dance. At first I focused on keeping slightly to her left. Perhaps I focused on it a little too much. It became something of an obsession, and I started thinking I should be enjoying the dance, but I wasn't. In fact I felt stiff and awkward. People always say to relax and let the music flow through you. How do you do that, though?

Celeste then smiled at me, and it was all I needed. Nothing else mattered. The drive to California didn't matter, Being Ray's delivery boy didn't matter, My mother's phone calls didn't matter. Nothing mattered but Celeste and me. There were no other crew members. There was no campground. There was no fire. There was no music.

It dawned on me there was no music. Maggie, Jake, and All Hands had stopped playing. I stopped dancing and looked around. They were putting their instruments away. The rest of the crew was preparing to call it a night.

"That's it?" I asked. "I thought we were just getting started."

"We have a long voyage ahead of us, Potts," Willow said.

"Don't want me falling asleep at the helm, do ye?" Helmsman asked.

"Course not," Willow answered for me. "Your turn to clean up, Potts."

"It's always my turn to clean up."

"Funny how it works out that way. Good night, Potts."

"Sure. Good night."

"Don't worry," Celeste said. "I'll help you. But just this one time. We don't want you to get spoiled."

"Thanks."

"So how's your face?"

"My face?" I touched my cheek where Celeste had slapped me. "Oh, you mean because of…at the cemetery. It's okay. It stung for a little while, but it's fine now."

"I'm sorry about that. It wasn't your fault your brother was in love with someone else."

Of course, all the good women fell for Ray over me. "Is that why?" Her comment stung me, but I did my best to hide it. "I was wondering what I had said."

"Are you enjoying your life among us Scallywags?" She smiled as she changed the subject.

"It takes some getting used to, but I have to admit that overall, I've enjoyed these past few days. Of course it would have been nicer to be able to stay in a hotel at least once in a while."

"Camping out is part of the whole experience."

"I guess. I've never been the outdoorsy type."

"You'll survive."

"You mind if I ask you something?"

"Be my guest."

"How'd you get involved in this pirate stuff?"

"I'm a tattoo artist. David Belasco was one of my customers. He sells period costumes, like pirate clothing. All my pirate garments come from Belasco's store."

"Belasco? Why does that name sound familiar?"

"He and Willow were once best friends. They started the Scallywags of Cannon Lake crew together, but they had a falling out. I think it was when David moved to California. I'm not really sure."

"Belasco got you into the whole pirate lifestyle?"

"I wouldn't exactly call it a lifestyle. But Belasco hired me as one of his models. Go to his website, and you'll see a few pictures of me modeling his fashions."

"I'll have to do that the next time I get a chance."

"This pirate lifestyle, as you call it, is a lot of fun. Going to the festivals, dressing up, and playing pirate. Of course we've never done it for an entire week like this before."

"I don't know. Going around saying 'Arrgh,' letting people take pictures of you. It's not really for me."

"Give it a chance. Anyway, I think we're done here. I'm going to turn in. You have a good night."

"Yeah, you too. Wait."

"What for?"

"Listen, maybe after all this is over, I was wondering if maybe you and I could get together sometime. You know, have dinner or something."

"Maybe. Good night, Ben."

"Good night, Celeste."

11

The sun hovered above the ocean horizon. It neither rose nor set, but rather waited. A half-dozen shipwrecks lay stranded on the rocky outcrops offshore. They leaned to one side or the other, as if attempting to outdo each other in impersonating the Tower of Pisa. There lay a ship graveyard. I stood on the rocky shore littered with bits and pieces of wreckage, a broken mast here, a rusted cannon there, a ship's barnacle-encrusted wheel. At the edge of the shore someone sat on a large flat rock staring out to the horizon. I recognized Ray. He and the sun seemed to be in silent communication with each other. I leaped from stone to stone, cautiously making my way to him.

"I don't know where she is, Ben," Ray said when I sat down beside him. Somehow I knew he referred to Caitlin Bishop. "I thought when people died they were met by all their loved ones who passed away. If she's here in the afterlife, why haven't I seen her?"

"I'm sorry, Ray," I told him. "I don't know. I'm sure you'll find her though."

"Where do I even look? I mean, do you know how vast the afterlife is? It's humongous, and there's no map available. There's no directory or any kind of information desk to go to. I could be wandering this place forever and still never find her."

"Come on, I'm sure it'll all work out. Anyway, I thought the whole point of these meetings was for you to guide me."

"I never said that."

"Then why do you keep popping up in my dreams like this?"

"They're your dreams, Ben. Not mine."

"But I'm on this quest for you. I'm traveling across the country to be your delivery service."

"I've been trying to tell you there's more to it than that."

"Like what? At least give me a hint of what I'm supposed to do."

"You'll know when the time comes. Keep doing what you're doing."

"You're not offering much help."

"Then I guess I might as well be on my way." Ray jumped to his feet and started leaping from rock to rock up the shoreline.

"Wait! I didn't say you had to go."

"Don't worry, Ben. I'll be around. I'm not deserting you."

He skipped away across the rocks. I watched him for a moment, then noticed something large out of the corner of my eye. It shot up out of the water and came down with a crash, smashing one of the old, abandoned, rotting ships.

"Ray," I called, "did you see that?"

I looked for him, but he was nowhere to be seen. I turned my attention to the bay. Something was out there, and it was big and dangerous. About twenty feet offshore, the water surface began bubbling, a little at first, and then it became more violent, like a cauldron about to boil over. From the midst of the angry gurgling something large and dark burst out, rocketing skyward. I looked up to see a giant tentacle towering overhead like a twenty-story building. An instant later it dropped on top of me.

I woke up to a relatively quiet camp. The fire had all but died out. Thin traces of orange glow quivered under the blackened firewood, as if the embers were desperately trying to find something left to burn. I heard Helmsman snoring and wondered how anyone could sleep through that noise. I had learned my lesson after the first night and made sure to place my sleeping bag as far from him as possible. The thought of asking Willow to leave me at a hotel became more tempting with each passing night, but I chose to make the best of the situation, at least for one more night. I turned on my side and somehow managed to fall asleep after a while in spite of Helmsman snoring like a jackhammer in an echo chamber.

When I woke up again, the sun began to peek out over the horizon. Several of the other pirates were already up and about their business. Redjack and All Hands were stowing gear; Willow and Helmsman were examining a roadmap. I spotted Celeste as she wandered off with her sketch pad. I thought about following her but decided she probably wanted to be alone. Besides, I needed to use the restroom.

After taking care of my morning routine, I thought about Emily. I still had not reached her, and from the looks of things I had a few moments to try to make another attempt. This time she answered.

"Hello?"

"Emily, hi, it's Ben."

"Ben, I really can't talk. I'm leaving for work."

"I only need a second."

"What is it?"

"Look, I screwed up, I realize that. I just…I don't want things to end the way they did."

"And how do you want things to end?"

"I don't know. Amicably? I mean I'd like to get together and talk about it over lunch or coffee or something."

"There's nothing to talk about. I'm sorry. I'm with someone else now. Let it go, Ben."

"But we were always so good together. I mean I always liked being with you and I thought you liked being with me too."

"I did. There's too much baggage, though."

"When you say too much baggage you mean my mother, don't you?"

"Look, Ben, you're a good guy, and you deserve to be happy. I want you to be happy, but I'm not going to sacrifice my own happiness. Not for you, not for anyone."

"Yeah, I get it. Listen, I do care about you, and if your happiness is somewhere else or with someone else, then I guess that's where you should be."

"Look, I really have to go. Take care of yourself. Okay?"

"Yeah, you too."

I pressed the end-call button and remembered the engagement ring still in my pocket. I reached in and pulled out the jewelry box to look at the ring. The whole thing suddenly seemed silly, running out, buying the ring, keeping it for as long as I did. Why did I even still have the thing? I needed to get rid of it. I considered burying it somewhere like I did with Caitlin's locket, but that didn't seem right. A trash can stood not too far away. I considered throwing it away. I wasn't so sure that I should. Maybe I should sell it. I probably wouldn't get much for it. No, it'd be too much trouble to try to sell it. I walked to the trash can and raised my arm to toss it in.

Again, I thought about selling it. I didn't want to lug it around anymore, though. I turned back to the trash can, and before I could change my mind again, I slam-dunked the ring and box into the can. I hated myself for screwing the whole thing up. Why did I even buy the stupid thing? Why didn't I give it to her when I first bought it? Stupid, stupid, stupid.

"Are you all right?"

I turned to see Celeste standing beneath a tree, drawing pad and pencil in hand.

"Were you eavesdropping?"

"No, I was sketching."

"Not me, I hope."

"I've already tried that. You're a terrible model."

"Yeah, I seem to be terrible at a lot of things. Maybe I'm just terrible at life in general."

"If that's what you want, sure."

"No, it's not what I want."

"Then change it."

How many times have I heard someone say "just change it" or something like that? "If you don't like the way your life is going, then change it." Every time I heard someone say something like that, I couldn't help thinking, "Sure, easy for you to say." How do you change the direction your life was heading when you felt like you had no control over where you're heading? I had to put that question to her. "Okay," I said. "So how—" But when I turned back, she was gone.

"There you are, Potts. Catch."

I turned in time to see something big and heavy flying at

me. I dodged, and the object struck the ground. I looked to see a cutlass sticking out of the ground, handle up.

"Are you crazy?" I yelled at Willow. "You could have killed me."

"Not likely," Willow said. "That blade couldn't cut through butter on a hot day in the Sahara. It's a prop sword."

"What am I supposed to do with it?" I cautiously plucked it from the dirt.

"In two days, Potts, we will be at the Palo Alto Pirate Festival, and we will be required to take part in a minor skirmish."

"A minor skirmish? What do you mean a minor skirmish?"

"Nothing to be concerned about. A friendly little exchange. Like when you played war as a kid. Lots of 'pow, pow, pow.' That sort of thing. It'll be fun, really."

"And we'll be using real swords?"

"Prop swords."

"I've never used a sword before."

"We thought as much. For the next couple days, you'll be learning the basics."

"You're going to teach me how to use a sword?"

"Not me. I'm the captain. That's not my job. That's a job for our master-at-arms."

"And who's the master-at-arms?"

"Crenshaw, of course."

I had little time to react, as Crenshaw leapt at me from behind a bush, screaming like a crazed banshee. I raised my sword to protect myself from his attack.

"That's it, Potts," Willow said. "Parry. Parry. Keep it up."

All I could do was keep my sword between myself and Crenshaw to prevent him from hitting me.

"You may want to counterattack every now and then too, Potts."

"Counterattack? How am I supposed to counterattack?"

"I'm certain you'll figure it out. I'll leave the two of you to your training. Don't be too long at it, though, we've got a long voyage ahead of us, and much to do."

"Willow! Wait, you can't leave now." But he was gone. My only recourse was to get Crenshaw to stop his vicious attack.

"Is this how you teach sword fighting?" I asked. "Attacking your trainee?"

"How do you teach a powder monkey to swim?"

"A what monkey?"

"You toss him into the ocean, and if he doesn't want to drown, he starts swimming."

"I don't know what that means."

"You want to learn how to fight, then start fighting back."

"This wasn't even my idea."

"Then prepare to die!"

"I thought we were getting along so well."

Crenshaw stopped in mid-swing, pulled a pocket watch from his vest pocket, looked at it, and said, "Your five minutes are up. Training is over. Time to board The Ship."

He turned and walked away. I dropped to my knees, trying to catch my breath.

"Come on, greenhorn, or ye'll be marooned here."

"Right behind you," I said, but Crenshaw didn't wait. He was already walking back.

The truth of the matter was I've never been an athlete. When I was a kid I was always picked last for any sports team, be it football, basketball, baseball, or what have you. I was always the worst player too, except for maybe Mary Ellen Grutsky, but she had some sort of rare blood disorder or something. As an adult I've been to the gym twice. The first time was when Chet Meyers, one of the guys at the office, tried to get five people to join so he could get a discount on his membership. Chet managed to talk me into joining. My first day at the gym, I decided to try the treadmill, thinking it should be simple enough. I managed to stay on it for maybe ten minutes before I slipped and fell off, spraining my ankle. The gym people called an ambulance to take me to the hospital as a precaution. They didn't want to get sued. The second time I went to the gym, I hobbled in on my crutches to cancel my membership. I don't think Chet Meyers got his membership discount either.

After exhausting my energy fending off Crenshaw's attack, as nonlethal as it was, it took a little longer for me to gather myself together and head back to The Ship. My breathing became labored, as if I had run a five-hour marathon through the Everglades or climbed Mount Everest while carrying a family of six on my back. I was sadly out of shape and reminded myself of that fact every time I paused to catch my breath.

When I reached The Ship, the engine was running. The doors closed, and ever so slowly The Ship began pulling away. They were marooning me, driving away and leaving me in a strange place with no way to get home. All my possessions were aboard The Ship: my wallet, my money, my credit cards, everything. They were leaving me with nothing. Perhaps it had been their plan the entire time. Perhaps they had intended to maroon me from the beginning. I would have no other choice but to call my mother and ask her for help. No! Not that. Anything but that. I would never hear the end of it.

"Stop!" I cried out. "Stop! Don't leave! Wait for me!"

The Ship continued to pull away. I ran to catch up. It moved slowly enough that I could jog alongside it, even though I was out of breath.

"Open up!" I banged on the door to get their attention. "Open up!"

Without stopping, the door slowly opened, and I prepared to leap into the stairwell.

But there stood Willow, blocking the entryway. "A bit out of shape, aren't we, Potts?" he said.

"Let me on board, please," I gasped.

"Crenshaw informed me that you were unable to last even a few minutes of swordplay. That's not good, Potts. This Saturday we have to be able to hold our own in the Battle Extraordinaire. Everyone has to do their part, and you're not ready."

"Are you going to let me on?"

"Two days, Potts. Only two days, and you're not ready. I blame myself, really. I should have foreseen this problem, but no captain is truly perfect. We all have our shortcomings. This is mine."

I couldn't run anymore. I began lagging behind. My breathing became strained.

"Pick up those knees, Potts. Come on. You can do this. You just have to want it bad enough."

When I looked up, Celeste appeared at the window, watching me. I couldn't let her see me fail. I had to succeed if only to prove that I was good enough for her.

I don't know how I did it. I don't know where I found the energy, but I pushed through it and forced myself to run as fast as I could to reach the door, and then, when I grabbed the side to pull myself into The Ship, Helmsman hit the brake. We had reached the exit to the campground, and he came to a stop sign. I couldn't stop as quickly as the vehicle, and I tumbled head over heels onto the pavement.

"Potts?" Willow's voice came to me through the haze. "Are you all right?"

No, I was not all right. I couldn't move. My breath came

in short, labored gasps. My knee had hit the pavement when I fell and hurt like hell. In fact there was a whole list of injuries; at least one elbow, my face, the heel of my hand, and several other parts of my body I was still trying to identify.

"Sorry," Helmsman called out through the window.

"Um, Redjack? Crenshaw?" Willow called. "I believe Mr. Potts could use some assistance getting aboard The Ship."

The men carried me on board and set me down on one of the seats toward the back of the bus. Spider tended to my wounds. Luckily I received nothing more than a few scrapes and bruises. It stung when she cleaned them, and I couldn't help wincing and yelping every so often.

"Potts, Potts, Potts," Willow said, as he approached. "At this rate you'll never be ready for Saturday's little get together."

"I have no idea what you expect from me," I said. "I'm not an athlete. I never was."

"It's no wonder, with that negative attitude of yours."

"I'm being a realist. Ow! That stings."

"You're not going to start crying, are you?" Spider asked.

"I'm not crying. I'm saying it stings."

"It would appear…" Willow leaned over me. "We are left with no recourse."

"You mean I don't have to take part in your little skirmish?"

"Of course you have to take part, but we need to kick up your training. Once Spider is finished with you, I want you to give me fifty push-ups."

"Fifty push-ups? How am I supposed to do that?"

"Don't tell me you don't know how to do push-ups."

"Of course I know how to do push-ups."

"Then you can do fifty of them right here in the aisle."

"Here? On the bus?"

"It's not a bus. It's The Ship."

"Your ship's floor is filthy."

"It's not a floor. It's the deck. And you're welcome to swab it first if you like."

"Swab it? With what?"

"I'm certain we can find you something."

"Hey, Ben," All Hands said as he came up the aisle. "That was one of the funniest things I've ever seen. You should have seen it."

"I'm sure it was a laugh riot," I said.

"It's a shame we didn't get it on video. We could make a lot of money with something like that."

"Maybe you'd like me to do it again so you can record it," I offered.

"Hey, would you?" he said. "We can get a camera at our next stop, and I'll videotape you doing it again."

"No, I'm not doing it again. I was being sarcastic."

"Geez, you don't have to get sore," he said before he returned to his seat. "It was just an idea."

"Ow!" I howled as Spider again touched a sensitive spot.

"You are such a big baby," she said.

"It stings," I told her.

"Well, I am finished, big baby."

"Thank you. I appreciate your help, but it does sting."

"Go do your push-ups."

"I'm not doing any push-ups."

All eyes turned to me. Even old Helmsman glared at me from his rearview mirror.

"What?" I said, "I'm not doing any push-ups. I don't care how you look at me, okay? I don't care what you say, what you do, or what you think of me. I'm not doing any push-ups."

No one said a word. Everyone continued staring at me, so I returned to my seat next to Crenshaw. I sat down and could hear his heavy breath rushing out of his nostrils. The next thing I knew, The Ship slowed down, pulled off the side of the road, and came to a stop.

"Now what?" I said. "Really? We're just going to sit here until I do your push-ups? Fine. We're going to be here a long time then."

"Oh, come on, Ben," Jake said. "All we're asking you to do is fifty push-ups."

"That's a lot of push-ups. There's no way I can do that many. I'd be lucky to be able to do five."

"Very well," Willow said. "Give us five push-ups, and we'll be on our way."

"I'm not doing any push-ups. We'll sit here on the side of the road and never make it to California. We won't deliver the last three items in the chest. Eventually we'll die, and the vultures will eat our corpses."

"I don't think there are any vultures around here," Jake said.

"Something will eat our corpses, I'm sure."

"Come now, Potts," Willow said. "It's not like we're making you do something the rest of us haven't done."

"All of you have done push-ups?"

"Yes, all of us."

"Right here, in this aisle?"

"Right in that spot."

"And how many did you do?"

"Fifty."

"All of you?"

"All of us."

"Except me," Jake said, "but I did have a doctor's note."

"True," Willow said, "Jake is the exception."

Due to Jake's twisted spine, I understood.

"I did fifty-one actually," All Hands said. "And Crenshaw did his with one hand tied behind his back."

I looked at Crenshaw, who gave me a quick grunt. I turned to look at the others, thinking Willow might be lying. I hoped one of them might have a tell that would expose the lie. My eyes met Celeste's, and I knew I had made a big mistake. I shouldn't have looked in her direction, but I couldn't help it. She looked disappointed. If it hadn't been for Celeste, I would have called Willow on his bluff. One look from her, though, I knew I had to step up to the plate and give it my best shot. "All right, fine, I'll do your push-ups," I said and stood up in the aisle.

They all cheered.

"But I'm not promising fifty. I'll do as many as I can."

"Bully for you, Potts," Willow said. "We'll keep count."

The others gave an affirmative, "Aye."

"All right," I said. I shook my arms out, staring down at The Ship's deck, wondering what disgusting substances might have stained it over the years. How many germs crawled on that surface? What sort of bacteria grew beneath my feet? The thought of lowering my face to that surface repulsed me, but I had to do it. I didn't want Celeste to think poorly of me. With one last deep breath, I bent down, placed my hands on the filthy surface beneath me, and prepared to do some push-ups. The smell of old rubber and dirty socks drifted to my nose, along with a slightly metallic odor. I could see scattered pieces of unidentifiable bits and crumbs and wished I had taken up Willow's suggestion of cleaning the floor before doing my push-ups. Never mind, if I didn't do the push-ups right then, I never would.

Slowly I let my elbows bend, lowering my face to the unsightly floor. I closed my eyes, thinking it might make it easier if I couldn't see what lay beneath me. When the tip of my nose came a fraction of an inch above the deck, I pushed myself up, breathing out as I did. One. My arms snapped straight, and then I lowered myself again, breathing in through my nose. The tip of my nose brushed the rubber floor lining, and I pushed myself up. I struggled more, but I made it. Two. My third push-up proved even tougher. I could feel my arms starting to tremble when I lowered myself for the third time. My breathing became more strained. I felt as if I couldn't get enough air into my lungs.

All Hands started chanting, "Potts, Potts, Potts," and one by one the others joined in until the entire crew chanted, "Potts, Potts, Potts."

I struggled to push myself up. The effort to straighten my elbows drained me, but finally I did it. Three.

As the chanting crew watched, I attempted my fourth push-up. I lowered my nose to the filthy rubber mat of the deck, fighting the urge to give up. Once my nose came within a few inches of the deck, I tried to push myself back up, but I couldn't straighten my elbows. Try as I might, my arms would not straighten. I collapsed on the deck. The chanting came to an abrupt halt, and my right cheek pressed against The Ship's deck. I could feel the dirt and crumbs clinging to my sweaty skin, but I didn't care because I couldn't move.

The Ship went quiet, except for my breathing, which, to me sounded like the last gasps of a dying manatee.

Willow leaned over me. "Potts?"

I didn't answer right away, so he said it again.

"Potts?"

"Yes?"

"I take it you're still among the living."

"No."

"Very well then. Crenshaw, would ye and All Hands be so kind as to help Mr. Potts to his seat?"

I felt my body being lifted and half-carried, half-dragged to my seat, dirt and crumbs still clinging to the side of my face. I sensed more than felt The Ship lurch forward and then back before it continued its journey. I asked myself whether Celeste would still consider going out with me if I threw up.

12

With time I began feeling better. My nausea dissipated, and my arms became less numb. Even though I felt better physically, my morale remained extremely low. I couldn't even do four push-ups. I seriously needed to get into shape, any shape, instead of a flabby blob. It's kind of hard to impress the ladies when you're a hopeless wimp, and more than anything I wanted to impress Celeste. I still had no idea how to do it.

As I contemplated the many possible ways I could impress Celeste, I felt someone nudge my shoulder. I looked over to see Celeste shove All Hands into Jake and perch on the edge of their seat.

"Hey, come on," All Hands protested. "Two people per seat, please."

Celeste ignored him and unscrewed the lid from a jar she held. From its cold, wet appearance, I knew the jar had been in the ice cooler. It contained a thick green liquid with the consistency of mud. "Drink this," she said and held the jar out to me.

"What is it?" I looked at it apprehensively.

"It's an all-natural homemade energy smoothie," she said. "It'll help you feel better."

"What's in it?" I asked and sniffed it. It had a faint smell of some kind of fruit, but it also smelled suspiciously like cabbage.

"Drink it," she said more firmly.

I took a sip and almost gagged. "This stuff's awful." Some of it dribbled down my chin. I wiped it off and looked closer at the jar to see if I could determine its contents.

"I didn't ask for your opinion," Celeste said. "I said to drink it."

"You don't mean you want me to drink it all, do you?"

"That's exactly what I mean."

I looked at the muddy green liquid once again, then looked at Celeste.

"Go on," she said.

I thought I'd better do what she said, so I took a deep breath and drank the rest of it as quickly as I could. I fought to keep it down and returned the empty jar to Celeste.

"There, that wasn't so bad." She screwed the lid back on.

"Actually it was," I told her.

She shook her head, took her jar, and went back to her seat.

I turned to see Crenshaw studying me. "What?" I said. "You ever try one of those? It's like drinking a shake made from old gym socks."

"I don't deal in poisons," he said. "Poison is a woman's weapon. When a real man wants to kill you, he uses a blade. A long, sharp, shiny blade."

"Poison? Wait. You're not trying to tell me Celeste poisoned me?"

Crenshaw said not a word. He took out his knife and began sharpening it.

Of course Celeste had no reason to poison me. She only wanted me to drink something to help me feel better. Granted, it tasted awful, but if you wanted to poison someone, you didn't give him something that tasted awful. You'd give him the poison in something that tasted good, so he'd willingly drink it unaware. Usually when you drank something that tastes awful, it's good for you. Right?

Some time passed. There was no telling how much time, but I felt ready to get off The Ship and do something. Sitting still on a long ride with nothing to do made me antsy. I couldn't keep still. I needed to get involved in some sort of activity. Maybe go hiking or swimming or kayaking. Maybe climb a mountain. Something other than riding in The Ship. My gosh, I felt like I had overdosed on caffeine. It made me wonder what was in that drink that Celeste had given me.

The thought occurred to me that it was some sort of potent energy drink, and the only one who could confirm it was resting her head on Maggie's shoulder with her eyes closed. I didn't have the heart to disturb her, so instead I tried to relax and focus on the scenery outside but saw only grass and rocks and shrubs and a few mountains in the distance. We were in the middle of nowhere with no possible escape.

A loud explosion burst the air, as if someone had fired a cannon, startling all of us. Maggie screamed. All Hands and Jake shouted colorful expletives. I joined them. Beside me Crenshaw sat poised at the edge of his seat, knife in hand, ready for action.

A few minutes later we stood outside, gathered around the shredded remains of the right front tire.

"That's not good," Maggie said.

"That's definitely not good," Jake said.

"Fix-a-Flat's not going to work on that," All Hands said.

"It would appear we have run aground, Helmsman," Willow said. "What have you to say to that?"

"Not to worry," Helmsman said, "we've got a spare."

"I'll help him." Redjack followed Helmsman to the rear of The Ship. "You may want to make yourselves comfortable."

"You heard what the man said." Willow waved his hand in the air with a flourish. "Let's break out the rum."

Within minutes Willow and the others were getting comfortable in their canvas chairs beneath a large beach umbrella, passing around a bottle of rum.

I couldn't sit down and didn't want any rum. Instead I grabbed a bottle of water and decided to walk around and explore the area until the tire got changed.

Crenshaw, however, had another plan in mind. "Where are you going?" He stepped in my path, holding a sword.

"I'm going to have a look around. Don't worry, I won't wander too far off."

"You're not wandering anywhere. We're going to continue your training."

"But I don't want to train."

"Too bad. Here." He tossed the sword to me.

Having no desire to attempt to catch it and end up cutting my hand, I let it fall to the ground.

"You need to learn how to catch a sword," Crenshaw said.

"Why?" I asked. "In case someone challenges me to a duel at work?"

"Pick it up."

I set my water bottle on a nearby rock, picked up the sword, and examined it as I imagined someone who knew something about swords might do.

"What are you looking for?" Crenshaw asked.

"The 'on' button?" I chuckled at my own joke.

Crenshaw didn't.

"This morning," he said, "I showed you how to defend yourself."

"Is that what that was?"

"Now I want you to attack me."

"Okay," I said, but he didn't have a sword, so I thought I should wait for him to arm himself.

"What are you waiting for?" he asked.

"Aren't you going to get your sword?"

"I don't need one."

"You sure? These things can hurt if I hit you."

"You have to hit me first."

"Come, Potts," Willow said. "Give us a demonstration of your sword-fighting skills."

"I have no sword-fighting skills," I told him.

"All you have to do, Potts, is hit Crenshaw with your sword. How hard can that be?"

"Yeah, Ben," All Hands said. "Give Crenshaw a good wallop."

"Give him a good thrashing," Jake called.

"Anyone want to take bets on this?" Maggie asked.

"No betting," Celeste said.

"Come on. Who wants to put their money on Potts?" Jake said.

Celeste lightly backhanded Jake's shoulder. "I said no betting."

"That's not a proper fighting stance," Spider commented.

"Potts," Willow said, "get into a proper fighting stance, for Pete's sake."

"A proper fighting stance?" I had no idea what it even

looked like, but I tried to stand the way I saw guys do in the old Kung Fu movies I loved to watch as a kid. I swayed from side to side, making little swirling motions with my sword, and making sounds like "Oooooooweeeeeyaaaah."

Crenshaw watched me a moment, shook his head, and asked, "What is that supposed to be?"

"My fighting stance," I said.

"Just attack me."

Okay, I thought, *if he wants me to attack him, I'll attack him*. I rushed at Crenshaw, giving my best war cry, which sounded more like a child throwing a temper tantrum. I raised my sword and swung at him.

Crenshaw ripped the sword from my hand and tripped me with his extended leg. I collided with the ground, getting a face full of dirt and dead grass. The Scallywags exclaimed, "Oh!"

Blinking the dirt from my eyes, I looked up to see a brown snake coiled about seven inches in front of me. He looked ready to strike, and I was in no position to move away.

"Come now, Potts," Willow said. "Have another go at it. Only this time you might want to stay on your feet."

I tried to say something, but my voice failed me.

"Ben," All Hands called. "Earth to Ben."

Finally I got the word out. "Snake!"

The snake sprang at me, but at the last second a blade swept in and crushed its head. Crenshaw scooped up the dead snake with the sword he had taken from me to examine it. "Nonvenomous," he said and flipped it into the bushes.

"Are you all right?" Celeste asked.

"I'm fine." I got to my feet, brushing myself off. I felt more humiliated than hurt.

Redjack approached. "Bad news."

"Don't tell me Helmsman lost his dentures again," Willow said.

"No. The spare tire is flat."

"That does put a damper on things."

"We're going to try to hitch a ride into the nearest town and get it repaired."

"And what're we supposed to do in the meantime?" All Hands asked.

Willow scratched his chin, looking as if he were deep in thought, and then a smile spread across his face. "Play bucket ball, of course," he said.

It wasn't long before a pickup came up the road. Spider and Celeste waved it down and convinced the driver to take Redjack and Helmsman into town to get the spare tire fixed. The driver tried to convince the women to join them, but they declined with as much courtesy as they could until Redjack had to step in and inform the driver that they needed to get going.

We gathered in the road and waved to Redjack and Helmsman, both sitting in the back of the pickup truck with the flat tire, waving back until they disappeared down the road.

I turned to Willow and asked, "What exactly is bucket ball?"

"It's a game we invented," he said. "In fact, it's how your brother acquired his nickname Longbucket."

"Hey," All Hands said, "I'll be a captain."

We all looked at him.

"A team captain, I mean."

"Very well, team captain," Willow said. "You shall have Crenshaw and Celeste on your team, and I shall take Maggie and Potts."

"Sounds good," All Hands said. "We're going to kick some pirate booty."

"Of course," Willow went on, "one of your responsibilities as team captain is to go get the bucket."

"Aye, aye." All Hands ran to The Ship.

"Careful how you step," Maggie called after him. "That thing's still on the jack, and we don't need it coming off."

"Aye, aye," All Hands called back as he climbed into The Ship.

"I'll ref," Jake said. "It's only fitting, since that's always been my job."

"It would seem I am the odd mate out," Spider said.

"Apologies, Spider," Willow said. "However, because Helmsman is not here, we could use a second referee."

"Okay, but no monkey business. I run a straight game. If I see monkey business going on, I'm blowing my whistle."

"Actually," Willow said, "we don't have any whistles."

"All right, then, I will yell at you in Mandarin."

"Fair enough."

"I have no clue how to play bucket ball," I said.

"It's very easy to learn, Potts. It's like football, only we use a bucket instead of a football."

"But if it's like football, why not use a football?"

"Whoever heard of a pirate playing football?"

"I don't know. Pittsburgh?"

"Ha. Potts, you amuse me, but that's baseball."

"Whatever. I don't get the bucket thing. I mean, why a bucket?"

"It was the only thing we had when we invented the game." All Hands tossed the bucket to Willow.

"Actually it was Longbucket who invented the game," Willow said.

"Ray?" I asked.

"Yeah, that's right," All Hands said. "He started tossing the bucket to people, and it evolved into a game, although he wanted to call it kick the bucket."

"We talked him out of that," Willow said, "and bucket ball was invented."

"All right, Scallywags," Jake said, waving everyone to him. "Gather round. We'll flip for bucket-off. You call it, All Hands."

"Heads," All Hands said when Spider flipped a coin into the air. "No, wait, tails. No, heads."

"Tails," Spider said when she caught the coin and slapped it onto the back of her hand.

"Hornswoggle!" All Hands said.

"We will receive," Willow said.

We started to walk to our end of the field when Celeste said, "Good luck," to me.

"Thanks, you too," I said.

"We won't need it."

"I will," I said more to myself as I followed Willow and Maggie to the designated end of the field. We stopped and turned to face the other team.

"Potts," Willow whispered to me, "get ready. I'm giving the bucket to you."

"Wait. What? No-no-no-no-no, big mistake."

"Too late."

Crenshaw had the bucket by the handle and tossed it as far as he could across the field to us. Willow and Maggie ran forward to catch the bucket. All Hands, Celeste, and Crenshaw charged at us, crying out, "Yaaaahhh!"

I didn't want to but forced myself to run behind Willow and Maggie. Willow caught the bucket, turned, and tossed it to me. I caught it purely by stroke of luck. Maggie blocked

Celeste. Willow blocked All Hands, but Crenshaw got past both of them and...

Whomp!

I lay flat on my back with Crenshaw on top of me. He rolled off and got to his feet with a wicked laugh. I wished I had gone into town with Helmsman and Redjack.

"Up you go, Potts." Willow held out his hand.

I took it and pulled myself to my feet. "I thought you were going to block for me," I said.

"I had All Hands," Willow said.

"I had Celeste," Maggie said. "She wasn't getting anywhere near you."

"But Crenshaw's the biggest threat. Someone has to block him."

"I thought you could slip past him," Willow said.

"He's bigger than me. He's faster than me. How can I slip past him?"

"Very well," Willow said. "I'll take Crenshaw from here on. All Hands is yours."

"Okay, I think I can deal with All Hands."

As it turned out, I was wrong.

On the next play, Maggie hiked the bucket to me, which I protested against as much as I could, but Willow claimed I was the best choice for quarterback. I simply had to toss the bucket to one of them. I never got the chance.

Celeste stayed with Maggie, and Crenshaw stayed with Willow. That gave All Hands an opportunity to come at me. I dodged to the left, dodged to the right, tried to find one of my teammates open, then...

Whomp!

I ended up on the ground once again.

"You okay, Ben?" All Hands asked as he got to his feet.

"Give me a minute."

"Come now, Potts." Willow trotted up to me. "Can't have you lying around all day. We have a game to win."

"Fine." With All Hands' assistance, I got to my feet. "But can we change this to a game of touch rather than tackle?"

"Touch? We're pirates. We're rough and tough and rugged. We never play touch."

"Okay, then you be the quarterback and I'll receive. How about that?"

"Are you sure? It's not easy to catch a bucket."

"I'm sure. Just throw the bucket to me."

"Maybe he can catch like Longbucket," Maggie suggested.

"What do you mean?"

"Interesting story, that," Willow said. "It's how Longbucket acquired his name. He was the best receiver we ever had. He could outrun everyone here and catch the bucket over half a field away. Of course I was pretty good at throwing the bucket that far, so we made a good team. Ye should have seen him, Potts. It was a spectacle to watch him catch the bucket. If you're half as good as your brother, ye'll do fine."

"I guess we're about to find out."

"That's the spirit, Potts," Willow said, slapping my shoulder.

We went into the next play. I ran as fast as I could, doing my best to get away from All Hands. I surprised myself when I somehow outdistanced him, and Willow threw the bucket. I watched as the bucket arced into the air and began falling. With every ounce of energy I had, I ran to catch the bucket. It came down quickly with me right under it. I reached for it, and it slipped right through my hands and hit the ground with a bounce. I stumbled and fell over. Behind me I could hear All Hands laughing when he grabbed the bucket and ran the other way. He made it all the way to the other end of the field to score a point for his team.

All Hands's team got the bucket next, and it didn't look good for us. Willow did well covering Crenshaw. Although Celeste was quicker, Maggie held her own. I, however, proved to be the weak link on the team. I had a tough time staying with All Hands. Because of me, he had all the time in the world to throw the bucket to one or the other of his teammates. For their team, scoring was not much of a problem, whereas with us, it was. I couldn't catch the bucket to save my life. Maggie did all right, but always had Celeste right there on her. She still managed to gain some yardage, but not enough to make a difference. Anytime Willow threw the bucket to me, it slipped right through my fingers.

Still, I enjoyed watching Celeste tackle Maggie. Oh, to be Maggie.

On the final play of the game, we had the ball. The score was 5 - 3 in their favor. Willow got us into a huddle. "Maggie," he said, "do whatever you have to do, but get open. Potts, keep All Hands busy. This will be our last opportunity to score, and we have to make it happen. Can I get an Arrgh?"

"Arrgh," Maggie and I said.

I have to admit it perturbed me that I was letting Willow and Maggie down. Although neither of them said anything or looked at me as if they were dissatisfied with my performance, I still couldn't help feeling I had failed them. I wanted to step up and prove that I could equally contribute to the team, but at the same time I knew I wasn't very capable athletically.

As I stepped up to the line, toe to toe with All Hands who looked at me with crossed eyes and mischievous grin, I became determined to give it everything I had. My mission became to get clear of All Hands and catch the bucket. Except I didn't know how I would do it.

"Yo-ho," Willow called out.

I looked at Celeste.

"Yo-ho!" Willow called out again.

Celeste glanced my way. It was all I needed.

"And a bottle of rum!" Willow called, and Maggie hiked the bucket to him.

I dodged around All Hands and ran as fast as I could. When I looked back, Willow was watching Maggie, who was doing her best to get open, but try as she might, Maggie couldn't shake Celeste. Finally Willow turned my way. I waved frantically, signaling I was open. He hesitated but Crenshaw was right on top of him, giving him no choice but to act immediately. At the last second, he threw the bucket.

It came right to me. I watched it arc into the sky and slowly descend, plummeting toward the earth. Quickly I maneuvered under it, and the bucket dropped into my hands.

"I did it!" I shouted, jumping up and down. "I did it! I caught the bucket."

Whomp!

All Hands tackled me. "Ben, you okay?" he asked as he got to his feet.

"You know," I said. "I'm really getting tired of being knocked to the ground."

"Sorry."

All Hands pulled me to my feet. I still clutched the bucket under my arm. I had managed to catch it but failed to score any points for our team. At that moment a car horn sounded, and we all turned to see Redjack and Helmsman waving to us from the back of an old pickup truck, repaired tire between them.

"It would appear our game has come to an end," Willow said. "All Hands, I believe your team has won."

"We won? We won? Finally." All Hands danced around, kicking up dust. He grabbed Celeste by the hands and twirled her around. "We won. We won! First time I've been on the winning team. Woo-hoo!"

Maggie stood, hands on hips, trying to catch her breath. "There's a first time for everything, I suppose."

Everyone else walked over to Redjack and Helmsman. I stayed behind, bucket tucked under my arm, grinning like an idiot.

13

By the time Redjack and Helmsman got the repaired spare tire onto The Ship's wheel, the sun had dropped down to the horizon. We needed to get a new tire to replace the old, shredded one but realized how late it had gotten. It was decided to spend the night where we were and move on in the morning.

The feeling all around was one of camaraderie, sitting around the fire, eating stew and drinking rum, listening to each other tell stories while Jake strummed his guitar and All Hands played his bongos. It all felt pleasant, with one exception; every time someone made me laugh I could feel all my new bruises from our bucket ball game, as well as the old ones I got earlier when I took a tumble while running to catch The Ship. I sat in my canvas chair nursing my wounds when Celeste came over and sat beside me.

"You okay?" she asked.

"I'll survive."

"They do tend to get a little rough, don't they?" She reached for my forehead and brushed aside a few strands of hair so she could examine one of my bruises.

"You didn't seem to mind." I turned to her, relishing the light touch of her fingers.

"I'm used to it. I grew up with three older brothers."

"You're a tomboy?"

"You could say that."

"I guess you pretty much have to be, to enjoy this kind of lifestyle. Me, I've never been the outdoorsy type. All this sleeping outside on the ground."

"If you want, I could talk to Maggie and Spider and see if they'd be willing to let you sleep on the bus with us women."

"Yeah, 'cause that would really help boost my male ego."

She shrugged and picked up a small stone. "It was just a thought."

"I appreciate the thought, but what I really need is a nice clean hotel room."

"It gets pretty expensive to put this group up in a hotel." She tossed the stone into a nearby bush.

"Actually I wasn't thinking about the whole group."

"Listen, if you think I'm going to spend the night with you in a hotel room—"

"No, no, that's not what I'm suggesting. I meant just me."

"So you're only thinking about yourself."

"You don't seem to have an issue with roughing it. None of you do. It's not for me. I'm too used to the comforts of a nice big, warm bed."

"I seriously doubt Willow would go for it, but you could ask. I know it must be hard for you to sleep among us commoners."

"That's not what I'm saying."

"Of course not." She got up and walked over to join Spider. Somehow I always managed to say the wrong thing. I seemed to have a knack for it. Try as I might to say the right thing, it invariably seemed to take a left turn.

I needed to go for a walk and clear my head. Also I realized I should call my mother. Some nearby brush gave me the opportunity I hoped for to duck away from the group.

"Oh, Benjamin, thank God you're alive," Mom said over the phone. "Are you on your way home? Something dreadful has happened, and I don't know what to do. I have no one to turn to. You're not here, and I'm in a terrible state."

"What happened, Mom? Are you hurt?"

"I'm not hurt, but I could have been."

"Tell me what happened."

"I went out onto my back patio this morning, and I saw a lizard there. It's one of those big lizards too. I have no idea how it got onto my back patio, but now it won't leave. I ran into the house screaming and closed the glass door behind me before it could get inside. You know how those things frighten me. It might jump onto my leg. I'd die of a heart attack if that ever happened."

It had to be a common garden lizard, probably no more than five or six inches in length. My mother always exaggerated when it came to lizards and frogs and other small creatures. When we were kids, Ray and I caught lizards to keep as pets, she'd insist that we kill them and then make us take a bath to scrub away "whatever vile diseases that disgusting creature may have been carrying."

"You must come home immediately, Benjamin. I won't be able to sleep tonight knowing that horrible creature is on my patio."

"I can't come home, Mom. I'm in the middle of the desert."

"The middle of the desert? What are you doing in the middle of the desert? Are you lost? Should I call 911 and have them send out a search party?"

"No, Mom, I'm not lost. We're camping out here for the night. We have to head into town in the morning to get a new tire."

"Benjamin, you listen to me. You must get away from those people and get to the nearest airport and take the first plane home."

"Mom, I'm not coming home yet."

"How can you do this to me?"

"I'm not doing anything to you, Mom."

"You've deserted me. I'm stranded here, trapped in my own house by a vicious brute on my patio."

"It's a lizard, Mom."

"Lord knows what that thing is capable of."

"It's capable of crawling on walls and eating bugs. That's what it's capable of."

"Oh, dear Lord, that's all I need. Some hideous monster gorging itself on bugs on my patio while I am trying to entertain."

"It won't bother anyone."

"I have my book club meeting tomorrow. You know I have my book club meeting every Friday. I'll be serving my famous blue crab beignets. The girls are always telling me how much they enjoy my blue crab beignets. But it will all be ruined because that beast will be freely scampering all over my patio with bits of bug spewing from its mouth."

"Mom, it'll be fine. Nobody will even notice the lizard."

"But I will. Please, Benjamin, just come home. I need you here near me, not roaming the country with a bunch of hoodlums."

"Why don't you ask one of your neighbors to come over and chase the lizard away for you? I'm sure someone will be glad to help you."

"I don't know."

"It won't hurt to ask. Try it."

"I'll think about it."

"Okay, I gotta go. I promise everything will be fine. I'll talk to you tomorrow."

"I pray that you're right."

I returned to the campsite. The crew members were already headed for their sleeping bags ready to call it a night. Several of them noticed me and wished me a good night. Celeste was not one of them.

"Potts," Willow said, "be a good man and tidy up before you turn in, will you? You seem to be good at it. Sleep well."

"Oh, come on," I said, throwing my hands in the air. Dirty plates, pots, utensils, and an empty rum bottle or two lay scattered around the dying campfire. I had once again been relegated to busboy.

A metal door clanked shut behind me. The smell of mold and mildew permeated the air as I walked down a dark, dank stone corridor. Two rows of prison cells stood on either side of me, all of them empty except one. At the end of the corridor a single occupant slumped in the corner of the last dark cell. A chain rattled as the prisoner rose and approached the cell door. His face became discernible when he stepped into the light.

"Ray," I said, rushing to my brother.

"Hello, Ben."

"What are you doing here?"

"Keeping the rats company." He kicked at a rat that scurried by, making the chain around his ankle rattle.

"They have you in chains," I said.

"I tried to escape yesterday, but they weren't ready to see me leave."

"But why are you in prison?"

"As Willow would say, 'That's a story.'"

I shrugged, letting him know I had plenty of time to hear it.

"I was searching for Caitlin. I searched every town I came across, every island I could find passage to, every tavern, every shop, everywhere I could think of. Then the other night I was about to give up, get a bottle of rum, and get as drunk as I could. And then I saw her."

"You saw her? Where?"

"She was leaving a dress shop with several other women."

"Did you talk to her? Did she remember you? What happened?"

"Some fat douchebag with bad breath bumped into me. He had the nerve to accuse me of stealing his wallet."

"You stole his wallet?"

"Of course not, but all he had to do was accuse me, and here I am waiting to be hanged."

"Hanged? For stealing a wallet?"

"I didn't steal it."

"Where's your lawyer? What's he doing?"

"I don't have a lawyer."

"No lawyer? How can they convict you if you don't have a lawyer?"

"I wasn't even given a trial."

"No trial? That's not right. We have to do something. I have to do something. I know, I'll go to see the governor. When he hears about this, he'll put a stop to it."

"Ben, the fat douchebag with bad breath was the governor."

"You stole the governor's wallet?"

"I didn't steal anybody's wallet."

"I can't leave you here."

"Then help me escape."

"What? How am I supposed to do that? You're in a locked cell with your leg chained to the floor."

"It's a dream, Ben, your dream. Maybe you can dream up some superpowers or something."

"I can't dream up any superpowers, can I? I mean, is that even possible?"

"Try it."

"This is too weird. Fine, I'll try." I grabbed hold of two of the bars on the cell door and attempted to pull them apart. It didn't work. I tried again, thinking maybe I needed to give it a little more time, but it was no use, and I gave up. "It's not working."

"Okay," Ray said, "I've got another idea."

"What?"

"Go steal the keys from the guard outside."

"Are you nuts?"

"He's probably asleep. He's lazy and not particularly bright. It'll be a piece of cake."

"You could have told me about the keys sooner."

"I would have, but I thought you could dream up some superpowers."

"Dream up superpowers? Yeah, right. If I could just dream stuff up, I'd dream up a beach full of beautiful women."

"Ben, go get the keys."

"Okay, I'm going."

As quietly as I could I crept out of the cellblock. Peering around the corner, I saw a greasy little man with a big black mustache, a balding head, and a bad comb-over. He reminded me of the bumbling sergeant in the old *Zorro* TV series. He slumped in a chair sound asleep, his feet propped on a table, his pudgy hands interlocked across his big belly. The keys rested on the corner of the table next to his feet. On the other side of his feet lay a pistol. I stepped around him and picked up the pistol, hoping not to wake him. I pointed the pistol at him and reached for the keys. In an instant he became wide awake. He leaped to his feet as I snatched up the keys.

He glowered at me then turned and ran for the exit yelling, "Prisoner escaping! Prisoner escaping!"

I aimed the pistol at his back but didn't have the heart to pull the trigger. Instead I ran to Ray's cell.

"What happened?" Ray asked as I fit the key into his cell door.

"We have to get going," I said. "The entire place is about to come down on us."

I swung the cell door open and went to work on the iron ring around Ray's ankle to free him from the ball and chain. It took me a few tries, but I finally found the right key, and we both ran out of the cell and down the corridor. We didn't get far before the sergeant appeared, followed by a half-dozen soldiers with muskets.

"The other way," Ray said. We turned and ran in the opposite direction.

Another half dozen soldiers appeared in front of us, forming a barricade to block our passage. Armed soldiers behind us, armed soldiers before us, we were trapped. At the sergeant's command they raised their muskets and prepared to fire.

"I guess it's the effort that counts," Ray said.

"I'm sorry, Ray," I said. "I blew it."

"You haven't failed, Ben. Give Sam my love."

I turned to ask who Sam was, but he was gone and the soldiers fired their muskets with a loud boom.

I sat up in my sleeping bag, looking around the dark campsite, half expecting to see myself surrounded by soldiers. I saw only Redjack, his pipe dangling from under his mustache, gripping a telescope attached to a tripod propped on his shoulder.

"Let's go," he said.

"Go? Where?"

"The show's about to start." He turned and trekked deeper into the pitch-black desert.

"What show?" I asked. He didn't respond. I got out of my sleeping bag and followed him anyway. After walking a dozen feet or so, I began wishing I had some sort of powerful flashlight with me as we moved away from the fading campfire. Having no other light source, I settled for the display screen on my cell phone to provide some illumination. I noticed Redjack carried no light himself. "Aren't you afraid of snakes?" I asked.

"Not particularly."

"You should be. I almost got bitten by one earlier today."

No response.

After a few minutes of walking, he stopped and set up his telescope. He looked into the eyepiece, making a few adjustments, then said, "This should do nicely."

I did what I could to scan the area for snakes with my cell phone, but it didn't offer much light, making my circumference sweep haphazard at best.

"What are you searching for, Ben?" Redjack asked.

"Snakes. Like I said, I almost got bitten by one earlier."

"I'm not referring to your search along the ground. I'm talking about why you're traveling with us."

"You know why. Ray asked me to deliver some stuff that he had in that old chest of his."

"Your brother may have given you the excuse, but each of us is on our own quest, and until we know what our quest is, we stand little chance of obtaining our goal."

"What are you, my therapist?"

"Have you considered why your brother wanted you to deliver those things for him?"

"He's dead. It's kind of hard to travel across the country and give stuff to people when you're dead."

"True, but I have to wonder if there may have been some other design behind it all."

"Like what?"

"I don't know. I'd have to think about it for a while."

We fell into silence for the next few minutes as I kept an ever-vigilant eye out for snakes and Redjack peered into his telescope.

"Come here," Redjack said after a while. "Have a look at this."

I walked over to the telescope as Redjack stepped aside. I peered into the eyepiece as a streak of light shot across the night sky.

"A shooting star." I saw another, then another, and then more shot past until it seemed they filled the sky. "Is that a meteor shower?"

"As a matter of fact it is."

"Wow. I've never seen one before."

"Incredible, isn't it?"

"It's amazing."

"Would you mind if I had a look?"

"Oh, yeah, sorry. It is your telescope." I stepped away to allow Redjack to see the meteor shower. "So how'd you know about the meteor shower?"

"I keep up with this stuff. It's one of my many hobbies."

"How many hobbies do you have?"

"More than any normal person probably should."

Once the meteor shower passed, Redjack pointed out some of the stars and constellations. I found it interesting, but eventually fatigue set in and I wanted nothing more than to return to my sleeping bag and grab some sleep before morning. I bid Redjack a good night, and again using my cell phone to keep an eye out for snakes, I returned to camp.

14

The next morning, we drove into Flagstaff. While Redjack and Helmsman busied themselves getting our shredded tire replaced, the rest of us decided to see what might be in the area.

The sound of kids laughing and playing drew us to a nearby public playground where a dozen or so kids were running around, climbing on things. There were five or six mothers sitting on nearby benches chatting with each other.

As soon as we approached, one of the children yelled out, "Hey! Pirates!" Half the kids on the playground came running up to us.

"Are you real pirates?"

"They aren't real pirates."

"Yuh-huh."

"They ain't got a ship. Real pirates have ships."

"Where's your ship?"

"The Ship," Willow announced, "suffered some damage in our travels and is now being repaired."

"You ain't got no ship. We're in the desert. You can't sail a ship in a desert."

"Good point," Willow said. "What be your name, lad?"

"I'm Josh, and this is Tyler, and that's Michelle."

"Pleased to meet you all," Willow said. "I am Captain Willow, and this is my crew, the Scallywags of Cannon Lake."

"Cannon Lake? Where's that?" Tyler asked.

"In Florida."

"Whatcha doin' here?" Josh said.

"We're traveling to California to attend a pirate festival."

"A real pirate festival?" Tyler asked.

"I wanna go to a pirate festival," Michelle said, jumping up and down with her hand high in the air.

"Yeah, me too," said Tyler.

"Here's an idea," Willow said, "why don't we have our own pirate festival right here?"

"Yeah," Josh said. He turned to the other kids on the playground who had been standing back. "Hey, come on, we're going to have a pirate festival."

All the kids ran to us yelling and screaming with excitement. They gathered around us chatting as only a pack of rambunctious children could.

Willow stood before them with arms crossed, assessing each child in turn. He summoned Crenshaw with a quick flip of his head.

"Listen up, mates," Crenshaw bellowed.

The children went silent.

"Captain Willow has something to say to ye."

"Thank you, Crenshaw," Willow said. "The first thing you have to do is learn how to be a pirate. To be a pirate, the first thing you need to learn is how to say 'Arrgh.'"

"Arrgh," the kids echoed.

"Come now, you can do better than that. Give me a really good 'Arrgh.'"

"Arrgh!"

"That's more like it. Come, one more time."

"Arrgh!"

"That be a fine 'Arrgh.' Now, the next thing is you must look like a pirate."

"How's this?" Josh asked as he scrunched up his face and shut one eye. "Arrgh!"

"Ooo." Willow placed his hand on his chest. "Ye gave me a start there, lad. But we have something even better. Eye patches." Willow held up one of his plastic eye patches and handed it to Josh.

"Eye patches for everyone," Maggie said as she and the other Scallywags pulled out handfuls of eye patches and handed them to the kids.

Celeste helped a young girl put on an eye patch then put one on herself, and they took turns saying "Arrgh" to each other.

I couldn't help laughing, which caught Celeste's attention. She smiled at me. I smiled at her, and then she turned back to the child.

"Now you all look like pirates," Willow said.

The kids cheered and bounced about with their hands raised high. Josh and some of the boys jabbed at each other with imaginary swords. A few of the boys fell to the ground, pretending to die in their most dramatic fashion.

Willow called for everyone's attention. "We begin each pirate festival with a parade of pirates." He led everyone in a parade around the playground. All Hands and Jake provided the music. Celeste, Spider, and Maggie shepherded a child in each hand. Even Crenshaw carried one of the smaller children on his shoulder. I took up the rear, doing my best to look inconspicuous.

While we marched in a circle, Tyler broke formation and ran back to walk with me. "Can I get a pirate hat?" he asked.

"A pirate hat?" I said. "I don't have any pirate hats."

"You can make one," he said. "My mom has a newspaper. You can make me one out of newspaper."

I looked to see his mother sitting on one of the benches under a tree. She waved to us, and Tyler and I both waved back. She appeared to be at least in her mid-thirties and looked like she had been through some rough times. She wore a pair of faded jeans and an oversized black T-shirt, and she held a cigarette, taking the occasional puff from it. A small dog sat in her lap, a folded newspaper beside her.

"She doesn't read it," Tyler said. "She uses it to fan herself when it gets hot. And it always gets hot."

"Do you think she'd mind?"

"Naw, she won't mind."

"I guess it won't hurt to ask."

Tyler ran to his mother, and I followed.

"Mom, look at me. I'm a pirate."

"Yeah, I see that. You got an eye patch and everything."

"I don't got everything."

"Hi," I said. "I'm Ben Potts."

"You all with the circus or something?"

"No, ma'am. We're on our way to California to attend a pirate festival."

"So, what y'all doin' here?"

"The Ship, I mean our bus, had a flat tire, and we're waiting for it to be repaired."

"Mom, he's gonna make a pirate hat for me."

"Is that right?"

"Your son suggested we might be able to borrow your newspaper to make him a pirate hat."

"Please, Mom, can we?"

"I guess so." She handed Tyler the newspaper.

"We really need only one sheet," I said.

"That's all right. Take the whole thing. Trust me, you're gonna need it."

"Thanks, Mom."

"But don't you be playing with any swords or knives or nothing. I don't want you hitting those other children either. You hear?"

"I won't."

"Thank you," I said. I followed Tyler to a nearby picnic table so I could fold his pirate hat.

It had been years since I had made a pirate hat out of newspaper, and I doubted I would remember how to do it, but I spread out a single sheet on the picnic table, and after a couple attempts, I finally figured out how to fold it properly. "And there you go," I said to Tyler when I placed his pirate hat on his head.

"Wow, Ben, thanks. Now I'm a real pirate."

He ran off to join his friends, hollering at them about his pirate hat. The other kids circled around to check out his new headgear. He pointed at me, and within seconds a dozen screaming children came running to me, all wanting pirate hats for themselves. Seeing no way of weaseling my way out, I made pirate hats for the kids until I ran out of newspaper. After I made the last one for a young boy who ran off with a loud whoop, a little girl about four years old appeared.

"I want a pirate hat too," she said.

"I'm sorry," I told her. "I don't have any more."

She folded her arms along the edge of the picnic table and stared at me with her bottom lip sticking out.

She looked so disappointed that it broke my heart, but I didn't know what to do. "What's your name?" I asked.

"Haley," she said.

"Haley, maybe you can ask one of the other kids if you can borrow their pirate hat."

"I want my own."

"I'm sorry. I don't know what else to do."

"Why don't you make her a pirate hat?"

I looked up to see Celeste standing next to me. She smiled and laid a sheet of newspaper down on the table. "Don't worry, Haley," she said as she slid onto the bench beside me. "We're going to make you a special pirate hat. We're going to put your name on it and everything."

I folded a pirate hat for Haley, and Celeste pulled one of her sketch pens from her pocket, wrote Haley's name on it, and drew a butterfly. "How's that?" she asked as she put the hat on Haley's head.

"Thank you," Haley said. She gave us a big smile and ran off to play with the other children.

I smiled at Celeste. "Looks like you saved the day."

"I only helped. You did most of the work."

"Where'd you get the newspaper?"

"From the gentleman over there." She pointed over her shoulder to an elderly man sitting on a park bench and drinking coffee from a foam cup. "He was nice enough to give me part of his. He doesn't read the want ads anyway, or so he claims."

"Thanks. I don't know what I would've done for Haley if you hadn't come along."

"It was sweet that you made pirate hats for all the kids."

"What could I do? Tell them no?"

"I don't think it's in you to deny these children."

"I can be mean when I want to be."

"I'm sure you can."

"I can be really mean."

"I don't doubt it."

"I once made a kid cry, in fact."

"I'm sure he deserved it."

Her smile made me think of a soft swirled ice cream cone that you get to eat on a hot summer day after mowing the lawn and trimming the hedges. "I'm sorry about last night," I said, "I'm not trying to be selfish or anything. I just don't enjoy sleeping outdoors that much."

"Fugget about it," she said in her best New Jersey accent.

It made me laugh. Celeste laughed with me, lightly slapping my arm.

"But, hey," she continued, "we have two nights to go, and then you can get back to your home and sleep in your nice comfortable bed. No more hard ground."

"True," I said. "I suppose I can put up with it for two more nights."

The Ship rolled up the road with Helmsman at the wheel. It pulled up to the curb, the door opened, and Redjack stood in the well.

"And *voila*! Here is The Ship!" Willow said to the children.

"That's not a ship," Josh protested. "That's nothin' but an old school bus."

"Is it, Josh?" Willow asked. "Is it really?" Willow placed two fingers to his mouth and gave a loud whistle.

The Scallywags bid a reluctant farewell to the children and boarded The Ship. We drove away, hanging out the windows, waving.

Some of the older children ran alongside the bus until we turned left at the corner. All Hands climbed up into the crow's nest to wave to the children, and I took the liberty of squeezing in beside him. We watched as they returned to their pretend sword fights and pirate adventures in their paper hats and plastic eye patches. I hated to leave, but we still had to get to Bakersfield, California, and then to Palo Alto.

We continued our journey with everyone in good spirits. Several conversations sparked up, creating a lively atmosphere. Celeste, Maggie, and Spider talked all about one thing or another. Jake and All Hands debated whether Superman could defeat the Hulk in battle and then whether Batman could take on Spider-man. Willow and Helmsman discussed our course and how much time our tire repair had cost us. Redjack sat in the back reading. How he could read in all that noise, I had no idea. Maybe he only pretended to read. I don't know.

Crenshaw, for his part, took the opportunity to lecture me on the pros and cons of a blunderbuss versus a musket. I could only think *blunderbuss* was a funny word, and musket made me think of the Three Musketeers, which made me think of chocolate, and then I wanted some chocolate, and I didn't hear another word Crenshaw said.

"So, Potts," Willow said as he slid in beside All Hands and Jake, forcing them to squeeze together against the window.

"Captain, not again," All Hands protested.

"Pipe down, matey," Willow said, "or you'll be swabbing decks for the rest of the voyage."

"I already swab the decks."

"Then I'll have ye swabbing the ceiling."

"I'm good," All Hands said, and he and Jake resigned themselves to their uncomfortable positions.

"Potts, I'm sure you're looking forward to the big festival tomorrow."

"I don't know," I said. "I have no idea what to expect."

"You are ready for our little skirmish, aren't you?"

"Of course not. I'm going to get killed."

"You won't get killed." Willow looked over at Crenshaw. "Will he?"

Crenshaw grunted. "It's very likely."

"I won't be a part of it," I said. "I can't. I'll be pummeled, pulverized, clobbered, pounded. I've taken enough of a beating in the past few days. I can't take any more."

"Oh, come, that's just first-time jitters. You'll do fine. Come tomorrow, when you're on that battlefield sword in hand, you'll be raring to have at 'em." He roared like a lion, swinging an invisible sword. "Raawwr! Raawwr! It'll be glorious."

"It'll be disastrous."

"Potts, you appear to be stuck on the negative. You must let go of those negative thoughts and learn to think positive thoughts."

"It's not in my nature to think positive thoughts."

"Nonsense. It's conditioning is all. You were conditioned to think negatively, and now you must take it upon yourself to recondition yourself to think positively."

"I don't know if I can do that."

"Of course you can, and we'll help you." He popped up to stand in the aisle, allowing All Hands and Jake to un-cramp themselves.

"Attention, crew," Willow said. "We are going to play a little game. It's called Let's Tell Potts What We Like About Him." Willow pulled me out of my seat and draped his arm around my neck. "It's a simple little game, really."

"The title needs work," Maggie said.

"The way we play is we each take a turn and tell our good friend, Benjamin Potts, one thing that we like about him. We are eliminated from the game when we are unable to think of anything or if we repeat what someone else has already said."

"I've got a better idea," I said. "Let's play I Spy instead."

"Sorry, we're playing my game," Willow said. "I'll go first."

"You always go first," All Hands said.

"Would you care to go first this time, All Hands?"

"Uh no, you go ahead."

"Thank you," Willow said. "What I like about Potts is he has a sense of humor."

"Blast it, that was going to be mine," Jake said.

"You can come up with something else," Willow said. "In fact, why don't you go next?"

"I couldn't possibly take All Hands's turn," Jake said. "I mean, we are going alphabetically, aren't we?"

"That was not stated, no."

"Blast it."

"I'll go," All Hands said. "I don't mind."

"Very well, All Hands. It is your turn. Jake will take his turn after you."

"What I like about Ben is that he's a decent guy."

"Blast it," Jake said. "I was going to say that."

"Then you should have gone first," All Hands said.

"Come, Jake," Willow said. "There is plenty to like about Potts."

"Okay," Jake said, "his breath doesn't stink."

"You see?" Willow said, "I knew you could think of something."

"I suppose that's something," I said.

"Crenshaw." Willow pointed to my fight trainer in black. "Your turn."

"Hmm," Crenshaw said, although it came out as more of a grunt than anything else. "I suppose he's a decent guy."

"Sorry, Crenshaw," Willow said. "All Hands has already said that. I'm afraid you've been eliminated."

Crenshaw grunted again.

"Spider, your turn."

Spider studied me for a moment. "He is not short."

"I'll accept that, but we really need to work on thinking of some really good compliments," Willow said.

"What you want?" Spider said. "I'm Chinese. We are not good at giving compliments. And we are not good at taking compliments either."

"Very well," Willow said.

"What I like about Ben Potts," Helmsman called over his shoulder, "is he's taking us on these treasure hunts that are kinda fun."

"It's not your turn, Helmsman," Willow said, "but thank you."

"Not my turn, he says. I'm seventy-six years old. I'll take my turn when I damn well please."

"It's Redjack's turn. Redjack, if you please."

"Very well," Redjack said. "What I like about Ben is he's a good listener."

"There you go, Potts, a fine compliment."

"I'm sorry," I said. "What'd he say?"

"Ha ha," Willow said. "There's that sense of humor I was talking about."

I chuckled. I thought it best not to tell him that I actually wasn't listening. Helmsman had mentioned the treasure hunt, or rather the reverse treasure hunt, and it started me thinking about Ray. It was Ray who had set the whole thing up. These people were Ray's friends. He belonged on The Ship with them, not me. I was nothing more than an outsider they tolerated for Ray's sake.

"Maggie," Willow said, "your turn."

"What I like about Ben Potts is," Maggie began, but she had to stop and think. "I like the way he dresses."

At that Willow, All Hands, Jake, and Spider gave an affirmative, "Arrgh!"

"They're not my clothes." No one heard me because they were all busy chatting among themselves about my pirate garb. "They're not my clothes," I shouted.

They fell silent.

"They're your clothes," I said more calmly. "You're letting me borrow them."

"I still like them," Maggie said with some humility.

"Look," I said, "I appreciate what you're trying to do. I do, but let's be honest. I don't belong here. Ray did. He was the fun brother. He was always the one everyone liked. I was just Ray's awkward little brother. If you were doing this with Ray, none of you would have any trouble coming up with something that you liked about him. All you can say about me is I'm a decent guy, I'm not short, and you like the clothes I'm wearing, but the clothes I'm wearing belong to you. Let's end the game here before it gets depressing."

"No," Celeste said, "the game's not over."

"I don't want to play the game anymore."

"I said the game's not over." She stood up in the aisle. "I haven't had my turn yet."

"It does seem only fair," Willow said. "Everyone should have at least one turn before we end the game."

"Fine," I said, "let's get this over with."

"What I like about Benjamin Potts," she said as she approached me. "Is that he's got a good heart. I saw it when he made paper hats for those kids at the playground. I saw it the other day when he helped an elderly woman pick up her change purse and all its contents that she had dropped. What I like about Benjamin Potts is that he is kind and caring. And maybe there are times when he says the wrong thing at the wrong time, but he doesn't mean to be cruel or hurt anyone. He's not perfect. Nobody is. But all in all, I like Benjamin Potts."

"Can I get an 'Arrgh?'" Willow said.

All the crew cried out, "Arrgh!"

"Then it's unanimous," Willow said. "We all like Benjamin Potts."

I heard what they were saying, but it didn't register right away. I was too busy gazing into Celeste's eyes. She gave me a little half smile and returned to her seat next to Maggie. I remained standing next to Willow.

"And who here believes Potts will prove himself tomorrow to be a true warrior at the big melee?"

Suddenly it went quiet. The only sound I heard was the labored rumbling of The Ship's engine.

"Hmm, maybe we should have quit while we were ahead. Ah, well." Willow patted me on the shoulder. "Try not to get hurt too bad tomorrow."

15

We arrived in Bakersfield sometime around four in the afternoon. As soon as we entered the city limits Jake began chanting, "Bring out the treasure chest, bring out the treasure chest!" All Hands and Maggie joined him, and they began clapping. The other crew members added their voices and claps until Redjack dug out the treasure chest from the rear storage and set it at my feet.

The clapping and chanting ended when I opened the chest and took out the envelope marked "Do not open until you are in Bakersfield, California." I held up the envelope so they could all see the writing on the front, moving the envelope from left to right as a magician might show a playing card to his audience. I even added some fancy hand gestures to build up the dramatic effect.

"Potts," Willow said, "open the envelope."

The expressions on their faces told me they weren't impressed with my antics, so I offered a little chuckle as an apology. I pulled the parchment from the envelope. It had the customary map drawn on it with the customary clue written in the corner. "Give the DVD to Sam," it said. Beneath, Ray had written another one of his bad poems, although it appeared to be more of a riddle this time.

"From Highway 58,
Exit not the Fake road,
Take a southpaw into the hard cold valley,
Go westward once it has been thoroughly burned,
Move clockwise ninety degrees into the capital of Michigan,
Then the Big Bad Wolf will huff and puff
but cannot blow it down,
Disembark at the birth year of Richard Renner."

"I have no clue what any of that means," All Hands said.

"We're supposed to figure it out," Maggie said.

"Perhaps if we take it line by line," Redjack suggested.

"Yes," Willow said. "Good suggestion, Redjack. Let us start with the first line."

"Okay," I said. "Exit not the Fake road."

"So, we don't want to exit onto the fake road."

"But which one is fake?" Jake asked.

"If we don't want the fake road," I thought aloud, "then we must find the real road."

"All Hands," Willow said, pointing. "To the crow's nest."

"Aye aye, Cap'n." All Hands scrambled to the crow's nest, taking the spyglass with him.

Jake grabbed for the map. "I still don't understand how we're going to figure out which one is fake."

"I don't think there are any fake roads." I pulled the map away from him. "We need to find the real road."

"You've lost me."

"If my guess is correct, you'll understand in a few minutes."

For several minutes we all remained silent, searching, hoping to see some sign indicating where we should go next.

"I cannot tolerate this infernal silence." Willow chopped the air with both hands. "I need some mood music, please."

Jake obliged him by playing an upbeat number on his mandolin while softly singing along. Maggie began tapping her feet, and Celeste and Spider joined in. Willow began singing along with Jake, and the group burst into full merriment, singing, clapping, and stomping.

"Hey, hey, hey!" All Hands called. "Stop the music."

The merriment stopped.

"You're not going to believe this," All Hands said. "Up ahead, I see Real Road."

"Real Road?" Willow said. "Really?"

"Really," All Hands said.

"That's the exit we want, Helmsman," Willow said.

"Aye aye." Helmsman maneuvered The Ship into the far-right lane.

"What's next, Potts?"

"Take a southpaw into the hard cold valley," I read.

"Hard cold valley?" Maggie asked. "We're in the middle of the frickin' desert. There're no valleys here."

"I don't think it's referring to an actual valley," Celeste said. "If the first line was a clue to a street name, then maybe this one is too."

"I think you're right," I said. "Hard cold valley?"

"Hmm." Willow placed his finger to his lips and began pacing up and down the aisle. "Valley Street? Valley Avenue? Valley Terrace?"

"I don't think Valley is actually in the name," I said.

"Then what is a hard cold valley?" Jake asked.

"There are several words that refer to places similar to a valley," Redjack said. "Gully, canyon, glen, to name a few."

"Exiting onto Real Road," Helmsman announced.

"Does anyone have a thesaurus?" I asked.

"Sure," Willow said, "I always keep one on hand just in case something like this should pop up."

"You actually have a thesaurus?"

"No, I don't have a thesaurus. I was kidding. Who travels with a thesaurus?"

"What do we need a thesaurus for?" Maggie asked.

"To look for words that mean valley."

"Maybe we should have All Hands call out the street names as we approach them," Celeste suggested.

"All Hands," I called.

"Potts, I'm the captain," Willow said. "I give the orders around here."

"You're right," I said. "My apologies."

"All Hands," Willow called.

"Aye, Cap'n," All Hands said, leaning down into The Ship.

"Do the thing they were suggesting."

"Huh?"

"Call out the names of the streets," I said.

"Make it so." Willow gave a dismissive wave.

"Aye aye, Cap'n." All Hands searched ahead with the spyglass. "Coming up to the first street."

We waited with all eyes on All Hands. Because he stood in the crow's nest, we could see him only from the chest down, not exactly what I would prefer to look at, so I focused on the top button of his vest.

"It looks like Douglas Street," All Hands said. He stuck his head down into The Ship. "Douglas isn't another word for valley, is it?"

"No," Maggie told him.

"Okay," All Hands said and returned to his lookout position. An instant later he poked his head back down. "What is a Douglas, anyway?" he asked.

"Never mind that," Willow said. "Keep a sharp lookout."

"Aye, aye, Cap'n." All Hands resumed his duties.

"Potts," Willow whispered to me. "What is a Douglas, anyway?"

"It's a name," I said.

"Very good, Mr. Potts," Willow said. "Carry on."

"Coming up to the next street," All Hands said. "Looks like Stonedale Highway."

"We're looking for a valley of some sort, All Hands, not a highway," Willow said.

"Over hill, over dale," I muttered to myself. I turned to Redjack. "Isn't a dale a valley?"

"I believe it is," Redjack replied.

"A dale is a valley," Crenshaw confirmed.

"And a stone is hard and cold," I said.

"Except we're in the desert," Willow said. "Stones get pretty hot in the desert."

"The hard cold valley," I said. "Stonedale, that's the road we want."

"We passed it," Willow said.

"We passed it?" I almost screamed. "We have to turn around."

"Helmsman," Willow bellowed. "Come about."

I don't know if you've ever tried to make a U-turn in a school bus, but it's not something they are made for. The tires screeched when Helmsman pulled hard on the wheel. Cars coming from the opposite direction stopped suddenly to avoid a collision. We all nearly lost our balance when The Ship leaned heavily to the right. All Hands almost toppled out of the crow's nest and into the street. Willow, who had been standing in the aisle, fell into his seat. Crenshaw fell onto me. It felt as if The Ship itself might topple onto its side. Somehow it managed to stay on all four wheels and complete the U-turn without any casualties or damage.

"Heading back to Stonedale Highway," Helmsman said. "Which way do we turn?"

"Take a southpaw into the hard cold valley," I read the instructions.

"Southpaw refers to the left hand," Willow said. "Take her to port, Helmsman."

"Port it is, Cap'n," Helmsman said.

"Wait, no," I said. "Turn right. Right."

"Port or starboard, Cap'n?"

"Southpaw refers to someone who is left-handed, Potts. Which means we turn left, which means port."

"But we made a U-turn, which means we're coming at it from the opposite direction. We need to turn right."

"Potts, you do have a point. Take us to starboard, Helmsman."

"Too late, Cap'n. We've passed it."

"Turn us about then, ye mud-munching bellyflopper."

"Aye aye, Cap'n."

"Wait," I cried, but it was too late. Once again Helmsman took us into a U-turn. This time I fell onto Crenshaw. Willow clung to his seat to avoid being flung to the side. I could hear All Hands behind me howling while he did his best to remain in the crow's nest. Jake held on for dear life but couldn't keep himself from sliding toward me in his seat. He never fully fell out of his seat, but found himself in a difficult position, his hands clinging to the seat near the window, his feet propped against the lower support of my seat. Once we were back on track, I jumped to help him right himself.

"Thanks, Ben," Jake said once he returned to a sitting position.

"We have to turn left this time, Captain," I said to Willow.
"Are you sure, Potts?"
"Yes."
Willow gave the order, "Take us to port, Helmsman."
"Aye aye, Cap'n."
I failed to notice that we were in the right-hand lane, which meant that when Helmsman turned left onto Stonedale Highway he did it from the right-hand lane, causing several cars to honk their horns and screech to a stop to keep from hitting us. Somehow we avoided a collision and headed down Stonedale Highway.

"What's our next clue, Potts?" Willow asked.

"Can you give me a minute? My heart is beating ninety miles a second."

"I'd like to give you a minute, but as we have no idea when we shall reach our next turn, I'd suggest we find out now before we have to go through something like that again."

"I don't think I could go through something like that again," I said.

"Then we'd best figure out what our next turn will be now."

"Right." I looked at the map and read the next line. "Go westward once it has been thoroughly burned."

"Once what has been thoroughly burned?" Maggie asked.

"Are we supposed to set fire to something?" Jake asked.

"No, we're not supposed to set fire to anything." I studied the map more closely. "No one is starting any fires."

"It's a clue, Jake," Celeste said. "When something is thoroughly burned, it becomes ashes."

"That's it," I said. "Ashes."

"All Hands," Willow said, "look for some ashes."

"Aye aye, Cap'n," All Hands said.

"No," I said, "we're not looking for ashes. We're looking for Ash; Ash Street, Ash Avenue, something like that."

"Yes, well, that would make sense," Willow said. "Did you get that, All Hands?"

"Aye, aye, we're looking for Ash Street."

"It could be Ash Street," I said. "But it could also be Ash Lane or Road or Avenue or something."

"Right, got it."

"Have you considered the possibility that it's not Ash?" Jake asked. "What if it's Cinder Street?"

"Cinder Street?" Willow asked, scrunching his nose.

"Yeah," Jake said. "As in 'burnt to a cinder?'"

"What kind of name is Cinder for a street?"

"I'm offering a suggestion."

"Cinder Street. Worst name for a street ever."

"I don't know. I'd live on Cinder Street." Jake slumped in his seat, sulking.

Maggie laughed. "Wouldn't it be funny if it turned out to be Cinder Street?"

A few of the Scallywags chuckled. I did too.

"Indeed," Willow said somberly. "A veritable laugh riot. Except there is no street in this country called Cinder Street, is there?"

"It was a joke, Cap'n," Maggie said. "I've never heard of a Cinder Street, but there are some pretty strange street names out there. Who knows, maybe there is a Cinder Street."

"What about it, All Hands," I called, "any sign of Ash?"

"I'm not sure," All Hands said. "We're coming up to Ashey Road. Will that work?"

"Ashey?" I asked. "Spell it."

"A-s-h-e," he said.

"The e is silent, All Hands," I said.

"Really? Ashe is spelled with an e?" All Hands scrunched up his nose as he pondered the point.

"Sometimes. When it's a name."

"Then this must be it coming up."

"Ashe Road coming up, Helmsman," Willow said over his shoulder. "Prepare to turn."

"Port or starboard, Cap'n?" Helmsman called back.

"Potts?" Willow turned to me.

"Go westward once it has been thoroughly burned," I read. "We have to turn westward."

"Which way is west?" Willow gazed out one side and then the other. "It all looks the same to me."

"Come on, you should know west from east."

"I'm a pirate, not a bloody Boy Scout."

"For crying out loud," Celeste said. "Turn to the setting sun."

"Ah, good thinking." Willow pointed out the left window. "Hard to port, Helmsman," he ordered.

"No, the sun is starboard side, Captain," Celeste said.

"Starboard? Are you sure?"

"Yes."

"It is starboard side, Captain," Redjack said.

"It's difficult to tell with all these trees." Willow peered out the starboard window trying to find the sun. "Very well, I shall trust in your wisdom. Hard to starboard, Helmsman."

"Aye aye, Cap'n." We made the turn onto Ashe Road without incident.

"Potts, what's our next clue?" Willow asked.

"Move clockwise ninety degrees into the capital of Michigan," I read.

"What does that mean?" Jake asked.

"Oh, these riddles." Willow slapped his forehead. "They're giving me a headache." He reached into his coat, pulled out a flask, unscrewed the cap, and took a swig. "Much better. Anyone else want any?"

"What's the capital of Michigan?" I asked.

"Lansing," Crenshaw said.

"Then that's what we're looking for, Lansing."

"All Hands," Willow called.

"Aye, Cap'n?"

"You want some rum?" He took another swig before holding the flask up.

"Oh, aye, Cap'n." All Hands held out his hand.

"Willow," I said, "we need to look for Lansing."

"Oh right." Willow quickly returned the flask to his coat pocket. "All Hands, keep an eye out for Lansing."

"Aye aye, Cap'n." All Hands saluted. "Can I still have some rum?"

"Later!" I said.

"I'll save you some, All Hands." Willow patted his coat pocket.

"What am I looking for again?"

"Lan-sing." I exaggerated my pronunciation.

"Aye aye."

"And exactly what do we do when we reach Lansing Street or avenue or whatever?" Willow asked.

"Move clockwise ninety degrees," I read again.

"Clockwise? That would be this way." Willow drew a quarter circle in the air with his finger. "We want to go this way." He drew the quarter circle again.

"Yes," I said.

"How do we know when we've moved ninety degrees?"

"It means to turn right."

"Lansing Avenue ahead," All Hands called down to us.

"Where away?" Willow asked.

"There away," All Hands replied, pointing as best he could.

"I see it," Willow said. "Helmsman, hard to starboard."

"Aye aye, Captain."

The Ship turned onto Lansing Avenue.

"Potts," Willow said, "what's next?"

"Then the Big Bad Wolf will huff and puff but cannot blow it down," I read.

"Can't blow what down?" Jake asked. "Lansing Avenue?"

"It's a reference to the Three Little Pigs," Celeste said. "It refers to the third pig's house."

"The brick house," Maggie said.

"Like the song by the Commodores?" Jake said. He began playing his mandolin and singing.

Crenshaw popped out of his seat growling as if he were about to leap over me to attack Jake.

"No disco on The Ship," Willow scolded.

Jake stopped playing and Crenshaw settled back into his seat, still growling.

"I guess we're either looking for a brick house or a street called Brick House," I said to Willow.

"All Hands," Willow called.

"Aye, Cap'n?"

"Brick house, whether it be the name of a street or an actual house. Let us know."

"Aye aye."

"Potts, please tell me we are near our destination."

"We are, Captain," I said. "Listen to this. Disembark at the birth year of Richard Renner."

"Richard Renner?" Maggie asked. "Who's Richard Renner?"

"Didn't he play for the 49ers?" Jake asked.

"No," I said. "Richard Renner was the star of an old TV show, *American Spy*. Ray and I used to watch it all the time when we were kids."

"Now all we have to do is figure out when he was born?" Willow asked.

"All we gotta do is Google it," All Hands said. "Ben's got a cell phone."

"I don't have internet access."

"A bit behind the times, ain't we?" Willow raised an eyebrow at me.

"I'm old fashioned. Don't any of you have a cell phone?"

"We're on a pirate adventure, Potts. We agreed there would be no cell phones among us."

"Hang on, I should know this. When we were kids Ray and I knew everything about this guy. I need to think. It's been ages. Okay, Richard Renner was born," I said as I tapped my fist to my forehead. "Richard Renner was born in 1947. Forty-eight? No, it was forty-seven."

"You're sure?" Willow asked.

"Yes."

"So the house number we are looking for is 1947."

"Yes," I said. "1947 Brick House Street, Lane, Avenue, whatever it is."

"Could it be Brick House Road?" All Hands called down.

"Yeah, it could be any of those; road, or street, or avenue, whatever."

"Because we're about to pass Brick House Road."

"What?" Willow cried. "Where away?"

"Starboard side," All Hands said.

"Helmsman," Willow nearly shouted into the old driver's ear. "Hard to starboard."

"Aye aye, Cap'n."

Helmsman turned the wheel hard, taking us into a right turn that felt like The Ship might tip over onto its side. Somehow we remained upright, but not without Crenshaw falling onto me again. Several others loudly cursed our driver as they too toppled over into their neighbor.

Willow fell into his seat, and poor All Hands scarcely managed to keep from falling out of the crow's nest, but we made the turn onto Brick House Road. Once we all righted ourselves, we watched the house numbers as we drove past them one by one at a crawl.

"House ho!" All Hands called out.

"Where away?" Willow asked.

"Ahead on the left," All Hands said. "Nineteen forty-seven Brick House Road."

"Prepare to drop anchor," Willow said.

"Dropping anchor." Helmsman brought The Ship to a stop in front of the house at 1947 Brick House Road.

16

The Scallywags crowded along the portside windows, curious to see the house our search had brought us to. Before us sat a modest, picturesque house. It reminded me of a cozy little cottage on some Caribbean Island. The exterior had been painted the soft pinkish beige of a conch shell with sky-blue trim. A healthy flower garden with a birdbath in the center and a garden gnome at the forefront gave a nice splash of color, creating an idyllic scene.

"And here we are," Willow said.

"I guess so," I said. "It looks nice enough. This should be easy."

"So," said Willow. "Who shall accompany you this time? Or would you rather go alone?"

"I don't care, really. If you want to come with me, that's fine. But you'll have to be respectful."

"Me? I'm always respectful."

Helmsman opened The Ship's door to allow Willow and me to disembark. Behind me the Scallywags chattered with each other as they leaned out the windows to watch.

At the front door I reached up to press the doorbell but hesitated. Once again, like at Caitlin Bishop's house, the thought of ringing someone's doorbell intimidated me. I then heard Celeste's voice in my head, "You have to face your fears, Ben." It gave me that extra nudge to stop overthinking things and do what I came to do. I pressed the doorbell, but no ringing could be heard.

"I think you should knock," Willow said.

"Give it a minute." I didn't feel ready to knock. Pressing the doorbell once should have been enough.

"Potts, I really think you should knock."

"I'll knock if they don't come to the door."

"I think it's been long enough. If they haven't come to the door by now you should knock."

"Okay, okay," I said, beginning to regret I had agreed to let Willow come with me. "I'll knock." I raised my knuckles, took a deep breath, and knocked as loud as I could on the screen door.

"Perhaps you should open the screen door and knock on the wooden door," Willow said.

"Let me handle this, please," I said through clenched teeth.

"Very well, but who's to say whether or not they even know we're out here?"

"Willow, please." I held up the flat of my hand.

The wooden door opened and a young girl about eight years old with long sandy-blond hair tied back with a pink scrunchie appeared behind the screen door. Her face made me think of a porcelain doll with large brown eyes, a button nose, and a slender chin.

"Can I help you?" she asked.

"Hi." I smiled as pleasantly as I could. "Is Sam home?"

The girl's eyes went wide, she slammed the door in our

faces, and then came the sounds of a dead bolt clicking and the little girl calling her mother.

"There you go, Potts," Willow said. "You've frightened the child."

"All I did was ask if Sam was home."

"Clearly that was enough to frighten her."

"Why would that frighten her?"

"Perhaps it was the way you asked."

"I asked as nicely as I could."

"You think it may have been because you have an ugly face?"

"Yes, Willow, that was it. It was my ugly face."

"Just so you know, I for one don't find your face all that ugly."

"Gee, thanks."

"My pleasure."

The lock on the door clicked again, and the door opened. This time a woman in her late twenties, an older version of the girl, appeared. Her shoulder-length, sandy-brown hair was held back from her forehead by a headband. She wore sweatpants and a faded orange T-shirt. The towel she had tossed over her shoulder gave the impression she had been busy with some housekeeping when we arrived. "What do you want?" she asked.

"Hi." I tried my best to appear as harmless as I could. "Is Sam home?"

"What do you want with my daughter?" She demanded.

"Your daughter?" I realized why the girl had seemed so afraid of us.

"It would appear," Willow mused, "that Sam is short for Samantha."

"Apparently," I said to Willow. I spoke to the woman at the

door. "My name is Ben Potts. My brother was Ray Potts. Did you know him?"

"Ray? You're Ray's brother?"

"Yes, ma'am. He asked me to give this to Sam." I held up the DVD with the girl's name "Sam" showing so she could see it.

She stared at the disc in my hand with a troubled look. "Where is Ray?" she asked.

"He died in a plane crash a couple weeks ago," I said.

"Oh, no, no, no." She placed her hand to her mouth as if to stifle a sob and glanced over her shoulder. "How am I going to tell her?"

"I'm sorry. Were Ray and Samantha friends or something?"

"She's his daughter," she said in a hushed voice.

"This is a revelation," Willow said.

"Ray has a daughter?" I didn't know what to think. I found it hard to accept the idea of Ray being a dad. On the one hand, he had never been very good with relationships. He always kept Mom and me at a distance, never allowing either of us to get really close to him. On the other hand, he had always been a bit of a ladies' man. I recalled one time when he was around seventeen, he thought he had gotten Debbie Farris pregnant. It turned out to be a false alarm, but from then on Ray swore that he would always take precautions to make sure he never ended up in that situation again. Now I found out Ray had a daughter.

"Potts, you're an uncle."

"I'm an uncle," I echoed. What the hell did an uncle do, anyway?

"Would you like to meet your niece?" She wiped the tear from her eye.

If I'm an uncle, did that mean I had to buy her presents for

Christmas and her birthday? What kind of presents did young girls like her want, anyway? Could I give her cash and a pat on the head? Would I have to go to birthday parties or have Christmas dinner with them? Or could I mail her a check? I mean, we lived on opposite coasts, for crying out loud.

"He would be honored to meet her," Willow said.

What would I even say to her? What if she didn't like me? What if I ended up saying something stupid like I usually did?

"Come in, please." She unlocked the screen door to allow us in.

I stood motionless, bewildered by the whole situation. Willow had to grab me by the shoulders and guide me inside.

"You must forgive him," he said to her. "He's in a state of shock. None of us knew that Longbucket was a father."

"Who?" she asked.

"My apologies. Longbucket was our sobriquet, or rather nickname, for Raymond."

"And who are you?"

"Again, my apologies. Allow me to introduce myself. I am Captain Willow, and that scurvy lot in the rusted old tub outside is my crew. We are the Scallywags of Cannon Lake."

"Are you? Well, I'm pleased to finally meet you. Ray told us a lot about you."

"Don't believe a word of it," Willow said.

"I'm Robin Evers." She gave us a big, welcoming smile. "And you've met my daughter Samantha."

"'Tis a pleasure, madam."

"Where is Sam?" I finally managed to utter. "May I meet my niece?"

"Of course," Robin said. "Sam, come here, please."

The young girl peeked out from around a corner. "Why are they dressed like pirates?" she asked.

"I don't know," Robin said. "If you come out here and ask them yourself, maybe they'll tell you."

Samantha drew away a little, not ready to leave her refuge, but after some coaxing by her mother she approached, caution in every step. She found a second refuge behind her mother.

"Hi, Sam," I said. "You don't have to be afraid. We're not bad pirates."

"My daddy was a pirate too," she said.

"Indeed, he was," Willow said. "One of the best."

"He wasn't really a pirate," Robin told her. "And they're not real pirates either."

"The devil you say," Willow protested.

"Willow, please," I said. I squatted down to get face-to-face with her. "Sam, your daddy was my brother. I'm your uncle."

"Uncle Ben." Willow snickered.

I ignored him.

"My name is Ben," I said. "This is Captain Willow. We're on our way to a pirate festival, which is why we're dressed like pirates. We stopped here on our way to the festival because your daddy asked me to give you something."

"What?" she asked.

I held up the DVD with her name written on it.

"Is it a movie?" she asked.

"I don't know," I said. "Why don't you play it and see?"

I handed the DVD to her.

She looked at it for a moment and then turned to her mother. "Can I watch it now?"

"Sure," Robin said.

Sam ran into the next room with the DVD in hand. We all three followed her as she plopped down on the floor in front of the television, removed the DVD from its case, and placed it into the DVD player. A moment later the video started playing.

Ray appeared on the screen. He sat in a hotel room playing a ukulele, singing some silly little song that made Sam laugh. She sang along with him, and they finished the song together.

"Hi, Sam," Ray said. "I'm sorry I can't be there with you. I really wish I could. I can't tell you how much I miss you."

"I miss you too," Sam whispered.

"But even though I can't be there with you," Ray continued. "I promised that I would teach you how to play the ukulele, so I'm going to keep my promise with this DVD. I hope you have your ukulele."

Sam jumped up, ran into another room, and returned with a ukulele, which looked very much like the one Ray held in the video. She sat back down on the floor before the television, ukulele at the ready. Beside me Robin smiled as she watched her daughter's eyes light up at the sight of Ray.

I too couldn't help seeing the love the daughter had for her father. We continued to watch as Ray demonstrated each chord on the instrument, and Sam emulated his actions, playing the chords as he did.

"When did she get the ukulele?" I asked Robin.

"It came in the mail about a week and a half ago." She wiped a tear from her eye. "It's the same one Ray used to play when he visited. He played that same song every time. He called it 'The Sunshine Song.' Sam loved to sing it with him. He promised he would teach her to play it on the ukulele one day."

"Potts," Willow whispered to me, "I recognize the ukulele. Longbucket often played it for us as well. Sometimes with Maggie and the boys and sometimes alone. And he often played that very song."

"So," I said, "he shipped the ukulele to her and charged me with delivering the DVD?"

"It would appear so."

"Why did he do that?" I asked. "Why didn't he mail the DVD along with the ukulele?"

"If he had," Willow pointed out, "you would never have met your niece."

"True."

Sam continued to play her chords with Ray, and I sat down on the floor beside her. I had never known that the young girl even existed. Ray never told me he had a daughter. Why did he decide to let me know now?

"Sam," I said.

She turned to me as Ray continued with his lessons on the television.

"When your dad and I were about your age, we wanted to start our own band. We were going to call ourselves the Banging Potts. A stupid name for a band if there ever was one. Anyway, we begged our mother, your grandmother, to buy us guitars because we needed to learn how to play. Instead she signed us both up for piano lessons.

"As it turned out, I had no musical talent whatsoever and gave up, but your dad was pretty good. Then one day he quit. Gave it up. When I asked him why, he said if I wasn't going to be a part of the band then he wouldn't have a band. Hm, I hadn't thought about that in years. I don't think he ever regretted it though. He eventually took up photography and was good at that too, so maybe it all worked out in the end." I then remembered that neither of us would ever see Ray again. "Or maybe not," I added quietly to myself.

Outside, The Ship's horn honked twice. I paid it no mind.

"Maybe," I said to Sam, "you've inherited your father's talent. Do you want to be a musician when you grow up?"

"I want to be a photographer," she said.

That comment made me smile.

"Potts," Willow said, "it's time to go."

I looked up at him, nodded, and got to my feet, giving Sam a quick kiss on her forehead. "Goodbye, Sam," I said. "I hope to see you again soon."

"Bye," she said.

I went to Robin, extending my hand. She brushed my hand aside and hugged me.

"Thank you," she said. "Being able to see her father again really means a lot, even if it is just a video."

"I'm sorry to have to be the one to tell you of Ray's passing," I said.

"I know." She gave my arm a reassuring pat. "Ray and I remained friends, and I know he loved Samantha more than anything. I can only imagine how hard it must have been for you and your family."

"That's another story altogether," I said. "It was good to meet you, Robin and Sam. I'd like to visit you both again if that's okay."

"We'd like that," she said and gave me another hug.

"Potts." Willow jerked his thumb toward the door.

"Sorry," I said to Robin. "We've got a long drive ahead of us."

"Take care, Ben," Robin said.

"My dear lady," Willow said as he took Robin's hand in his and kissed it, "it has been a pleasure, but the tide waits for no one, so we must depart. Fare-thee-well." He turned to Samantha. "Adieu, daughter of Potts, adieu."

We left the home of Robin and my newfound niece, Samantha, and with a heavy heart I boarded The Ship behind Willow.

As Helmsman drove us away, I watched out the window to see Robin and Samantha standing outside their door waving to us. All the Scallywags waved back until we turned the corner and could no longer see them.

We continued toward Palo Alto, and the Scallywags chatted away among themselves while I sat in silence. My thoughts filled with Sam and Ray and how Ray and I had lost our father when we were young, and now Sam had lost her father at a young age. I wished I could do something for her. I just didn't know what.

Willow plopped down in the seat across from mine, once again shoving All Hands and Jake against The Ship's side. He handed me a flask of rum.

I took a swig and handed it back to him. "Thanks," I said.

"What's wrong, Potts?" he asked. "You should be in high spirits. You've discovered you have a niece."

"I know. The problem is I don't know how to be an uncle. What am I supposed to do? She's lost her dad. Am I supposed to take on the role of some sort of surrogate father to her?"

"Bah! You think too much, mate. This is a time for celebration." Willow rose to address the Scallywags. "What say ye, mates? How do we celebrate this prodigious occasion?"

"A song," Jake said. "Music is ideal for celebrations."

"Aye," Maggie agreed. "Let's have a song."

"Marvelous," Willow said. "Get out your instruments, and let's have some music."

All Hands brought out his bongos and Jake his mandolin. They debated which song to play. Jake wanted to play a song called "The Ships Sail Out Tonight," while All Hands wanted to play a song called "We Merry Band of Travelers." Maggie suggested a song called "To the Sea, to the Sea." Finally they all agreed on "Little Pirate Girl," a song that Redjack recommended in honor of Samantha.

Jake and All Hands played while the entire crew sang a

lively tune that put everyone in a jovial mood, clapping their hands as they sang. After the second verse, I clapped with them, and with encouragement from Willow I even sang a little of the chorus, which was all I could grasp.

When the song ended, Willow whispered something to Helmsman, who nodded in agreement. Willow turned to us, smiled, and cried out, "Prepare to fire the cannons."

"Enemy vessel to port," Helmsman announced.

"Fire a warning shot," Willow said.

We pulled up alongside an RV, and Helmsman honked the horn. The woman sitting in the passenger seat looked over at us, as did a boy and a girl riding in the back. The entire crew rushed over, crowding around the windows, All Hands and Jake were leaning on my shoulders, and they all cried out, "Arrgh!"

I remained reluctant to join them, but as we approached a second vehicle on our starboard side, the crew implored me to join in, and finally I gave in. We rushed to the windows on The Ship's starboard side, Helmsman honked the horn, and when the people in the next vehicle looked at us, we all cried, "Arrgh!" I felt uncomfortable with it at first, but after a few times I laughed and actually began enjoying myself.

17

We reached Palo Alto later that evening and pulled into the campsite. After signing in, we drove The Ship through the dark, searching for a place to set up camp, passing several campsites and dozens of people, all of whom were dressed as pirates. They sat about campfires or strolled through the grounds chatting and laughing, and some were even singing.

As we passed, many of them waved to us in welcome. The Scallywags leaned out the windows and waved back, exchanging hellos, and joking with them. All Hands perched in the crow's nest, waving as if he were in a parade, calling to several of the people. It felt as if we were returning home after a voyage.

"Do you know all these people?" I asked Jake.

"Nope," he said. "We're an Atlantic Coast-based crew. This is the Pacific Coast. Usually we don't travel so far to attend a festival. It gets expensive."

"But you're acting like you're seeing old friends you haven't seen in a long time," I said.

"We have something in common. We're all pirates."

The crew found a spot to its liking, and Helmsman parked The Ship.

As we disembarked a man and a woman approached us. "Ahoy, mateys, where might ye hail from?" the man asked.

"Florida," All Hands said.

"Ye drove all the way from Florida?" the woman said. "That be quite a drive."

"Then welcome," the man said. "I be Rigby, and this be Sasha. We're with the Pirates of Preciado Beach."

"The Pirates of Preciado Beach?" Willow inquired. "Who might your captain be?"

"Captain Belasco heads our crew," Sasha said.

"Belasco?" Willow almost growled the name.

"Aye," Sasha said. "Do you know him?"

"Do I know him?" Willow waved his hand in the air as he sucked in a deep breath through his nose. "Do I know the villain who stabbed me in the back?"

Sasha and Rigby looked at each other for a moment before Rigby turned to Willow. "Are you Brian Willow?" he asked.

"Captain Willow to you, sir," Willow roared.

"Apologies, Captain Willow," Rigby said. "Captain Belasco talks about you at times. I understand there's some kind of rivalry between the two of you."

"Rivalry?" Willow bellowed. "That's putting it mildly. We are sworn enemies, your captain and I."

"We just came by to welcome you and to invite you over for a drink if ye've a mind to," Rigby said.

"Lies!" Willow said. "You came here as spies. Admit it. That scoundrel of a captain of yours sent you here to spy on us."

"Why would we be spying on you?" Sasha asked.

"You know very well why." Willow stabbed the air with his finger.

Celeste took Willow's arm. "Umm, excuse me, Captain." She led him away from the visitors. "Perhaps it would be best if I handled this. You don't want to get yourself all upset before dinner, do you? It's bad for the digestion."

"You may have a point, my dear," Willow said. "Very well, I shall allow you to deal with these vermin. My mouth is developing a nasty taste from just looking at them." Willow reached into his coat and pulled out his flask as he walked away.

Celeste walked back to Sasha and Rigby. "I apologize for that. I'm Celeste. David, your captain is an old friend of mine."

"So you're Celeste," Sasha said. "I'm pleased to meet you. The captain talks about you as well."

"As much as we appreciate your kind offer," Celeste said, "we've only just arrived and need some time to settle in."

"Of course," Rigby said. "We completely understand."

"Perhaps we could accept your invitation another time," Celeste offered.

"Certainly, you'd be most welcome anytime."

"Thank you," Celeste said.

"I suppose we'd best get back to our camp," Rigby said. "We'll see you all in the morning. Have a good night."

The Scallywags bid the two a good night as they returned to their own camp.

"And you may inform that villainous captain of yours," Willow called after them, "that his day of reckoning is at hand. The gauntlet has been thrown down. He shall be groveling in the dirt, begging for my mercy before tomorrow comes to an end."

"A little much, don't you think, Cap'n?" Jake asked.

"Not in the least bit," Willow said. "I thought I was the model of restraint."

Willow paced, mumbling curses against Belasco and his

crew. Meantime, the rest of us set about making camp. Once I had the chance, I went in search of a private spot where I could call my mother. I wanted to tell her that we had arrived safely in California and inform her she had a granddaughter. I had no idea how she would take such news, but I thought she at least had a right to know. Of course all that news got shoved to the back burner once she answered her phone.

"Ben, you must come home right away," Mom wailed. "Do you hear me? Right away."

"What is it this time, Mom?"

"I don't know what to do. You must tell me what to do about him, Ben."

"About who, Mom?"

"Mr. Esteban."

"Mr. Esteban? Is he another one of your fish?"

"Certainly not. He's the gray-haired Hispanic man who lives down the street."

"Okay, yeah, I know who you're talking about. What happened?"

"I did as you suggested and asked someone to help me with that horrid beast that has been prowling about on my patio."

"You mean the lizard?"

"You know exactly what I mean."

"I'm glad to hear that. Good for you."

"No, it's not good. Wait until you hear what happened."

"Okay, what happened?"

"I was in the front yard tending to my azaleas when Mr. Esteban came by and said hello. I returned his greeting, and we began talking."

"Uh huh."

"I mentioned the creature on my patio and asked him if he wouldn't mind chasing the beast away. He said he'd be happy to."

"So did he get rid of the lizard?"

"Yes, he did."

"So there you go."

"But that's not all. After he chased the beast from my patio, he invited me to come over to his house for a drink sometime."

"That was nice of him."

"It's not nice, Benjamin. It's not nice at all, and I have no idea what to do."

"Simple. Accept his invitation."

"I'm not that sort of woman, Benjamin."

"What sort of woman?"

"The sort of woman who would accept such invitations from a man like Mr. Esteban."

"Why? Is he married?"

"His wife passed away a few years ago."

"So he's a widower. You're a widow. I still don't see a problem."

"Benjamin, do you not understand what 'having a drink' translates to?"

"It translates to having a drink, Mom."

"For all I know he intends to drug me then use me in all kinds of perverse ways."

"I doubt that's going to happen."

"You never know."

"Mom, maybe he's lonely and wants some company."

"You're very naive, Benjamin."

"And you're paranoid."

"Very well, I will accept Mr. Esteban's invitation. Be prepared to get a phone call from some strange doctor when I end up in the intensive care unit at the hospital in a drug-induced coma after being treated as a sex toy by that man."

"I'll be sure to send flowers."

"You are heartless, Benjamin, heartless."

"That's me, heartless and naive."

"Come home, Benjamin, please."

"Bye, Mom. I'll call you tomorrow." I hung up. After I did, I realized I forgot to mention Samantha. Mom should know that she had a granddaughter. I thought I should call her back and tell her, but I couldn't deal with her anymore right then.

Later the Scallywags and I sat around the campfire after having eaten dinner, chatting about one thing or another and passing the rum around, when All Hands decided to ask me a question.

"Ben," he began, "what happened between you and Longbucket?"

"What do you mean?" I asked.

"You didn't know that Longbucket had a daughter, did you? You didn't know that he often dressed as a pirate and attended festivals with us either. I mean, you don't seem to know much about him beyond when the two of you were kids. Why?"

"All Hands," Maggie said, "it's none of our business."

"It's okay." I accepted the bottle of rum when Redjack offered it to me.

"You don't owe us any explanation, Ben," Celeste said.

"No, but maybe I need to talk about it." I took a good swig of rum and passed the bottle to Crenshaw before saying more. "I guess," I continued, my face scrunching and tightening because of the rum, "if it was anything, it must have been the motorcycle trip."

"Which motorcycle trip are you referring to?" Willow asked.

"When we were teenagers, Ray and I always talked about traveling the country together on motorcycles."

"I didn't know you could ride a motorcycle, Ben," All Hands said.

"I can't, but I was going to learn," I said. "Anyway, when Ray turned twenty-one, he bought a motorcycle. Mom was furious. She kept telling him that he had to return it, but he refused. She said she was going to call the man who sold it to him and have him come and take it back. Ray wasn't about to let that happen. Ray came to me and said he was leaving, and if I wanted to come with him I could. He knew where I could buy a cheap motorcycle. It was in good condition too.

"I told him I would have to think about it. I was only nineteen at the time. Mom, of course, begged me not to listen to Ray. She said he would get me killed and told me I had to stay with her. She said she needed me to stay with her because she couldn't bear to be alone. In the end I told Ray I couldn't go with him because Mom needed me. Ray took off alone, and I hardly ever saw him after that. He would occasionally send us a postcard or email to let us know he was okay. He never really told us what he was doing or who he was spending time with. I saw him maybe only four times in the past ten years, even though he had an apartment in Orlando. I don't know. I've often wondered what would have happened if I had bought that motorcycle and taken off with him. I'll never know."

"But here you are, Potts." Willow spread his hands with a sweeping gesture. "Traveling with us across the country. Perhaps this is your chance to make amends for the past."

"No, I don't buy it. Come Sunday I'm going to have to fly back to Florida and return to my old life. This is nothing more than a brief getaway."

"Is it?" Spider asked. "Or is it an opportunity?"

"I'm not Ray. I don't have his self-confidence. I don't have what it takes to start a new life like that."

"Ah, Potts," Willow said, "you have so much to learn. But come, let us think of more positive, life-affirming subjects. We're here in California, looking forward to a day of fun and merriment tomorrow."

"I guess so."

Redjack appeared in front of me toting the treasure chest. I hadn't even seen him leave the campfire. He set the chest on the ground at my feet. In all honesty I had almost forgotten about delivering the next treasure item until then. After discovering I had a niece and having reached our destination, the thought of delivering the remaining items didn't seem to be a priority, yet two items remained. As the Scallywags gathered closer, asking each other who the next recipient might be and making suggestions like a long-lost brother or Ray's adopted son, I opened the trunk and removed the next envelope. It read, "Do not open until you are in Palo Alto, CA." I opened the envelope and pulled out the parchment. It had no map this time, only the instructions, "Deliver the baseball cards to Zuleida."

"Who's Zuleida?" Maggie asked. "Anybody know a Zuleida?"

No one had any idea who Zuleida could be. The parchment offered no other clues to go on, not even one of Ray's bad poems.

"Here is another mystery." Willow held up a finger and wiggled it as he spoke. "Longbucket does enjoy challenging us, does he not?"

"I don't think you can get much enjoyment out of something once you're dead," All Hands said.

"That may be, but I don't believe we will figure this mystery out tonight. Let's clean up our dinner dishes and retire to bed for the night."

"Wait," I said, "you mean I'm not going to have to clean up by myself?"

"No, Potts, tonight we work as a crew, for tomorrow we shall fight as a crew."

I sat speechless. I couldn't figure these people out, but I began to appreciate their eccentric ways. I stuck the baseball cards and Ray's instructions into my pocket, which meant only one more envelope and item remained inside the treasure chest. After I closed and secured the lid, Redjack carried the chest back to the cargo hold and returned to help clean up.

18

I found myself on the deck of a wooden sailing vessel surrounded by men fighting and killing each other. The sounds of clashing swords, curses, screams, and the occasional gunfire erupted to a deafening level. A second vessel lay alongside. Ropes and grappling hooks bound the two ships together. Fire and smoke enveloped everything. I was in the midst of a pirate attack, but which ship or crew I belonged to, I didn't know. In my right hand I held a cutlass but felt no desire to use it.

"Let's go," someone yelled in my ear.

Startled, I turned to discover Ray standing next to me.

"Go?" I yelled back. "Go where?"

"We can take the dory and row to shore," he said.

"But what about the battle?" I asked. "Aren't we going to help?"

Ray looked at the fighting going on around us and smiled. "It's not my fight," he said.

"Not your fight?" I cried. "Then what are we doing here?"

"I stopped by to pick up a little something," he said.

"What could you possibly need to get in a place like this?"

"Nothing much. Just this." He held up a gold ring with a large diamond on it. The diamond sparkled in the firelight.

"A ring?" I said. "We're in the middle of a pirate attack so you can steal a diamond ring?"

"Be happy for me, Ben," he said. "I'm getting married."

A grime-smeared pirate with bloodshot eyes and a black mustache charged at us crying out, "Yaaa!" He raised his cutlass, ready to strike us down. Ray shot him, and the man fell backwards onto the deck.

"Married?" I asked. "To Caitlin?"

"Yep. Granted I haven't asked her yet, but she's gonna say yes."

"But you're dead. You're both dead."

"That doesn't mean we can't be happy."

"And she's already married."

"That's the beauty of it. The afterlife means a new beginning. Once she died, she was no longer married to that jerk."

A second pirate charged at us yelling, "Die, you pigs!" I thrust my cutlass at him, stopping him in his tracks. He turned, reeled for a moment, and fell into an open hatchway.

"That being the case," I said. "Of course I'm happy for you."

"Thanks, Ben. You don't know how much this means to me."

Ray started climbing over the ship's railing but a third pirate charged at us. "I'll eat your gizzard!" he cried.

I kicked over a nearby barrel that rolled into him. He tripped and fell over the side of the ship, howling all the way down.

"I wish I could be there for the wedding," I said as Ray climbed down into a small rowboat that waited in the water below.

"I wish you could too," he said. "I'd ask you to be my best man if I could. You know that, right?"

"Yeah," I said. "I know that."

"Well," he said as he untied the line holding the dory to the ship. "I have to get back to Caitlin and pop the question to make it official. Take care of yourself, Ben."

I gave a small wave. When he began rowing away, I remembered the reverse treasure hunt. "Hey, wait!" I called after him. "Where is Zuleida? I have to give her the baseball cards."

"Keep your eyes open," he called back as his boat slipped into a developing fog. "You'll find her."

His answer failed to assure me.

I gazed into the fog, hoping he would say something or do something that might provide more help. After all, he was the one who entrusted me to carry out the whole treasure hunt thing, but nothing came. Only silence. Too much silence. When I turned around, I found myself surrounded by angry, bloodthirsty pirates directing their swords and pistols at me. I attempted a friendly smile.

"Arrgh!" they roared as they charged at me.

I awoke to find myself still surrounded by pirates, but these particular pirates were sound asleep, and I didn't mind them as much. I settled down and eventually fell back asleep.

As the sun rose, I awoke for the second time to discover Crenshaw standing over me holding a sword in each hand.

"Practice time," he said.

Crenshaw and I fenced while All Hands, Jake, and Maggie rehearsed a few of their songs. Willow helped Redjack get out his swords and other blades. Celeste and Spider were busy with Spider's jewelry. Redjack and Spider planned to share a vendor booth at the festival. Helmsman busied himself under The Ship's hood, checking the oil and other fluids.

"Ahoy, mateys, be ye the Scallywags of Cannon Lake?" someone called to us.

I turned to see a man with a long staff approaching us. At the top of his staff perched a small skull with strings of beads and feathers hanging from its crown.

"Ahoy yourself, sir. That we are," Willow said. "And who might you be?"

"I be Bilgewater Bill, the master of ceremonies for this year's event."

"Pleased to meet you, sir," Willow said, shaking the man's hand. "I'm Captain Willow, and this scurvy lot is my crew."

"Welcome, all of you," Bill said. "You seem to be the talk of the camp this good morning. Everyone be talking about how ye lot drove all the way here from Florida. Is that true?"

"Aye, it is."

"And you drove across the country in this old heap?" Bill walked up to The Ship to get a closer look.

Helmsman stepped in front of Bilgewater Bill prepared to defend his baby. "Now don't ye go bad mouthing The Ship. She may not look like much, but it's what's on the inside what counts, and she's got the heart of the Kraaken inside her."

"No offense intended, mate," Bill said to Helmsman. "If she's made it all the way here, she must be a sturdy machine."

"That she be," Helmsman said. "Redjack and I put a lot of time and hard work into her."

"And who might Redjack be?" Bill asked.

"That would be me, sir." Redjack ambled up to Bill.

"Pleased to meet you." Bill shook Redjack's hand. "And as

much as I would enjoy meeting each and every one of you, I actually came here to take you to The Commodore."

"The Commodore?" Willow asked. "And who might The Commodore be?"

"He is the head of the events committee. In fact he and I started this festival a few years back."

"And he has requested an audience with us?" Willow asked.

"Did you not make a request when you registered for this event?"

"That I did."

"For us to grant your request, there are certain matters we require to be worked out."

"Then I suppose we'd best go see The Commodore," said Willow.

"Aye," said Bill. "If ye'd care to follow me."

Willow, Celeste, Crenshaw, and I followed Bilgewater Bill through the festival grounds. The others remained behind to prepare for the festival. As we passed the vendors and others also preparing for the day's event, many called out greetings to our little band. The Scallywags returned their greetings.

"There are three things I must brief you on regarding your meeting with The Commodore," Bill said to Willow.

"I'm all ears," Willow said. "Brief away."

"First, if ye really want The Commodore to grant your request, it always helps to offer him a gift."

"A gift?" Willow asked. "What kind of gift?"

"He likes muffins."

"We don't have any muffins."

"That's okay. The promise of a muffin will suffice. Second, when ye address The Commodore, he prefers to be referred to as 'Your Cuddliness.'"

"'Your Cuddliness?'"

"He likes to think of himself as a big cuddly bear."

"He does have his ways, doesn't he?"

"Yes, he does."

"And what's the third thing?"

"If he asks you to sing a song for him, your best option is to sing his favorite song, 'Dancing Queen' by ABBA."

"His favorite song is 'Dancing Queen?'"

"Not really, but he thinks it's funny to have pirates sing it."

"I'm not even sure if I know all the words."

"Oh, just fake it. He doesn't care."

We came to a large tent. Upon entering I first noticed a portly fellow sitting on a large chair atop a dais. His round belly, long gray beard, and big smile made him look something like a piratical Santa Claus. About a dozen other pirates, men and women of varying ages, scurried about or filled out paperwork or sat at a table counting money into cash boxes.

The Santa Claus-looking pirate looked over some documents while talking to a small pirate with glasses.

Bilgewater Bill tapped his staff on the ground and cleared his throat. "Presenting," he announced, "the Scallywags of Cannon Lake out of some part of Florida."

"Oh good," the Santa Claus-looking pirate said. He handed the documents to the man he had been talking to and shooed him away. "You're better at that sort of thing than I am, anyway, Bartleby. You can sort it out on your own."

The man referred to as Bartleby stepped away from the dais and moved to a table off to the side where he busied himself with sorting through several documents.

Willow stepped forward and bowed to the overweight man sitting on the dais, whom I concluded had to be The Commodore. "Good morning, Your Cuddliness," Willow said.

"None of that bowing stuff," The Commodore said. "I ain't no king."

"Beg pardon," Willow said. "I'm a bit rusty on the protocol of addressing commodores."

"It's like talking to anybody else, only a bit tangier."

"I wish to offer you a gift," Willow said, "a muffin."

"Ooo, you brought me a muffin?"

"No. I don't have any muffins on me, but I promise to bring you one as soon as possible."

"I suppose as long as you bring me one before noon it'll be all right."

"Consider it done."

"What can I do for you?"

"I believe you summoned us," Willow said.

Bilgewater Bill crossed to sit in a chair on the dais next to The Commodore.

"Right, you're here because I summoned you, and I do appreciate your promptness." The Commodore paused for a moment before he turned to Bilgewater Bill. "And why did I summon them?"

Before Bill could answer, the tent flaps rustled behind us and three more pirates entered. Two I recognized; we had met them the previous night, Rigby and Sasha. The third, a tall, handsome black man, I had never seen before. He looked and moved like an athlete.

"Belasco!" Willow cried in a rage and started toward the man.

Crenshaw stepped in front of him, and Rigby and Sasha stepped in to protect their captain. I jumped in to assist Crenshaw, and Celeste stepped up to Willow to try to calm him.

"I'll tear you limb from limb," Willow threatened Belasco.

"Captain, no, please," Celeste said. "This is why we're here, to settle this matter."

"Willow," Captain Belasco said, "it's been a long time. Have you gained some weight? Best lay off those johnnycakes."

"I'll johnnycake you, you traitor," Willow said.

"And Celeste," Belasco said, "you're looking as lovely as ever."

"Thank you, David," Celeste said. "It's good to see you again, even if it is under such circumstances."

"Don't concern yourself with Willow," Belasco said. "He's merely blowing off some steam."

"Blowing off some steam?" Willow said. "You stole Louise from me."

"Louise is much happier than she has ever been," Belasco said. "And you know it."

"Excuse me," The Commodore said. "Remember me?"

"My apologies, Your Cuddliness. Good morning," Belasco said to The Commodore.

"Now who might you be?" His Cuddliness asked.

"I am Captain Belasco of the Pirates of Preciado Beach," Belasco said. "And these are two of my crew members, Rigby and Sasha."

Rigby tilted his hat to The Commodore. Sasha curtsied.

"And what may I do for you?" the Commodore asked.

"If I'm not mistaken," Belasco said, "you summoned us."

"I seem to be doing an awful lot of summoning today," The Commodore said.

"They are here in regard to a request for public battle between the Scallywags of Cannon Lake and the Pirates of Preciado Beach," Bill informed him.

"Ooo, I'd like to see that," The Commodore said. "When is this battle to take place?"

"Perhaps we should set it for twelve-thirty this afternoon at the tournament field," Bill offered.

"Splendid idea." The Commodore clapped. "And we can let everyone watch. How does that grab you?"

"I am more than satisfied with that." Willow almost bowed to The Commodore but caught himself.

"My crew and I shall be happy to oblige," Belasco said. "However, I wonder if the captain here would be willing to make our competition a little more interesting?"

"How so?" Willow asked.

"A side bet," Belasco said.

"Ooo, a side bet. Will it involve amputation?" The Commodore asked, listening with interest.

"What sort of side bet?" Willow asked.

"My crew has been craving Mexican food the past two days, and we recently discovered a nearby Mexican restaurant called Don Miguel's. They claim to have the best chimichangas in town."

"We've been to Don Miguel's," The Commodore said. "Bill and I took our families there last week. Their chimichangas are excellent. Right, Bill?"

"You mean that place up the road there? Yeah, great food. Loved their chimichangas."

"Then how about this?" Belasco said. "The losing team buys dinner for the winning team. What say you, Captain Willow?"

"Very well," Willow said. "Agreed."

"Shall we shake on it?" Belasco extended his hand.

Willow pondered Belasco's hand for a moment before he grasped it and shook it.

"I hope you've brought enough money, mate," Belasco said. "My crew can get awfully hungry."

"I'm hardly concerned," Willow said. "We will humiliate you."

"That's yet to be seen."

"Fine, fine," The Commodore said. "Now that that bit of business is done, shall we move on to something more important?"

"You mean we're done?" Willow said.

"Quite so."

"That's a relief." Willow wiped his brow with the back of his hand. "I thought you were going to ask us to sing a song for you."

"Splendid idea!" The Commodore's face lit up. "Do you know 'Dancing Queen' by ABBA?"

Crenshaw, Celeste, and I gave Willow evil looks. We were almost out of there, but he had to open his mouth.

"We'd be only too happy to," Willow said, smiling uncomfortably. He began singing the song.

I kept quiet, hoping he'd be content with doing a solo, but he nudged me to join in. As much as I hated to, I started singing along. Willow nudged Crenshaw on his right. Crenshaw grunted his disapproval, so Willow nudged him a second time, and Crenshaw unwillingly began singing with us. Celeste, who stood on Crenshaw's right, laughed into her hand.

Willow motioned to her to join in, but she couldn't stop laughing. Crenshaw turned to her, giving her his meanest look, but singing a disco song robbed the look of its effectiveness. Celeste made a couple of attempts to join but laughed too hard to do it with any conviction. When she finally managed to stop laughing, she apologized over and over and then went back to laughing again.

The Commodore seemed to enjoy our offering of entertainment. He tapped his toes and bobbed his head to the rhythm. Bilgewater Bill and everyone else present laughed and applauded when we finally ended the song.

19

After our meeting with The Commodore, Crenshaw became relentless about our sword practice. Forty-five grueling minutes of lunging, parrying, and getting swatted by the flat of Crenshaw's sword followed. Finally I couldn't take another second of it and fell to my knees, begging for a breather. Crenshaw begrudgingly granted a five-minute break for me to get some water and catch my breath.

I had other plans, though, and when Crenshaw's attention turned to a neighboring pirate band practicing swordplay, I slipped away. I hoped I might be able to disappear amid the festival crowd and escape the wearisome bouts with Crenshaw's bulldog-like drills.

Strolling through the festival, I came across the booth that Redjack and Spider Lau shared, selling their merchandise. Thinking it might be as good a place as any to hide, I grabbed a chair in the back corner and prayed Crenshaw wouldn't come looking for me.

Redjack and Spider assisted people who expressed an

interest in their wares while I lazily sat in the corner, sipping water.

An attractive redheaded woman in her mid-thirties approached me. "Excuse me," she said. "I was looking at your daggers and was wondering if you made them yourself."

"No, ma'am," I said. "Redjack makes the swords, not me."

"I was wondering if you have any daggers with a sinister-looking squid adorning the handle."

"A squid?" I asked. "You mean like the squid's head is the pommel of the dagger, and its tentacles wrap around to form the handle? Something like that?"

"Yes," she said. "I would love to acquire a dagger like that."

"Redjack," I called.

He turned to me. I directed his attention to the woman. As if someone had flipped a switch, Redjack's usual stoical expression changed into one of stupefaction. He stepped over to her. I could see his lips moving as if he were searching for something to say.

"You look familiar," she said. "Have we met before?"

"Yes," he said. "It's been a few years, but we met at a pirate festival in North Carolina."

"That's right," she said. "I remember you. Redjack, right?"

"Yes," he said. "You're Rebecca. You asked me if I had any daggers with a sinister-looking squid on the handle."

"Yes," she said. "I'm still looking for a dagger like that."

In response Redjack drew the dagger from the sheath on his belt and presented it to her handle first.

"Incredible." She took the dagger and examined it more closely. "This is exactly what I've been looking for. Did you make this?"

"Of course," he said. "I made it after I met you in North

Carolina. I had hoped you would show up at the same festival the following year, but I never saw you again."

"That's because six months later I got a job offer out here in California."

"I suppose it's lucky for both of us that my crew and I traveled across the country to attend this festival."

"Yes, it is." Rebecca laughed and then took a moment to study the detail on the dagger. "I can't believe you actually made this for me. Thank you."

"It was my pleasure," Redjack said.

I wanted to stay and see how things between Redjack and Rebecca played out, but I spotted Crenshaw working his way through the crowd and thought it best if I made myself scarce. I ducked behind a nearby tent, looking for a shortcut to another part of the festival in hopes of losing Crenshaw. I searched for somewhere to lie low until the coast was clear.

I spotted the perfect hiding place, a fortune teller's tent. The very thing I needed, a small, dark, enclosed space where I could keep a lookout for my pursuer. Above the entrance a sign read, "Madame Zuleida Knows All, Sees All, Tells All." Something about the name sounded familiar. Zuleida? I reached into my pocket and pulled out the parchment with Ray's clue written on it. I read it again. "Deliver the baseball cards to Zuleida." The same name. Could it be a coincidence? I doubted it, so I decided to check it out.

Bells jingled when I passed through the tent flap. A strong scent of incense filled my nostrils. I couldn't see anything inside the tent at first and stumbled around until my eyes adjusted to the dim light.

"You come to seek answers from Madame Zuleida," someone said. A woman stepped into view dressed in full gypsy garb. "Come, sit. Madame Zuleida will tell you all you wish to know."

I sat in a chair on one side of a small table.

She sat in a chair opposite. She produced a deck of oversized cards and began shuffling them. "The spirits are astir today," she said. "They are prepared to speak. Ask what you will." She set the cards face down one by one on the table.

"Did you know Raymond Potts?" I asked.

"You wish to know if the spirits know someone by the name of Raymond," she said. She flipped the first card over so that it lay face up. "The spirits say 'yes.' They know your friend Raymond."

"No," I said. "I'm asking if you knew him, and he wasn't my friend. He was my brother."

She flipped another card over. "The spirits seem to be bewildered. Wait. What?"

"I want to know if you, Madame Zuleida, knew my brother Raymond Potts," I said.

"Me?" she asked. "But the spirits are astir. I speak only for the spirits."

"My brother, Ray, wanted me to give these to you." I pulled the stack of baseball cards from my vest pocket and held them out to her.

She looked at the baseball cards in my hand a moment before she placed the deck of tarot cards on the table. She accepted the baseball cards, removed the rubber band, and placed them one by one on the table before her. "Carl Clemente," she read each card in turn. "Dale Pettigrew, Lou Gamble." She stopped and looked at me. "Raymond Potts," she said. "Your brother was Raymond Potts?"

"Yes."

"I am sorry." She set the baseball cards down. "Your brother died, didn't he?"

"Yes."

"And he knew." She held up a finger for emphasis. "But he refused to believe. How I wish the spirits were wrong that day."

"What do you mean?"

"Two months ago your brother came to me. He told me of a dream he had. He dreamed he was going to die, and he asked me to speak with the spirits to confirm or deny whether his dream would come true or not. The spirits confirmed his dream. He found it all curious but still refused to believe. He told me when he was a boy he had a dream foretelling his father's passing, and even though that dream came true, he remained skeptical." She paused. "May I ask how he died?"

"A plane crash."

"The spirits gave no specific details of how it was to happen."

"It wouldn't matter." I knew Ray too well. "He wrote me a letter saying he refused to let fear and psychic predictions control his life."

"He made a bet with me." Madame Zuleida held up the baseball cards. "If the spirits were proved correct, he would give me these baseball cards, but if the spirits were proved to be wrong, I would give him a bottle of scotch."

"Scotch? Not rum?"

"He liked his rum, sure, but I like my scotch." She reached under the table and pulled out a bottle of scotch. She set it between us and produced a small stack of paper cups. She took two paper cups and placed them next to the bottle. "Shall we?" she asked. "In your brother's memory."

"Okay," I said.

She opened the bottle and poured a little scotch into each cup. She handed me one of the cups and took the other for herself. "To Ray," she said, and we tapped cups.

"To Ray."

We both emptied our cups. It took me two gulps to empty mine. I wasn't much of a scotch drinker, but Zuleida tossed hers back like water.

"I've been collecting baseball cards since I was a child," she said, crushing the paper cup in her hand, "My father was a big baseball fan, and since he didn't have a son, he took me to watch the Yankees play and bought me candy and baseball cards. I still have my collection from my childhood. Collecting baseball cards became something my dad and I did, a sort of father-daughter bonding time."

"It's unusual for a fortune teller to collect baseball cards, isn't it?"

"It's unusual for a grown man to dress up like a pirate."

"A week ago I would have agreed with you, but despite all the bumps and bruises, these past few days have actually been fun. Strange, but fun."

"How does dressing like a pirate cause bumps and bruises?"

"Never mind, it's a long story."

She picked up one of the baseball cards, turned it over in her hand, and gave a big sigh. "I can't accept these." She gathered the cards and shoved them at me. "They belonged to your brother. You should keep them."

"No, he wanted you to have them." I shoved them back at her. "Besides, I was never much of a baseball fan. I wouldn't know what to do with them."

"All right. Thank you." She gathered the baseball cards and tucked them into her pocket. "Tell you what. Since you're here, why don't I read your fortune? On the house."

"Sure, if you want."

"Who knows?" she said as she shuffled her tarot cards. "Maybe there's a beautiful woman or lots of money in your future."

"Maybe," I said.

One by one she laid her tarot cards face down on the table. Behind me came the jingle of bells as someone entered the tent.

"I'm sorry," Zuleida said. "I'm with someone. Would you mind waiting outside, please?"

"We were just leaving, ma'am," Crenshaw said as he grabbed my shoulder. "Come on, Ben, we've got a battle to win."

"Is everything okay?" Zuleida asked.

"Sorry, Zuleida," I said. "It was nice meeting you, but I have to go." Crenshaw pulled me up from my seat and started dragging me from the tent by the collar. "Bye."

"Bye, Ben."

As Crenshaw and I emerged from the tent, I thought I heard Zuleida say, "Oh, that's not good, not good at all." I may have been mistaken, but still I wondered what she saw in the cards.

Maybe one day I'd find out.

20

At the south end of the fairgrounds, the battlefield had been roped off to prevent people from wandering onto it. On either side stood bleachers filled with spectators. A canopied platform had been raised at one end of the field where The Commodore sat with about eight or ten other pirates, male and female alike. At opposite ends of the field, thin white rods had been planted in the ground. A flag waved from the top of each rod. One bore a white skull and crossbones on a blue field; the other bore a white skull and crossbones on a red field.

Crenshaw and I found the Scallywags gathered at one end of the field beneath the blue flag, preparing for the upcoming battle. Each of them donned a harness made of Velcro straps, on the front of which was a cloth pouch. Crenshaw and I both had to put on similar harnesses. Across the field Belasco's crew had gathered beneath the red flag. Once our harnesses were securely in place, a single water balloon was placed into the pouch, and we were each handed a foam rubber sword.

Bilgewater Bill stepped into the center of the field. He called for everyone's attention and introduced both our crews. He explained the game as a variation of capture the flag. The object of the competition was to capture the opposing team's flag before they captured yours. He went on to explain that if someone's water balloon broke during the battle, that person was eliminated. If we wanted to eliminate a player from the game, we had to burst their water balloon with our foam rubber sword, which meant defending our water balloon was imperative.

"The battle shall commence at the blast of my conch shell," Bill announced.

Willow assigned me the task of defending our flag with Redjack and Crenshaw. Willow himself would lead Celeste, Maggie, Spider, and All Hands in an attempt to capture the enemy's flag. Jake and Helmsman would lead the crowds in cheering for us.

Bilgewater Bill looked to Willow and Belasco. "Captains," he said. "Are you ready?"

"Ready," Willow responded.

"Ready," Belasco said.

"Let the battle commence." Bill blew into his conch shell, sounding a blast similar to that of an elephant hitting puberty.

"Death to tyrants and traitors!" Willow cried out.

"For glory and chimichangas!" Belasco returned.

The two crews charged to the center of the field, foam rubber swords at the ready. Willow and Belasco met in the center as the others paired up against each other. Redjack, Crenshaw, and I could do nothing but watch as the ten of them whacked each other with their foam rubber swords, doing everything they could to burst their opponent's water balloon while defending their own.

Spider became the first to be eliminated. Her opponent, an older man with a neatly trimmed white beard, proved to be quite formidable. Although Spider was a skilled combatant, he managed to outmaneuver her and break her water balloon. I started to rush in to avenge Spider, but Redjack stopped me.

"Hold steady," he said. "Keep to your post."

"Our job is to protect the flag," Crenshaw said. "Unless all of our offensive team are eliminated, we remain here."

At that point the pirate who took out Spider jumped in to assist in the battle against All Hands, who battled Rigby. They appeared to be evenly matched, but All Hands had his hands full fighting off two opponents. Moments later two things happened. First, Celeste managed to eliminate Sasha. All Hands got eliminated almost at the same time. Aside from Willow, only Celeste and Maggie remained.

Rigby and his teammates converged on the women. I became eager to rush in to protect Celeste, even though she seemed capable enough to hold her own against her opponent.

Again Redjack had to restrain me with a hand on my shoulder. "Easy," he said. "Trust your crew mates."

Willow and Belasco appeared to be in a stalemate, and I wondered why none of the others jumped in to help their captain. When I posed the question, Crenshaw explained that most likely Belasco had ordered his crew to leave Willow to him. The two captains fought ferociously against each other, neither giving the other any opportunity for a final blow. Maggie made a successful lunge against Rigby, striking his water balloon, causing it to break, but it cost her, because it left her open for an attack from the silver-bearded pirate, who quickly burst her water balloon.

Then, Celeste stood alone against two opponents, the silver-bearded fellow, and a red-headed woman with fierce eyes.

I could not restrain myself any longer at that point. Despite Redjack's protests, I charged across the field, a berserker unfettered.

No more would I stand by while my crewmates were eliminated from the competition. No more would I tolerate watching while the woman I wanted to cuddle while watching *The Princess Bride* fought to defend her lovely yellow water balloon, so I charged across the field, sword at the ready, intent on taking out the pirate with the well-trimmed white beard. In my mind I told him, *You will not burst her water balloon. You will not burst her water balloon.*

I was too late. As I drew near my target, his sword slipped in, striking Celeste. I couldn't reach her in time. Celeste fell to the ground, water splattering her clothes, and she cried out in defeat. I wanted to rush to her aid, cradle her in my arms, tell her it would be okay, but I had no time. The man with the well-trimmed white beard spotted me. Our eyes met, and heedless of all else, I charged at him. He readied himself. Perhaps Crenshaw had trained me better than I thought, perhaps my desire to avenge Celeste invigorated me, or perhaps I got really lucky. Whatever it was, I somehow managed to dodge his attack and thrust my sword into his chest, causing his water balloon to pop like a humongous unsightly boil.

Before I had a chance to gloat over my success, the woman came at me with a war cry like a Valkyrie with a vengeance. I had no time to think. I kicked my right leg out behind me, dropped my left hand to the ground, and thrust my sword at her when she lunged. I had no idea where that maneuver came from, maybe some old kung-fu movie I saw as a kid. Somehow it worked. Water sprayed my face, and she looked down in astonishment.

Everyone stared at me in amazement. Even Willow and

Belasco had ceased their futile attempts to eliminate each other. The game board once again became even, yet we had the advantage.

"Ben."

I turned to see Celeste sitting on the ground like a young girl on a Sunday picnic. Her eyes sparkled in the sunlight. "Go get their flag," she said.

At the other end of the field waited three of Belasco's fiercest-looking pirates. The first man looked as tall and round as an oak tree. He had a baby face and a thin brown goatee. Beside him stood a short musclebound man with a clean-shaven head and a black Van Dyke beard. The third, a Black man, smiled as I approached. He had an athletic build, dreadlocks, and a single gold tooth that glittered in the sunlight. Behind them their red flag fluttered in the gentle California breeze, beckoning me to come claim it.

I felt no need to rush at them, so I took my time crossing the field. I estimated that my chances of getting past all three of them and claiming their flag on my own was slim to none, but I had made a commitment, and I couldn't turn back.

"Is it your plan to take on the three of us alone?" Dreadlocks asked when I walked toward them.

"No," someone behind me said. Redjack and Crenshaw jogged up to stand beside me, Redjack to my left, Crenshaw to my right. "It is our plan to take you on as a crew." Redjack winked at me.

"Now here is a proper challenge," Dreadlocks said. "Come forward then and let us claim our victory that much sooner." His crewmates laughed.

We stood facing them like an old samurai movie showdown, waiting to see who would make the first move. I sneered at Dreadlocks, trying to look menacing.

He chuckled.

My heart pounded. The crowd cheered us on. It felt good to command such support, yet one false move, one failed attempt, and not only would I be eliminated from the battle, but I would also lose the crowd. I didn't know what to do. *Should I attack Dreadlocks and chance it or wait for him to make the first move? Maybe I should let Redjack or Crenshaw lead.*

"We attack on your command, Ben," Redjack said to me.

My command? I didn't want to command. The only reason I got as far as I did was because I wanted to protect Celeste, and now I was the guy in charge? Something was terribly wrong with that scenario.

"Ben," Redjack hissed.

"Humph," Crenshaw grunted.

Dreadlocks gave me a questioning look.

"Come on, lad," Van Dyke said. "What are you going to do?"

"I smell pizza," Oak Tree said. "Anybody wanna get pizza after this?"

I had to make the first move. Whether I failed or succeeded, it was up to me. Screw it, I decided. Now.

"Attack!" I cried out, moving in as fast as I could.

Dreadlocks stood ready and lunged at me when I charged at him. I anticipated his maneuver and parried his attack. Spinning in the opposite direction, I moved into his attack zone and struck his water balloon with the butt of my sword. His balloon splattered onto both of us, so I slipped past him and made a final dash toward their flag. I snatched it from the pole and held it aloft for all to see.

The crowds cheered. Redjack cheered. Crenshaw cheered. Willow cheered. In fact all of the Scallywag crew cheered. Celeste cheered.

I smiled at her and waved the flag. She signaled for me to wave it to the crowd. I waved the flag and noticed a familiar face among them. Ray stood smiling at me. I almost burst into tears knowing that he had been there to share the moment.

"Hi, Mom, it's Ben."

"Benjamin, I'm afraid I can't talk now. I'm on my way out the door."

"Really? Is everything okay?"

"Yes, Jorge has invited me out to dine with him."

"Jorge? Who's Jorge?"

"Jorge Esteban. Remember? I told you about him yesterday."

"Mr. Esteban? This is a turn of events."

"I did as you suggested and accepted his invitation to have a drink with him."

"And he didn't drug you?"

"Certainly not. Jorge would never do such a thing."

"And now he's taking you out to dinner?"

"Yes, he told me about this new Mediterranean restaurant in town. It sounded lovely, so we decided to make a date of it. He's outside in his car waiting for me right now. I don't want to keep him waiting."

"Okay, but I have to tell you something."

"Very well. Make it quick, please. Jorge is honking his horn."

"Okay, real quick, you're a grandmother."

"What? Benjamin, what have you been doing?"

"Not me, Mom. Ray."

"What do you mean?"

"Ray has a daughter, Mom. I met her yesterday."

"Ray has a daughter?"

"Her name is Samantha."

"I have a granddaughter?"

"Yeah, you have a granddaughter. She's a sweet kid. We need to set something up so you can meet her."

"Yes, I would like that. Very much."

"Her mother's name is Robin, and they live in Bakersfield, California."

"Goodness, California is such a long way away."

"Yeah, I know. Look, I'll arrange everything, okay? And I'll make sure we take a plane when we go to visit."

"Of course, we'll take a plane."

"Okay, I'll be home tomorrow, so I'll see you then."

"I'm glad to hear that. You be careful, Benjamin. Call me when you get home tomorrow."

"I will, Mom."

"Imagine that, I have a granddaughter."

"You have a granddaughter, Mom."

"Hmmm."

21

I spent the rest of the day wandering through the festival, sometimes with one or two of the Scallywags, sometimes alone. I fired a cannon with Willow, sang a few sea shanties with Maggie, sold some knives and swords with Redjack, and sold jewelry with Spider. I ate some calamari with Jake and some conch fritters with All Hands, threw some knives at a wooden target with Crenshaw, played ring toss with Helmsman, and danced a few jigs with Celeste. I wasn't very good at the dancing, but I still enjoyed it.

Several hours later, as the sun began to set and all the festivalgoers headed home, the Scallywags mingled with some of the other pirate crews they had met throughout the day. It reminded me of a fraternity. They didn't know each other, but being pirates, they welcomed everyone with open arms.

Exhausted and alone, I ambled through the campsite and back to The Ship. As much as I wanted to collapse into my sleeping bag and pass out, I still had one more thing to take care of. With lantern in hand I climbed aboard The Ship, trudged down the aisle of seats, passed the spiral staircase that led up to the crow's nest, and finally pulled back the curtain to reveal the cargo hold at the rear. I dragged the treasure chest out a little, opened it, and removed the final envelope, which read "Open when all other items are delivered."

I opened the envelope and read the parchment inside. Like the previous parchment, no map adorned this one, only the message, "The puzzle box is for you, Ben." I took the puzzle box from the treasure chest, closed the chest, and disembarked.

Night overtook the campground. Campfires sparked up. Pirates milled about, sharing food and songs and stories. Some pirates meandered from one campfire to another. I walked through the campground in search of the Scallywags. I walked near a grove of trees and a rustling sound caught my attention. I turned to see All Hands lurking about as if hiding from someone.

"What are you doing?" I asked.

"Shhh," he said, putting his finger to his lips. "Be vewy, vewy quiet. We're hunting ninjas. Heh-heh-heh-heh."

"Who's *we?*" I asked.

Two people sprang out from the tree grove with swords raised for attack. I recognized them as two of Belasco's crew. One was the large Oak Tree guy. The other was the young redheaded woman.

"Ninjas!" he yelled.

"Die, ninjas, die!" she yelled.

"Whoa, wait a second," I cried, putting my hands up to defend myself.

"Guys, relax," All Hands said. "It's Ben."

They stopped and lowered their weapons.

"You sure he's not a ninja?" Oak Tree guy asked.

"Positive," All Hands said. "Ben, you know Big Steve and Kelly?"

"Only from the battlefield," I said.

"Big Steve Obermann," Oak Tree guy said, offering his hand.

I shook it and said to the girl, "Then you must be Kelly."

"Cannonball Kelly." she grabbed my hand and pumped it vigorously.

"You need a new nickname," All Hands said. "Cannonball Kelly is lame."

"Is not," she returned.

"Is too."

"Kill the ninja!" I spun around to see Jake rushing at me, sword in hand.

"Jake," I warned him. "Don't even try it."

"Oh, hi, Ben," he said, hiding his sword behind his back. "Thought maybe you were a ninja."

"I'm not a ninja, and you know it."

"Sorry," he said.

"That's okay," I said. "Where is everybody? Don't tell me they're all hunting for ninjas."

"No, just us," All Hands said.

"The others are over there, somewhere," Jake said, pointing.

"Now if you'll excuse us," Kelly said, "we've got some ninjas to find."

"Good luck," I said before the four of them skulked off.

A little farther on I came across Redjack and Crenshaw with three of Belasco's crew.

Crenshaw sliced a watermelon in half with a sword.

"Nice cut," the guy with the dreadlocks said.

"Hey, guys," I said as I approached. "What're you up to?"

"Look who's here," Dreadlocks said, "the hero of the day."

"Good evening, Ben," Redjack said. "We're testing some of our swords."

"I don't believe we've been introduced," Dreadlocks said.

"No, we haven't," I said.

"I am Jean-Paul Thibaudeau. They call me Mr. Tibbs. I'm the first mate of the Pirates of Preciado Beach."

"Pleased to meet you, Mr. Tibbs."

"Now," Mr. Tibbs said. "This man with the dark beard is Walt 'Dead Eye' Ramos, and this fellow over here is the esteemed Mike Silver."

"We were rather impressed with your skills this afternoon," Mike said. "How long have you been studying swordsmanship?"

"Hmm." I thought about the question for a moment. "Since Wednesday."

"Wednesday?" Mike asked in surprise.

"Yes," I said. "Crenshaw has been teaching me for the past few days."

"You mean to tell me," Mr. Tibbs said, "that we were bested by an amateur?"

"Is this true, Crenshaw?" Mike asked.

"It's true," Crenshaw said. "He was a terrible student."

"Indeed," Redjack said. "We were as surprised as you."

"Years of practice only to be outdone by a dilettante," Mike Silver said. "There's irony for you."

"Irony indeed," Mr. Tibbs said. "Luck is probably more like it."

"You must share your secret with us," Mike Silver said. "How did you manage to defeat us?"

"To be honest," I said. "I don't know myself."

"As I said," Mr. Tibbs affirmed, "luck."

"I won't deny it."

"Okay, here we go, next target." Walt Ramos placed a two-liter plastic bottle of cola on the stand.

"Come on, Walt," Mr. Tibbs said. "That's a waste of a good beverage."

"We have another bottle," Walt said. He drew his sword back and swung, slicing through the bottle. Soda splattered us and the two halves of the bottle fell to the ground. The pirates all laughed and applauded. I laughed, wiped the few drops of soda from my cheek, and left them to their fun.

I continued through the camp and wondered where Celeste had gone. I thought maybe Maggie or Spider might know. As I contemplated where they might have gone, I heard a familiar snoring sound. I was hardly surprised to discover Helmsman sound asleep in a hammock strung between two small trees. He looked peaceful in his slumber, despite his snoring being anything but. Up ahead I heard someone singing, but not in English. At least it didn't sound like English; it sounded more Asian.

I followed the sound and discovered Spider Lau, Maggie, Rigby, and Sasha sitting around a table. Spider sang while the others sat listening. A bottle of rum stood on one corner of the table with four shot glasses, one in front of each person. The table held a plastic cup and a handful of dice were scattered across its surface. I approached when Spider ended her song.

"That was a song my mother sang to me," she said, "when I was a little girl in China."

"That was beautiful." Maggie tapped her finger on the table and her head bobbed. Her words were slurred. "Absolutely beeyou-tee-fool."

"Beautiful, beautiful," Sasha echoed. She leaned her head against her arm, which was propped up on the table.

"My mother used to sing to me too," Rigby said. "She would sing a song called 'Shut Up and Go to Sleep Before I Smack You in the Head.'"

Sasha sat bolt upright and burst into a fit of laughter, and then her head sank onto her arm again.

"Whose turn is it?" Maggie asked.

"It's Sasha's turn," Spider said.

"My turn." Sasha popped up in her seat as if she had just returned to life. She scooped up the dice, dropped them into the plastic cup, shook the cup, and smacked the cup upside-down onto the table. She lifted the cup to reveal the dice, and the women all leaned in to look.

"Four sixes." Sasha raised her fists in triumph. "I win."

"You don't win," Rigby said.

"I don't?"

"We have to add up the points to see who wins," Spider said.

"How many points do I have?" Sasha asked.

"Who knows?" Maggie slurred. "Who cares?"

"Everybody drink," Rigby ordered.

The four lifted their shot glasses, tossed them back, and slammed the empty shot glasses down onto the table. Rigby picked up the bottle of rum, removed the cork, and refilled each glass in turn.

"Now what?" Sasha asked.

"Now you have to reveal something about yourself that none of us knows," Maggie said.

"My boobs?" Sasha asked. "You want me to reveal my boobs?"

"I've seen your boobs." Rigby grinned. "Plenty of times."

"Maggie and Spider haven't seen them." Sasha started raising her blouse. "Maybe they'd like to see them."

Spider held up her hand for Sasha to stop. "Thank you, no."

"We're good." Maggie shook her head.

Sasha dropped the hem of her blouse looking like a scolded child.

"You have to tell us something about yourself that we don't know," Rigby said.

"Okay." Sasha scrunched up her face and gazed up. After a few moments she said, "When I was ten I liked the boy who lived down the street, but I was too shy to tell him how I felt, so I stole his bicycle. The way I figured it he would have to talk to me to get it back."

"Did your plan work?" Maggie asked.

"No, they reported it to the police, and when my father found the bicycle in our garage I was grounded for a month."

"Poor Sasha," Spider said.

"Grounded?" Maggie said. "That's nothing. My dad would have whooped my behind for stealing a bicycle."

"My dad would probably have let the cops throw me in prison," Rigby said.

"Hey, guys," I said as I approached.

"Ben Potts," Rigby said, "how are you?"

"I'm fine," I said. "I see you've all been drinking."

"A little bit." Maggie held her forefinger and thumb apart about half an inch. "A teeny tiny little bit."

"But don't worry." Sasha waggled her finger. "We're not driving anywhere."

"We're just going to sit here and play our game." Spider slapped the table for emphasis.

"What game are you playing?" I asked.

"Who knows?" Maggie said. "Something with dice."

"And rum." Rigby tapped the bottle with his finger.

"Dice and rum," Sasha said.

"It is called the game of dice and rum," Spider said.

"Sounds fun," I said. "I was wondering if you knew where Celeste is,"

"Oh, Ben, Ben, Ben," Maggie said. "You might as well give up. The two of you are never going to be together."

"There are plenty of other fish in the sea, Ben," Sasha said.

"Yeah, well, I'd still like to see her."

"The last time I saw her," Rigby said, waving his finger as if trying to pinpoint her exact location, "she was riding off on Captain Belasco's motorcycle."

"Motorcycle?" I asked. "Where was she going?"

"Don't know," Rigby said. "You'd have to ask Captain Belasco."

"And where is he?"

"He's in that tent over there." Maggie pointed to a nearby tent. "With Captain Willow."

"With Willow?"

I found it odd that Willow and Belasco, who, as far as I knew, hated each other, would be spending time together. Maybe they were locked in mortal combat, trying to kill each other. I pushed aside the tent flap with some apprehension, surprised to find Willow and Belasco sitting side by side in canvas chairs drinking rum, eating chimichangas, and laughing.

"Potts," Willow said as I peered in through the tent flap. "Come in and join us."

"If it isn't the great swashbuckler," Belasco said.

I entered the tent and sat down in an empty canvas chair. "I can't stay long," I said. "I have to get up early tomorrow for my flight back to Orlando."

"Nonsense." Willow poured some rum into a cup and handed it to me. "Have a drink with us."

"Try a chimichanga." Belasco offered one wrapped in paper. "They really are good."

"Thanks." I took a sip of the rum and bit into the chimichanga.

"Am I right? It's good, huh?"

"Yeah, I mean, I'm no big Mexican-food connoisseur, but it's very good."

"Ha!" Belasco slapped his knee. "I told you, the best chimichangas in town."

"Except," Willow said, "neither Potts nor I have tried every chimichanga in town, so we can neither confirm nor deny that."

"Then you'll have to take Don Miguel's and my word for it," Belasco said.

"I don't know Don Miguel, so I don't know how trustworthy he is," Willow said. "And as for you, I shall never again trust your word for anything."

"That hurts my feelings."

"Good. I want to hurt your feelings."

"Is this about the woman you stole from him?" I asked.

"What woman?" Willow cocked his eyebrow.

"I would never steal a woman from my friend," Belasco protested. "Besides, we have different tastes in women."

"But I thought you said he stole your woman, Lois or something."

"You mean Louise?" Willow said. He and Belasco looked at each other and laughed. "Potts, Louise is not a woman."

"I don't understand."

"Louise," Belasco explained, "is a golden retriever."

"A dog? You stole his dog?"

"I didn't steal her, no."

"That's exactly what you did." Willow wagged his finger at Belasco. "You stole her from me, and it broke my heart."

"I gave her to a loving family. A family with kids and a big yard for her to play in. You lived in a tiny apartment, and you were never there. Poor Louise was depressed and lonely. She needed a place to run around and play, and the Wallace family had a place for her to do that."

"I miss her though."

"You can visit her anytime you wish, and I know you do visit her almost every weekend."

"All this over a dog?" I asked.

"Potts, Louise is more than just a dog. She's a very special dog. She's special to me, anyway."

"I'm sure she is," I said. I tossed back the remainder of my rum. "Well, I should probably call it a night."

"Potts, it has come to my attention that we never finished Longbucket's reverse treasure hunt."

"Reverse treasure hunt?" Belasco said. "What's that?"

"Longbucket made a request of Potts. He asked him to deliver five items. We delivered three of them on our way here, but as I recall two still remain."

"Actually," I said, "all the items have been delivered."

"They have?"

"This is the final item." I reached into my pocket and revealed the puzzle box.

"But if you still have it," Willow said, "how have all the items been delivered?"

I pulled out the piece of parchment from my pocket and handed it to Willow.

"'The puzzle box is for you, Ben,'" he read. "Why did he give it to you?"

"I don't know," I said. "I always hated these things, because I could never solve them."

"What about the other thing? The baseball cards?"

"As it turns out, Zuleida is a fortune teller here at the festival."

"You met her and gave her the baseball cards?"

"Yup."

"Without me? Without the Scallywags?" Willow leaned over to me. "Potts, I thought we were in this together."

"Sorry," I said. "I was wandering the fairgrounds and stumbled across her tent. If I had known you wanted to be there that badly, I would have made sure you were included."

"Don't give it another thought, Potts. It was your quest, not ours. We were only there to assist."

"Come to think of it," I said. "I never did thank you for your help. I do appreciate what you and the Scallywags did for me."

"Glad to be of service. And speaking for the Scallywags and meself, we enjoyed having you on board for the voyage."

"I rather enjoyed it myself," I said. "It was kind of fun."

"Perhaps we should do it again next year."

"By all means," Belasco said. "You must come back next year. We must have a rematch. It would be an insult to me and my crew if you didn't."

"We'll have to see," I said. "I can't make any promises right now."

"I'm sure you'll be able to make it happen one way or another, Potts," Willow said.

"If you'll excuse me, I need to get some sleep." I rose from the chair. "I was hoping for a chance to tell Celeste goodbye. Do you have any idea where she might be?"

"Celeste borrowed my motorcycle." Belasco poured himself another glass of rum. "She said she had something to take care of, and I don't know when she'll return."

"It's just as well, I guess. Anyway, thanks for the rum and the chimichanga. Good night."

"Good night, Ben," Belasco said. "I do hope we see you again next year."

"Potts." Willow rose to shake my hand. "Take care of yourself. It's been a pleasure."

"You too, Captain, and I'll see you back in Florida."

22

I left the tent and started back to The Ship, where I planned to bunk down for the night. Walking through the campground I got lost in thought about Celeste. I really did want to see her before I left, but without knowing where she had gone or how long she'd be away, it didn't look very promising.

An engine roared from somewhere on the grounds. I didn't pay much attention at first, but it became louder. I couldn't help wondering what it was. Looking up, the first thing I noticed were her shapely, tanned legs as they straddled the motorcycle, Belasco's motorcycle, I guessed. Her outstretched arms formed a V that gripped the handlebars. Her long chestnut hair and puffy white blouse billowed behind her as she approached. She had a sly grin as if she intended some mischief. Only God knew what kind of mischief Celeste could get into once she put her mind to it.

She braked in front of me. "Get on," she shouted over the rumbling of the motorcycle.

"What? Listen, I don't have time."

"Then stop wasting it and get on," she said.

"I have an early flight tomorrow." I climbed on behind her.

"I know. Hang on."

I wrapped my arms around her waist, and together we roared off, winding through the campground, dodging pirates, tents, campers, and other vehicles. We passed All Hands and Jake as they emerged from behind a group of trees, still hunting ninjas, I assumed. They waved as we passed. I smiled back, afraid that if I tried waving, I would lose my grip and fall off. A minute or so later, we left the grounds and sped onto the main road.

"Where are we going?" I yelled into her ear.

"Hang on. You'll see," she yelled back.

A thousand stars sparkled above us. White lines zipped by beneath us. I had never ridden a motorcycle and had no idea how much experience Celeste had riding one either, but I didn't worry about it. Instead I enjoyed the ride, holding her waist, the wind blowing her hair into my face, her scent filling my nostrils. She smelled like lavender and perspiration. I vowed to ride motorcycles more often.

We turned into a parking lot, and to my pleasant surprise we pulled up to a hotel. It was the last thing I expected to see, but I was glad to see it. Neither a high-priced resort nor a cheap flophouse, it appeared to be more of a hotel for business travelers.

"What are we doing here?" I asked as she parked the motorcycle.

"I booked us a room for the night," she said.

"A room? For us?"

We entered the lobby where a young woman in a white blouse and green vest typed away on a computer behind the front desk. An elderly couple stood before the desk, several suitcases at their feet, arguing over which credit card to use. Thinking we would need to check in, I turned to the front desk, but Celeste walked toward the elevators, so I followed her. We took the elevator to the third floor and walked down the hall to a room at the far end. Celeste produced a card key and passed it through the slot on the door handle. The door opened, and we entered our room.

Inside, green appeared to be the dominating color scheme. Green carpet, green curtains, green bedspread, topped with green pillows. It looked like a leprechaun's paradise.

"There's only one bed," I said.

"King size," she said. "You want to take a shower first?"

"Yeah, sure."

She smiled and turned toward the large screen television, snatched up the remote control, and turned it on. I watched her for a moment before I went into the bathroom, closing the door behind me.

The soap and hot water took me to another place. I always loved my showers; the feeling of being wet and clean made me feel new. I had my own ritual when I showered. I started with my arms and shoulders and worked down, methodically scrubbing every part. I would then shampoo my hair, wash my face, and plunge myself under the water spray to rinse everything away. As I got to the final step of my ritual, I heard the swish of the shower curtain and the jingle of the curtain rings. I looked over my shoulder to see Celeste step onto the wet tiles.

"Mind if I join you?" she asked.

I gawked at her naked form, unable to speak at first, but with some effort I managed to say something. "Not at all." It came out more as a squeak than an actual sentence.

She drew closer, wrapped her arms around my neck, and

pressed her lips to mine. The wonderfulness of feeling her wet, naked body against mine as we kissed was like the first time I went to Disney World and rode Space Mountain as a kid. It was like that first bite of banana cream pie after I'd been craving banana cream pie for days. I wanted to plunge my face into that delectable dessert and gobble it up.

I had a moment, then, when I questioned it all. I pulled away. "Are you sure this is what you want?" I asked.

"I paid for the room," she said.

"Yeah, but I mean, don't you love Ray?"

"Ray's gone. Whatever might have been is also gone. I need to move on."

"But does that mean I'm the rebound guy?"

"Is that a problem?"

I thought about it for a moment. "No," I said, "not really."

"Then shut up and make love to me."

I won't go into any great detail about that night. I'll only say I'd never had a night like it before or since. Celeste did things I thought women would never do. I was sure the people in the rooms next door heard everything. Finally we both collapsed, trying to catch our breath, and ended up falling asleep in each other's arms.

I sat up in the sand, facing the ocean. Beach stretched out in both directions as far as I could see. Behind me a line of trees and brush ran parallel to the shore. The ocean roared as waves crashed, stretching toward me, the water almost touching my toes. Seagulls shrieked and hovered above the water, searching for fish. I closed my eyes and inhaled it all, letting it fill my lungs. The place offered such peace that I wished I could stay forever.

A shadow crept in. Even with my eyes closed I felt it blocking the sun. I opened my eyes to discover a familiar silhouette standing over me.

"Careful; you know how easily you get sunburned."

"Ray?" I shaded my eyes with my hand.

"Who else?" He sat down in the sand beside me. He looked out at the ocean, dusted the sand from his hands, and sighed. "Finally," he said. "A little bit of peace."

We sat for a few moments relaxing like two guys on a well-deserved vacation. The only things missing were margaritas and hot girls in bikinis.

"Now what?" I asked. "I completed your quest. I delivered all five items like you wanted."

"Not quite. There's still the puzzle box."

"Your note said it was for me."

"It is for you."

"I have it. Mission complete."

"Except you still have to solve the puzzle."

"The puzzle? You mean I have to open the box?"

"Of course."

"That's not going to happen."

"That was the point of giving you the puzzle box. You have to figure out how to open it."

"Come on." I put my hands to my face, groaned, and collapsed onto the sand. "I suck at stuff like that. You know I suck at it."

"Yeah," he said and laughed. "You always got so frustrated anytime you had to solve anything you thought was difficult. You remember that time you threw my Rubik's cube at the wall?"

"Then why?" I asked, sitting up. "Why would you give me some stupid puzzle box to solve? Are you doing this to irritate me?"

"You remember when we were kids and you had that little pirate figurine? You called it Shorty something."

"Shorty McPhee, the shortest pirate what sailed the Seven Seas."

"That's it. Shorty McPhee, such a stupid name for a pirate."

"No, it isn't. He was short, and his name was McPhee."

"It's a stupid name, Ben."

"Whatever. Longbucket is a stupid name."

"I can't argue with that." He laughed. "But that was Willow's idea, not mine."

I chuckled. After having spent a week with Willow, I had grown to like him and his eccentric ways.

"Anyway," Ray continued, doodling in the sand, "what I was saying was you remember one day your little pirate guy, Shorty McPhee, disappeared? You looked everywhere for it, and you never could find it."

"Yeah, I remember. I thought that Boyd kid next door stole it."

"He didn't steal it."

"You took it, didn't you? I should have known."

"Yeah, I took it and hid it."

"Where? I looked in every crack and crevice of the house and never found it. Where'd you hide it?"

"Open the puzzle box."

"Fine." I shook my head. I hated puzzle boxes.

"Take care of yourself, Ben." He patted my shoulder and started to rise.

"One more thing before you go."

"What?" He sat back down.

"Zuleida told me you had a dream that you were going to die."

He nodded, his eyes fixed on the ocean. "I did."

"If you knew you were going to die, why would you get on a plane?"

"Because it was just a dream, and there was nothing in the dream that told me how I was going to die." He dug a small hole in the sand. "There have been only two times in my life when I had dreams predicting someone's death. The first time was when Dad died. Remember?"

"Yeah."

"I never experienced any other dreams after that. I figured it was a coincidence until I had a dream predicting my own death. I wanted to know if it was a dream or if I was really seeing the future."

"But Zuleida confirmed your suspicions."

"Ben, she's a fortune teller at a pirate festival. You really think she has psychic powers?"

"I don't know. Maybe."

"I went to her because I was curious, and she was the closest thing to a real psychic I knew of. Even then I remained unconvinced."

"So you got on the plane anyway."

"How else was I going to know the truth? Besides, like I said in my letter, I refuse to let fear and psychic predictions control my life."

In the distance something caught my eye. I heard a faint "Yoo-hoo" like an echo. I turned to see a woman with long dark hair and wearing a yellow sundress standing on the beach, looking at us.

"Sorry, Ben," Ray said. "Looks like it's time for me to go." He stood, brushing the sand off the seat of his pants.

"Who is that?" I asked.

"Caitlin, of course."

"You've found Caitlin?" I got to my feet.

"Yeah."

"So what happened?" I waved to Caitlyn, and she waved back. "Did she agree to marry you?"

"She did."

"That's awesome." I grabbed Ray and hugged him.

"Ben, Ben, come on. You're embarrassing me."

"Don't give me that. My brother's getting married." I broke the embrace and stepped back. "When's the wedding?"

"This is the afterlife, Ben. Time is irrelevant."

"Can I come?"

"I'll see what I can do." He gave me a quick half-salute, half-wave before he turned to join Caitlin.

I stood watching him walk away, fighting back the tears, because for the first time I realized I would never see my brother again.

In the morning Celeste took me to the airport on the motorcycle. We kissed one last time before parting. Of all the kisses I enjoyed with her, two really stood out for me: our first kiss in the UFO store, and our last one, at the airport.

"Take care of yourself, Ben Potts," she said, then roared away, to pursue other free-spirited adventures, I imagined.

We had talked about getting together back in Florida in a week or so, or rather I talked about it. Celeste gave a few noncommittal "Uh-huhs." As much as I wanted to be with her, a part of me knew it would never happen. She was the wild creature that needed freedom in order to live and thrive, and I was the domesticated pet in need of security and comfort.

Deep down I knew I would have to let her go. I hadn't fully learned how to do it yet, but I was working on it. Still, I would always love her and would never forget the one night we shared in Palo Alto, California.

Inside the airport as I searched for my gate, a young boy ran up to me. "Are you a pirate?" he asked.

I had almost forgotten I still wore the pirate garb the Scallywags had given me. My own clothes remained stowed aboard The Ship. "I guess I am," I told him.

"Mom, look, a real pirate," he called to his mother.

"I see, Randy," his mother said. "Now don't bother the man."

"It's okay. He's not bothering me," I said.

"Can I get a picture with him, Mom? Please?"

"You'd have to ask him."

"Can I, huh?" he asked.

Strange how only a few days ago I would have done everything to avoid such a situation and usually did, when I traveled with the Scallywags. Of course, at the time I could gracefully bow out and let the others take the spotlight. This time I stood on my own. "Sure, why not?" I said.

On the plane I had been lucky enough to get a window seat. Gazing out at the clear blue skies, I never felt more relaxed or prouder of myself. At that moment I remembered the puzzle box, which I still had in my pocket. I took it out and examined it, hoping to find some clue that would help me open it. Nothing presented itself. I attempted to solve it several times, only to be unsuccessful each time. Nothing I did worked.

I got frustrated and cursed under my breath, but then I remembered I wasn't alone. I looked over to see an elderly woman sitting in the seat next to me. She had a look of concern on her face. I smiled at her and apologized.

Deciding that getting angry or frustrated wasn't the answer, I returned my attention to the puzzle box. I took a few deep breaths and ran my fingers along the surface of the box. To my surprise, something clicked. A small, wedged piece of the box slid to the side, and the box opened.

The plane engines roared louder and we started down the runway. The flight attendants began their safety procedure routine, but I didn't hear a word they said. I became fixated on the small pirate figurine in my hand, Shorty McPhee, the shortest pirate what sailed the Seven Seas. I smiled as I turned the figurine over in my hand. It all suddenly fell into place.

"Thank you, Ray," I whispered. "You helped me rediscover my inner pirate."

Arrgh!

THE END

Acknowledgments

I would like to acknowledge several people and give them a big thank you. First, my niece, Shannon Beatty, who took the photo of me I'm using as my headshot. I've used this photo on numerous occasions. Second, I would like to thank my beta readers: Carol Jones, C. C. Gallo, Angie Mayo, Beverly Gilewitz, and Dr. Bonnie Benson, all of whom gave very helpful feedback. A big thank you to my editor, Jason Letts, whom I found through Reedsy. He did a great job, and his comments challenged me to write better. Finally, I want to thank you, the reader, the ones who have read and enjoyed this little tale of mine. May it help you find your own inner pirate, if you haven't already.